THE
GEOGRAPHY
OF PLUTO

THE
GEOGRAPHY
OF PLUTO

A Novel by

CHRISTOPHER
DiRADDO

Cormorant Books

Canada Council
for the Arts
Conseil des Arts
du Canada

 ONTARIO ARTS COUNCIL
CONSEIL DES ARTS DE L'ONTARIO
50 YEARS OF ONTARIO GOVERNMENT SUPPORT OF THE ARTS
50 ANS DE SOUTIEN DU GOUVERNEMENT DE L'ONTARIO AUX ARTS

Canadian
Heritage
Patrimoine
canadien
Canadä

The publisher gratefully acknowledges the support of the Canada Council for the
Arts and the Ontario Arts Council for its publishing program. We acknowledge
the financial support of the Government of Canada through the Canada Book
Fund (CBF) for our publishing activities, and the Government of Ontario through
the Ontario Media Development Corporation, an agency of the Ontario Ministry
of Culture, and the Ontario Book Publishing Tax Credit Program.

LIBRARY AND ARCHIVES CANADA CATALOGUING IN PUBLICATION

DiRaddo, Christopher, 1974–, author
The geography of Pluto / Christopher DiRaddo.

Issued in print and electronic formats.
ISBN 978-1-77086-364-4 (pbk.). — ISBN 978-1-77086-365-1 (epub). —
ISBN 978-1-77086-366-8 (mobi)

I. Title.

PS8607.I69G46 2014   C813'.6   C2013-9078932
                                          C2013-907894-0

Cover design: Angel Guerra/Archetype
Cover photograph: Vincent Fortier (vincefortier.tumblr.com)
Interior text design: Tannice Goddard, Soul Oasis Networking
Printed and bound in Canada by Friesens.

MIX
Paper from
responsible sources
FSC
www.fsc.org
FSC® C016245

CORMORANT BOOKS INC.
10 ST. MARY STREET, SUITE 615, TORONTO, ONTARIO, M4Y 1P9
www.cormorantbooks.com

For my mom and dad

"And I asked myself about the present: how wide it was, how deep it was, how much was mine to keep."

Chapter 1

I shook the snow from my shoulders and walked into my apartment, throwing my keys onto the table as I closed the door. I could already hear the next day's hangover in the darkness. Steadying myself against the wall, I undid my laces and removed my boots with the sides of my feet. I tossed both boots onto the mat in the corner, but then stepped into a puddle by the door. "Shit," I muttered, jumping away from the wet spot. I flipped on the lights overhead, locked the door, and pulled the offending sock from my foot.

I walked down the hallway, turning on more lights as I went. The apartment was exactly how I had left it earlier that evening: everything tidy and in its place. The shower curtain was pulled out over the tub, the kitchen sink empty of dishes that were now stacked neatly in wooden cupboards. I had dusted, quickly vacuumed, and changed the bedsheets before leaving.

I knew I was being excessive. I hadn't planned on returning home with someone, but then who plans that sort of thing? I figured, though, I might as well be prepared. Just because I was a mess, didn't mean my place had to be.

There was a flashing red light on the phone in the kitchen. Two messages. "Hi, Will," the first one crackled. It was my mom. "Just checking in. I don't remember what you were doing tonight." I could hear her running a list in her head. "It's nothing important. You can call me tomorrow … Good-bye," she added stiffly, signing off as if sending a signal into space.

Delete. Next message.

"Hey there, tiger," a voice sang with a jovial drunkenness I recognized well. It was Angie. "Belated Merry Christmas!! I meant to call you the other day, but it's been crazy here. I wish you had come. New York is such a blast! Anyway, it looks like we'll be back in Montreal on the fourth, so we'll do dinner or something and I'll tell you all about it. Maybe I'll give you a shout tomorrow, or you can call me here at Nancy's — you've got the number. Take care, babe! And be sure to wish your mom a Merry Christmas for me! Happy New Year!"

I erased the second message. It was 11:15 p.m. I picked up the phone and dialled.

"Hello?"

"Hey, did I wake you?"

"No, I'm up watching the news," my mom answered with a rasp. "Is everything all right?"

"Yes, everything's fine," I said, hoping the booze in my body wasn't audible. "Sorry if I'm calling too late, but I thought you might be up."

"No, it's fine," she said, clearing her throat. "You just never know what kind of call you're going to get at this time of night. How was your evening?"

"It was okay," I admitted. "I went out for a drink with a friend." Silly, lying to my mother at this age. "I just got in. How was your night?"

"Oh, fine. I didn't do too much. I watched some movie on TV, one of these cheesy Hallmark Christmas ones." I could hear the newspaper shifting on her lap. "I wanted to know if I'm going to see you before New Year's," she said. "You know, for meals and such ..."

"How about tomorrow? I can stay over too, if you like."

"That'd be nice," she said, pleased. "*Singin' in the Rain* was on today. I taped it. Maybe we can watch it together?"

"Sure."

"I suppose it's because of the holidays, but one of my channels has been playing nothing but classics all week. You should take a look at the schedule while you're over and let me know if you want me to tape anything else for you."

"I will."

My mom was up now. I could hear her moving around her apartment, opening and closing kitchen cabinets. "What would you like for dinner then? Spaghetti? Steak? I have steaks."

The mere mention of food made me realize I hadn't eaten dinner. "Either sounds good," I said, diving towards my collection of home-delivery flyers. "Oh, before I forget, Angie wishes you a Merry Christmas."

"That's nice. Did I tell you she sent me a Christmas card?"

I was surprised and a little envious. "I didn't get a Christmas card!"

"Well, you see her all the time ... Will, why don't you invite her over for dinner tomorrow too? It's been ages since I've seen her."

"Angie's in New York for the holidays."

"Well, when she's back, then. I'll save the spaghetti for a night she can come."

I mumbled an affirmation, my concentration now on finding something to eat. I was flipping through the flyers, looking for chicken, humming along to whatever my mom was saying. There was something comforting about these aimless conversations I continued to have with my mother since I'd moved out several years ago. If nothing else, our voices made up these sweet harmonies that were sung to each other in *um*s and *ah*s as we carried on with our days.

"Well, I just wanted to call and say hi," I yawned. "I should let you get to bed."

"Don't stay up too late now," she ordered as if I were still a teenager.

"I won't. Good night."

"Good night, dear ... love you."

I hung up the phone.

I was too tired to order in so I opened the fridge to find whatever comfort food was in there. It was pretty much empty, so I took out a yogurt cup, mixed it in a bowl with a chopped banana, and collapsed onto my couch. I stared at the walls as I ate.

My apartment was small, but comfortable. It had taken a while before it felt that way. I remember the morning I first moved in, how a neighbour's cat had run in with all the boxes and peed in a corner of the bedroom. It was weeks before the smell was gone. I'd also painted most of the walls as the previous tenant had been fond of pastels. But in the end, after months of living here, it began to feel like home; as much my home as the place on the other end of the phone line, where I grew up and where my mom still kept a bed for me.

I had been staying in that bed a lot lately. Over the last three months I had been troubled by another imprint that lingered on my walls and furniture. Although he had never lived here, Max's indelible presence could still be felt in the apartment, his scent burnt into the wood like waves upon waves of incense. It spooked me, sometimes, being alone in this space. It reminded me too much of who I used to be, who I was when we were together. Sometimes it felt as if I were the thing that didn't belong in the room. That this was someone else's house, a happier person who was long disappeared, and I was living in his place as a squatter.

I finished the bowl of yogurt and got up to start rehydrating. I had only gone out for one drink, but that had quickly turned into four. It was the holidays, after all, and I had felt the need to take advantage of the time I had off from teaching geography at James Lyng High School — even if my partner-in-crime was AWOL in the streets of New York. I had been counting on Angie too much lately. The last few months had seen us hitting the bars in a way that I hadn't in almost ten years, since I was nineteen. I guess that's what happens when the most important relationship you've been in dissolves: you get out of the house as much as possible.

On this particular night I had braved the cold and gone to Sky. Sky bar and its three floors had been, at one point in our lives, the heavenly body we circled like satellites. It had since fallen on hard times as newer establishments had sprung up and eclipsed its brilliance. I myself hadn't been in more than two years. I was surprised to find it had gone through some major renovations. Gone were the centralized bar and grimy pool tables that Angie and I used to play on. In its place, Sky now boasted two wooden barges on which smooth-faced twinks served cocktails, and a series of minimalist couches at the back that no one sat on. Many of the faces were still the same, however — the boys at the bar sitting like birds on a wire. At first I thought that to be a comfort (at least some things never change), but then with each drink I began to wonder if it wasn't sad. Don't we all come here to find a reason to stay home?

I had found someone, or at least I thought I had. And inasmuch as I tried to excise the thought of Max with each drink, I kept seeing him in the bottom of my glass — my old life dissipating with every sip.

How can you lose something you thought was forever?

Chapter

2

I grew up in a two-bedroom apartment on Hôtel-de-Ville in the Plateau, an ever-expanding neighbourhood of university students and large families of varying ethnic origin. We moved in when I was three; a year after my dad died. This was back before the area became gentrified, before the trendy bars, shops, and restaurants opened, before the rents rocketed and the buildings turned into condos. Back then it was a place where a single mother and her son could find a place cheap and large enough to live in, close to all the amenities necessary for city dwellers who didn't have cars, yet far from the bustle of commercial downtown.

It was also three blocks from where my mother's sister Mary lived at the time. She had helped us find the place. It was a tight fit, but we made good use of it. It was one of six apartments in an old complex that looked like an abandoned prison from the outside. Its brick was oppressive, bleak, and grey, and framed by weathered lampposts and black power lines. The six balconies on the building's facade were battered, covered in splintered wood and chipped paint. Tenants' belongings were left out on them, exposed to the elements in a crude introduction to the lives of those who lived inside: rusted hibachis, broken toys, wet garbage bags. Outside the building's heavy door stood a large tree with limbs that remained bare year-round, save for one branch that gave birth every spring to an animated row of yellow leaves.

Inside, the apartment walls were paper-thin and water-stained. The smell of cooked foods was buried deep in the carpets — curries and casseroles Mom tried to mask with scented candles and air freshener. At night we could hear the laugh track from our neighbours' television, broadcasting the French variety shows. We could hear the flush of their toilet, the run of their sink. The apartment was full of furniture from our first home. My mother had refused to throw anything out. Every room held the old stuff like trophies. Even when the place was clean it still looked like a mess. Glass vases, ceramic figurines, and handmade doilies crowded tabletops. A ratty ottoman sat on the floor next to my mother's chair. The ottoman had once belonged to my dad. We had had two living rooms in our home back then.

Mom seldom left the apartment unless it was to go to work or shop for groceries. She was a librarian at the Atwater Library, working an ever-changing schedule I couldn't keep up with. When I was young she would bring home book after book for me, hardcover English translations of *Astérix & Obélix*, *Tintin*, and *The Smurfs*. As I got older, the books changed: Judy Blume, Hardy Boys, and the odd *Choose Your Own Adventure*. I wasn't into these teen paperbacks as much, but not wanting to hurt her feelings I would pretend to read them, leaving them by my nightstand and advancing the bookmark to mark my progress.

I was at an age where I only wanted to watch TV. I would stay up at night, flipping through the late-night television shows. The one luxury we could afford was cable. Mom had subscribed to the local service, hoping I would stay around the house more. I did stay home most nights; not to watch TV, but because I had nothing else to do. I was in high school and didn't have many friends. Mom would shuffle around the apartment, nervously picking things up and putting them down somewhere else; making sure the clutter was in its place. There was some logic to where things went that would escape me once I moved out. When she acted this way, fixing and straightening everything, I wouldn't be able to relax until she went to bed.

"What was that?" my mom yelped, startled at the sound of a loud bang from over our heads. It was a Friday night in late September and I was fifteen years old; the two of us were in the living room watching television. "I hope it's not Mrs. Tremblay. Do you think she's had a fall?"

The bang had been followed by the bustle of feet running from, and back to, the location of the noise. "I'm sure she's fine," I said. "She probably dropped something." Still very much a kid, I was sprawled on the couch wearing sweats and tube socks, my gangly feet upon the coffee table.

"Maybe it was Mr. Tremblay," she said, turning her head towards the ceiling. "If he fell then she wouldn't be able to help him get up."

"Or maybe she knocked him down," I said, my eyes fixed on the last five minutes of some show. "You know, had enough of his old-man ways and took a swing at him with the Candlestick in the Conservatory. Maybe you should go help her hide the body."

"William," my mom chastised, suppressing a chuckle. "Don't joke about such things."

"Listen," I said, the bustling replaced by a frantic scrubbing. "The noise is coming from the kitchen. She probably dropped a jar and it spilled open or something ... Or maybe she's cleaning the blood off the floor."

"You're bad ..."

Mom went on with her knitting, glancing at a crossword by her side. She was adept at multi-tasking and could watch television and be busy with a project or two at the same time. She also made long lists of things to do that she would rewrite once enough of them were checked off. She must have been around thirty-seven then, still young and active, but when I look back I see her at fifty: small and thin, with a greying brown bob and a love of costume jewellery.

"So, how are you liking your job?" she asked once the show was over, making an overstitch. I had started my first part-time job, working under the table in the kitchen of a halfway-decent restaurant on St. Laurent. The place was located on the trendiest stretch of the Main, popular with both suits and wannabe starlets. I was underage, but we needed the money and my mom had a friend who knew the owner. All I did was wash dishes twice a week and listen to the cooks talk plainly about the women they'd screw. "Make any new friends?"

"Well, there's this one girl. Angie," I said, still watching the TV as the local newscast chimed on.

"Angie? Sounds pretty. Is she Italian?"

"I don't know if she's Italian, Mom," I grumbled. Angie was a couple of years older than me. The niece of the owner, she worked behind the bar. She was friendly with me in a way the waiters never were. She was a tomboy, slim and athletic, with long black hair she kept tight in a ponytail. I never saw her in a dress or anything the slightest bit feminine, just jeans and a T-shirt or the black uniform we all had to wear. Sometimes, when she'd reach up to get a bottle from the top shelf, I'd notice the waistband of her underwear. She wore Fruit of the Loom boys' briefs, which I found strange yet amusing. She was only three years older than me, but already she possessed a wealth of knowledge about many subjects — politics, cars, recent music and film, and places in Montreal I had never heard of. I knew almost nothing about our city. I was at an age where I still found myself watching the odd cartoon after school to distract me from my homework.

"How old is she? Does she go to school?"

"No. She's eighteen. She works full-time. She dropped out when her brother died." Angie hadn't told me this. I had learned it from one of the cooks on his cigarette break. "Leukemia."

My mom stopped knitting and shook her head. "That's terrible."

"It was misdiagnosed. They initially thought …"

"Oh, Will," she pleaded. "I don't want to hear any sad stories."

I stopped. She went back to her knitting. The local news began to report on a string of downtown robberies, the anchor in a serious blue suit with black bushy eyebrows. "Why don't you see what else is on?"

Yawning, I began to flip through the channels, looking for something we could watch, when I came across what appeared to be a bunch of men parading around in full-length gowns. My eyes grew wide and my whole body seized. Immediately I switched the channel, but not before having taken everything in. There were at least four of them on the screen, caked up in powder and wigs, belting out some song in a dark nightclub. And alongside them, among the flashing yellow bulbs, had been two buff men in nothing but red satin short shorts.

"Wait, go back," my mom started, keying in to the music but not the images. "Was that a musical?"

"I don't think so," I said, refusing to flip back. "It's in French." I knew that was enough for her to lose interest. My mom may have loved musicals, but the last thing she would have wanted to see was some brash American classic dubbed into French. Wordlessly she nodded, and went back to her knitting.

I, however, was curious. I had glimpsed enough flashes of skin to get me wide-eyed and alert. I knew I couldn't go back to the channel until she was out of the room.

I picked up the TV *Guide* under the guise of checking what was on and looked for the film's title. *Personne n'est parfait*, it said in the time slot with no additional information. "It doesn't look like there's anything on," I said, faking a yawn and switching back to the news.

Twelve anxious minutes later Mom rose from her seat. "Well, I'm off," she said, kissing me on my forehead. "Don't stay up too late."

It seemed as though it took forever for her to get to bed.

I waited until she was in her room with the door closed before I changed the channel. Instantly I was greeted by two men in bed: one dark-haired and fussy, the other light-skinned and sleepy. The sleepy one was topless, rolling over to expose his hairy chest and give his partner a good-morning kiss on the cheek. I was mesmerized.

I had missed the first twenty minutes, but it didn't matter. I had trouble understanding the film. It had undoubtedly been dubbed in France, and the French accent, much different from the Quebec one, was not something I was used to. I turned the volume down low so my mom wouldn't hear.

I recognized some of the actors, although I didn't know who they were. All but one. I remembered Matthew Broderick from *Ferris Bueller's Day Off*. In this movie, however, Matthew Broderick played a gay man.

I knew the word gay, and what it meant. I had been called it a number of times too — in the schoolyard, in gym class, on the street. But until now it had only been a slur; an insult I would try to ignore. This time it was different. The word was real, tangible. It had a shape, and I got to see what it looked like. Midway through the film, Matthew Broderick was kissed fully on the mouth by another man. Kissed in a haystack. Soft. Mouth open. Wide and down. Matthew closed his eyes and in that darkness I was kissed with him. The kiss set off something inside of me, and in those few perfect seconds I felt my body swell in a way it never had before.

I watched the film until the final credits. When it was over I got up and turned off the TV. I walked into my room, closed the door and clicked on the small table lamp on my desk. I opened the window to let in some air. Outside I could hear voices, neighbourhood boys in the night circling street lamps like buzzards on bikes.

Rummaging through my knapsack I took out a mix tape Angie had made me the week before and popped it into my stereo. Music sprang from the small speakers and I turned the volume down. Angie had filled both sides of the cassette with songs by bands she thought I should know about, bands with names like The Smiths and The Cure. "Your homework for tonight," she had said as she handed the tape over. The cassette was all decorated in silver pen, with shooting stars and kaleidoscopic curlicues on the jacket. I didn't know anything about music. All I knew was the popular stuff they played at our school dances. Angie's music was the opposite of all that. It was slower and pensive, with melodies that were wistful or brooding. At first I had found it cold, but its sound had begun to grow on me.

As I listened to the music I stood in front of the mirror, staring at myself for what felt like the first time. I saw a geeky teenager in a child's clothes, with unkempt greasy hair and traces of adolescent acne. I took off my shirt and stared at the concave of my chest. It wasn't ready; it was small and blank, an empty canvas all pale and smooth and nothing like the buff men in the movie. I began to brush my hair. I parted it a number of ways: on the left, on the right, in the middle, trying to unearth the hesitant young man beneath. Not bad, I thought. Maybe I'd try again tomorrow in daylight.

I turned around and looked at the walls of my bedroom decorated with magazine pages and pictures of pop stars and Hollywood actors. There was a poster Mom had brought home from the library a couple of years earlier advertising its 1991 Open House, and one of the furry Expos mascot waving fans into the Olympic Stadium. I couldn't remember why I had put them up.

I began to feel cold so I closed the window, shut off the music and slipped into bed. As I lay there, the yellow light from the street lamp climbing into bed with me, I thought again of the kiss on TV. I had jerked off to the thought of men before, but it was always to headless torsos. On this night, however, I reached below and allowed myself to think of a full-on kiss and whom I might share it with. I thought of Steve, this boy in my biology class whose bare arms I would sometimes stare at. I thought of Paul, this French boy with a strong jaw from the neighbourhood who commandeered our street on weekends for hockey games. And I thought of Pascal, one of the waiters from work who I had walked in on changing in the back, his flat furry stomach disappearing into his jeans. I thought of these boys, their lips, their hands, and then I thought about their hands touching me — broad, furry hands, worn and enveloping like those of my manager, who'd clasped mine firmly with his the day he hired me.

When I came it was thunderous, the sensation blaring through my head and body. This time it wasn't the image of a man that pushed me over the edge, but the idea of him, the imagined feel of his body pressing up against my own. It was electric.

Coming down, I was worried the riotous force of my orgasm had caused me to make a noise my mom, asleep in the next room, might have heard. Shaken, I quickly cleaned up with a tissue and threw it under the bed. I immediately fell asleep.

THE NEXT DAY WAS SATURDAY. It was a bright, beautiful day with a clear sky and a warm breeze. I wasn't working so I woke up late. Mom had already gone to her job. She had left a note on the kitchen table letting me know she'd be home around five and if I was hungry I could help myself to the leftover stew in the fridge. I spent most of the day listening to Angie's tape, scanning the dial on the radio to see if I could find more. I replayed the movie in my head, wondering what the English version was called and where I could find others like it. I went through things in my room, every drawer. I took all the juvenile posters off the wall, emptied my closet and bureau, and made piles of things to either toss or give away. I put everything in black garbage bags that greeted my mother when she got home from work.

"What's all this?" she said.

It was clothes she had once bought for me, remnants of toys I had held on to. Classic action figures, kids' books and pictures. "Stuff I don't want anymore," I told her. "I want to paint my room."

She came in and surveyed my room with wonder. I had stripped it of artifice. It was plain, fresh and ready to be plied with whatever I chose.

I felt like sharing what was happening to me with my mother, but I knew she wouldn't understand. And although I knew that Angie was somehow connected to all of this I wasn't sure if this was the time to talk to her about it either.

This knowledge was mine. It was the first thing I would ever truly own, and, for now, I wanted to keep it for myself.

Chapter

3

New Year's Eve came and went. I decided not to go out and rang in 2006 at home, reading, planning the homework I'd be assigning in over a week's time. The holidays had me on a different timetable — up until all hours, sleeping in late. Soon I would have to force myself back into the regular rhythm of the workweek. It was not something I was looking forward to.

Angie returned from New York on the Wednesday and I asked her, as requested, to join my mother and me for supper the following evening. Being a big fan of my mother's cooking, Angie dropped everything to come, including a dinner invitation from her own parents who had hoped to exchange Christmas presents with her.

I, too, love my mother's cooking, in particular her pasta sauce. I have such fond memories of the large aluminium pot that would sit on the back element of the stove, churning away inch after inch of deep red liquid until it was thick and flavourful. The sweet aroma of tomatoes and herbs would build throughout the day and fill our apartment. My mother had first learned the recipe from her sister, Mary, and although she says her sauce is never as good as her sister's, I believe it to be perfection.

"That was delicious, Mrs. Ambrose," Angie said once we were done, taking the initiative to get up and clear the plates.

"No, Angela, please sit down," my mother said, rising from her seat. "You're a guest."

Angie protested, but then sat back down as she was told. My mother took the plate from her and, placing it on top of her own, headed over to the sink.

Mom knows that Angie is a lesbian. Even though I, and every one of her friends, call her Angie, my mother insists on addressing her by her birth name. I suppose it's out of respect for Angie's parents, but I think it's also a subtle way of feminizing her, the verbal equivalent of applying blush to the cheeks of this boyish girl who in the summer sits at her dinner table in sneakers and a tank top. On this particular night, Angie was looking masculine in jeans, and wearing a black, short-sleeved "The Eagle NYC" T-shirt. She had cut her hair over the holidays, and now sported a thicket of short black curls on her head. I thought she looked great, but still took a moment to tease her about how much she looked like Betty Rizzo from *Grease*. A sarcastic "Peachy keen, jellybean" was her comeback.

I sopped up the remaining sauce on my plate with a piece of bread and then, popping it into my mouth, got up to help. I knew my mom wouldn't let me help either. "No. Go and sit down in the front," she said as I approached from behind with glasses and cutlery. "Please. You've helped enough today." All I had done was put up some blinds she had bought. "One more thing off the list," she added, and turned around to make a check mark on the paper square stuck to the fridge.

I left the dishes next to the sink before collapsing on the couch by the table. For some reason I am always tired at this address. There is something about the place, the food, the glow of the lights and the heat from the stove that lulls me into a state of drowsiness whenever I am over. All I felt like doing was taking a nap.

"You know, I think I do like those blinds," I yawned from where I slouched. Mom had bought these navy-coloured vertical blinds to replace the tattered brown curtains that had hung in the living room. At first I had been unsure about her choice, but that afternoon, with the retreating sun coming through the open slits, the blinds had given the room more light. "Well done."

"I like them too," she said over the spray of water. "So Monday's the big day?"

"No, Tuesday. One extra day before we have to go back to the gulag."

"But Will, you like your job!"

"I do, I do …" I acknowledged, petting the cat who had come up to see me. I had bought my mom a cat almost three years ago, about a month before I left home. I had figured that in order to leave, to start my life, I needed to leave something behind. Something besides my bedroom, which she kept furnished with my stuff, old school projects, photo albums, and childhood mementos. I wanted to give her something that would keep her company, someone she could talk to, so I got her a black and white tabby she named Elizabeth. My mom had once confessed to me that, although thrilled to have a son, she had hoped for a girl when she was pregnant. She told me that she would have named her daughter Elizabeth. I laughed so hard the day one of my mother's co-workers — who shared the same name as our cat — came over for lunch only to become mortified once my mother began to shoo "Elizabeth" out of the kitchen.

"What are you teaching when you get back?" asked Angie.

"We're doing the characteristics of a metropolis this semester," I said. "Stuff like population density, neighbourhoods, and city services. Their big assignment will be to imagine and create their own city on another planet."

"That's interesting," commented my mom. "Why another planet?"

"Just trying to make it more appealing. Most of my students seem more interested in the outer reaches of space than the realities of their own planet."

"Mrs. Ambrose," Angie started, standing by the fridge. "Will tells me it's your birthday next Saturday."

"I'm going to be fifty."

"Fifty!" Angie blurted, looking at me. "Will didn't tell me that." Angie's exclamation was suffused with the polite amount of surprise, but I felt she was putting it on a bit thick. My mom looked much older than her years and we all knew that. "That's a big deal. Are you going to do anything special?"

"We haven't discussed it yet," my mom said, casting a glance at me from across her shoulder. "My sister is coming to visit, though." Her only sibling, Mary, now lived in Venice, Florida, with her husband, Joe. It had been two years since her last visit and my mom was excited to see her. "I don't know what we'll do when she gets here. We'll definitely make some meals. She's a great cook."

"You must have been so young when you had Will," Angie said. "My parents are in their sixties."

"Yes, but you're the youngest," I said to Angie. Right away I wondered if that had been insensitive. I hadn't considered her younger brother, the one who had died. I had never known Marco. To me, Angie had only two older siblings, both of whom I had met. Marco was an invisible third who existed only in stories.

"Tell me, Angela," my mom said. "Your parents didn't mind you spending the holidays in New York, away from home?"

"I didn't give them much choice," Angie said, almost apologizing. "But I'm thirty-one, and that's more than old enough to do what I want. My mom wasn't too keen on the idea since she wanted the whole family together but, in the end, she saw it as a great opportunity. I mean, how often do you get to stay in someone's apartment for two weeks in New York rent-free?" Angie and her friend Carol had been dog-sitting at a friend's place in Brooklyn over the holidays. I had been invited to join them, but opted instead to stay in town. I couldn't imagine leaving my mother alone at Christmas.

"It must be beautiful there this time of the year," my mom said. "All the lights and decorations. And all the people out, doing their last-minute shopping and on their way to fancy dinners and parties." I could see her picturing the bright lights and fast cars. "I've always wanted to go to New York City."

More surprise from Angie. "You've never been?"

"Are you kidding?" I said, moving to a horizontal position on the couch. "She's never been anywhere. Like me."

"I had the chance to go, once, when I was a teenager," my mom remembered. "With an aunt and uncle who were going down to visit. But in the end I got nervous and backed out."

"What happened?"

"It all seemed too much hassle."

I hadn't heard this story before, but it didn't surprise me. My mom had always talked about wanting to travel, picturing herself in exotic places and situations. She often spoke about going down to visit her sister in Florida, but it was always Aunt Mary who came up. One Mother's Day I tried to get my mom to come with me to Ottawa for the day to check out the annual Tulip Festival. She had seen an article in the paper the week before and went on and on about how nice it would be to go. Her interest dwindled once I offered to rent us a car.

"Well, that's what you should do for your fiftieth," Angie said. "You should take her to New York, Will."

"No," said my mother.

"Why not?" Angie rose from where she sat at the table, grabbing a cloth by the stove to dry the plates now crowding the dish rack. She proceeded to list for my mother her favourite places in the city: Coney Island, the Guggenheim, and 42nd Street. "You of all people have to see a show on Broadway at least once in your life."

"One day, perhaps. Thank you, Angela," my mom responded. She had listened attentively and would pretend to consider the idea. "Speaking of musicals," she continued, looking up at the clock in the kitchen, "the classics continue. *My Fair Lady* is on tonight. Would you like to stay and watch it with me?"

"Oooh, *My Fair Lady*!" Angie swooned. Angie is such a fag. She has this enormous crush on Audrey Hepburn. I can't count the number of times she has made me sit through her films — her favourite being *The Children's Hour*. One Halloween she even convinced me to play Fred to her Holly Golightly (we often dressed up as pairs). It had sounded fun at the time, but I looked nothing like George Peppard and it soon began to wear thin once I had to explain to everyone who I was.

"We can't," I answered for both of us. "Angie and I have plans."

"You're going out?" she asked, surprised, taking her hands out of the sink and drying them.

"I told you we wouldn't be able to stay late. Remember? That's why we came early."

"It's our friend Izo's birthday," Angie explained.

"Izo? That's a funny name."

"Rizzo and Izo!" I joked.

Angie rolled her eyes. "It's short for Isabelle, Mrs. Ambrose."

"But maybe I'll come back tomorrow? For lunch?" I said to please her and then looked at Angie. "But we are supposed to meet them soon. What time is it?"

"Where's that watch I gave you?"

I couldn't bear to tell my mom that I thought I had lost it. For Christmas she had given me this beautiful black watch. It was sleek and simple. It was analog, with hands and a crown. My mom told me that she figured it would come in handy whenever I gave tests in class. I could picture her at the store, in front of the counter, envisioning me at my desk looking down at the watch and then saying with authority, "All right, everyone, pencils down!"

"I left it at home."

"Can you stay for some coffee? There's cake."

I squirmed in my silence. Mom knew not to push it. "All right, okay, you two get out of here. Have fun."

I summoned a burst of energy to propel me off the couch. Angie put down the dishrag and the two of us grabbed our sweaters and jackets.

"I don't understand how you don't freeze in that." My mother said, looking at the two spring jackets I was layering on top of my black sweater. "You're lucky you haven't caught a cold."

I hadn't owned a proper winter coat in more than two years. I could never find one I liked, the most affordable being gargantuan and unflattering, so instead I opted for layers, piling two thin jackets on top of a thick wool sweater that the cold would still penetrate. "Believe me, I'm fine, Mom."

We both kissed my mom goodbye and headed out the door.

OUTSIDE WE WERE GREETED BY the slicing cold. Angie took a few obligatory steps past the building before lighting up. She took in a drag from her cigarette and exhaled as if she had been holding in the air all night.

"Aren't you a little old to be hiding that from my mother?" I teased.

"Oh, shut up," she said innocently. "I'm not going to smoke in front of your mom, Will. I'm already a disappointment to my own mother, don't make me out to be one to yours, too."

"I'm sure she knows you smoke, Angie. Oh, give me one." And with a greedy hand I dove into her coat pocket.

She chuckled and helped to retrieve the pack. "What are you doing? Do you really want to start up again?"

"One here and there … it can't hurt."

We walked briskly towards Laurier Metro, skating halfway.

"So, really, how was New York?" I felt that Angie had held back while telling us about her trip over dinner.

"It was incredible. We went out every night and I spent way too much money. Carol got wasted at this dive in the East Village on our first night. We met a bunch of these cool boys at this boy bar that played the best music. It was all on this jukebox in the corner of the room. Can you believe it? All these great albums on a jukebox. Why don't Montreal bars have jukeboxes? Where are all the jukeboxes?"

Within several cold minutes, enough to smoke most of our cigarettes, Angie and I were inside once more, our legs and hands burning as we entered the Metro and peeled off our tuques and scarves. Downstairs, on the platform, we waited for the train. There weren't many people around: a man made use of a public telephone, a woman read a newspaper on a bench, and across the tracks a gang of boys in oversized jackets hung out. I could hear the echoing rumble of an approaching train but couldn't tell from which direction it was coming.

Angie looked at me as a train on the opposite side of the tracks pulled into the station. "So, you'll never guess who's going to be there tonight. Geneviève!"

"Geneviève?" I searched. "Mel's girlfriend?"

"Ex-girlfriend. They broke up over the holidays." Angie couldn't hold in her excitement and began to do a little dance. "She's an Aries!" A Sagittarius herself, Angie was an ardent believer in astrology and regularly studied the positions of the planets and their influence. Each new love interest was always flung through the stars to check for compatibility. It seemed that Geneviève was a perfect match. "Come here," she said, and pulled me towards a map of the city on the subway wall. "See." She pointed to an intersection of streets that made up the corner of Drolet and Rachel. "This is where she lives."

"How do you know where she lives?"

"Shut up, I know everything. See, this is where she lives. So if you don't see me for the next little while it'll be because I'll be at her place ... or over here," she said, pointing to the block in Little Italy that she called home. She then drew an invisible line with her finger connecting the two. "Both places. Back and forth, back and forth, until my knees give out."

"Confident much?"

"I'm going to ask her out, Will, and she is going to say yes."

I may have teased Angie about her confidence, but that's because I knew she had it in abundance. Angie was notorious among the Village's dykes for being a great lay. There was never a lack of women wanting to climb into her bed. Why couldn't I be more like that?

I stared at the city map beside my friend and looked for my own points of interest. This map was not unlike the ones on the walls of my classroom. It had the same kinds of icons, the same lines, the same legend in the corner. But on this one I saw something more elusive. This map charted the years of my life as if they were just another feature on a crowded transit map. I could see in the spot where Angie had pointed out her own address all the conversations and beers and dinners that had taken place. And then there was her old place too, near the hospital. How many nights had I crashed on that couch? Where my mother lived — and where I'd grown up — I could see all the hours spent in my bedroom with the door closed, music playing. And then I saw all the lost hours at Max's place, on Montgomery, located a ways over and a block from the green circle that was the Frontenac Metro station. How many times had I biked those streets in between his home and mine on Édouard-Charles, a stubby, almost-forgotten block located west of Parc Avenue?

It's a cliché to call a city boulevard an artery, but I could clearly see the metaphor on the map. Blue and red lines thrown across the black and beige like a person's circulatory system, the bus stops and Metro tunnels spread out from a central hub. All these horizontal, vertical, and diagonal lines taking people in all directions, and I felt immobile, trapped beneath them as if by some invisible net.

"What's the matter, Will? You're so quiet."

"Nothing," I said, coming to. But then, feeling the need to say something more, I added, "I suppose I feel a bit guilty about leaving like that. My mom would've loved it if we had stayed and watched the movie with her."

"I know your mom, Will, and she doesn't lay nearly as much guilt on you as my mother does."

"No, I don't mean that," I said. "She doesn't make me feel guilty, I do. I know she'd like me to be around more. And the truth is I enjoy spending time with her. It's just ... I don't know. I feel so distracted these days. Not very present, even when I'm with her."

Angie turned around and leaned up against the wall. "What's up?"

"Nothing," I lied again. I had learned not to talk to Angie about Max. Each time I brought him up she would get annoyed. Although I knew she had my best interests at heart, I could hear the frustration in her voice when she offered me advice. My recovery couldn't happen fast enough. "I just have a lot on my mind. Work stuff."

"Well, if you don't feel like you're spending enough quality time with your mom, then make the time."

"You're right," I said, putting my hands in my coat pockets and looking at the tips of my sneakers. "I should do something special for her fiftieth."

"New York!"

"You know my mom, Angie. She'll never agree to go to New York."

Angie considered it. "Well, there must be *something* you know that she'd like. What about getting her tickets to see *Cats*? I heard it's coming to town this summer."

"Andrew Lloyd Webber, Angie?"

"They're not for you, selfish!"

"You're right." My mom would never buy a ticket to a show she wanted to see. She'd see the posters and ads, read the interviews and reviews in the newspapers. She might even clip the articles for me, but she'd never go by herself. "It's a great idea."

The two of us went quiet for a minute, checking out the crimson faces of the people coming down the stairs. Angie then turned back towards me, hands in her pockets, and looked at me askew. "You sure you're okay?"

"Yes, sure, I'm fine," I said. "Peachy keen, jellybean."

Angie stuck out her tongue.

Soon enough the train arrived. We rode the three stops to Berri Station, talking more about Geneviève than anything else, and got off to walk towards the Village.

AFTER PULLING OUT SOME CASH at the ATM we headed over to meet Angie's friends at Adonis, a seedy male strip club at the far end of the Village. Adonis is a funny place: small and dingy with exposed brick walls that remain hidden within the club's dark shadows. The regular crowd is a mix of older men, young hustlers, and drug dealers, but for the past few weeks Thursday nights were Ladies' Night, the only time women were allowed. Drinks were cheaper and the dancers more eager to take it all off for the gender many of them preferred. But word was out among the ladies-who-lez that this was the place to start Thursday evenings. Two pitchers of beer cost a ridiculous twelve bucks, shooters were a dollar. Women could come by early in the night and get a buzz going before hitting the clubs. On this particular Thursday the place was packed with lesbians. It was Izo's birthday and she had invited a large group of her friends. As Angie and I walked in we could see that her gang had commandeered three tables near the back of the bar. About a dozen dykes, many dressed like young boys with clipped hair, tight T's, and baggy jeans, were crowded together — much to the confusion of the bar's older patrons who often mistook these girls for young twinks.

"Will! You sassy homosexual!" Izo yelled, pulling me in to kiss her on the mouth. "Where the fuck have you guys been?"

"Okay, you're drunk," I said, taking a seat and looking at the numerous pitchers on the table. "I'm seriously going to need to catch up. Where's the waiter?"

"We had dinner at Will's mom's place," Angie explained, sitting down in an empty seat beside Geneviève. "You're lucky we came at all. We could be watching *My Fair Lady* with her right now."

"Hot for Will's mom, Angie?" Izo ragged. I could tell from Angie's returning glare she had told Izo of her plans for Geneviève, and it was clear that Izo would now do her best to embarrass her friend.

"What did Will's mother make you?" Franny asked.

"Spaghetti." Angie rubbed her belly. "It was delicious."

"I love spaghetti! You have to invite me over one day, Will," Franny said.

"Me too," said Carol.

Geneviève remained quiet and watched Angie out of the corner of her eye.

Over the next hour we got blitzed, our tables crowded with packs of smokes, dirty ashtrays, and empty shot glasses. More of Izo's friends arrived and staked out tables nearby. The girls ran the room. The din of our conversations besieged the action on the stage. The men stripping seemed confused as to why there were so many women in the bar who were not paying them any attention. It caused a few of them to lose their erections.

If indifferent, these girls were not repulsed by the parade of naked men before us. They were curious, and shared criticisms as if judging a beauty pageant. Together we'd analyze their bodies, comment on choreography, wardrobe, and song selection. Many of these girls had never before seen a penis in the flesh. Together, they ganged up on me with questions: "Do you prefer cut or uncut men?" "Does size matter?" "What if it's too big?" "What about balls, what do you do with those?" I didn't know how to answer them. What is it I like about a man's body? I knew I didn't quite care for the sculpted muscles and hairless pelts these strippers wore on stage. In reality, what I wanted was much more than a body part. I wanted roundness, softness, depth.

About an hour after we arrived, I saw what I was looking for. A gang of three girls and one boy entered the bar and sat down at a nearby table. We all noticed them, except for Angie and Geneviève who were deep in conversation. I could tell the girls were straight by the way they dressed and the way they watched the Latin dancer remove his briefs. But it was their friend who stole my attention. My gaze kept being drawn from the action on the stage to the table where he sat. He was tall and attractive: lean, handsome, with smooth pale skin and a dark mess of waves on his head. Emanating from his cheeks were blushes of red — from either the beer or the bar. He reminded me of a Raggedy Andy doll, lopsided in his seat.

I turned back to our table to where Angie was busy courting Geneviève. Reaching for her smokes, Angie opened up the pack and offered one to her love interest. Coyly, Geneviève removed a cigarette and drew it to her lips. Angie took one out for herself and snapped her Zippo, cupping the flame as she lit Geneviève's smoke. Sometimes I think the only reason left to smoke is so someone else can light your cigarette for you. I have always marvelled at the way Angie has girls eating out of her hand. She knows what to do, what to say, where to place her arm. In many ways she is such a better fag than I. She knows how to charm members of the same sex. Knows how to be one of the guys. I watched her body language as she leaned into the conversation, conveying interest, straining to listen over the loud music. Then, subtly, she placed her right hand on top of Geneviève's left knee. And that was it. You'd have thought the entire world had stopped, the look Geneviève had on her face.

There was a big round of applause. The next dancer had revealed his cock, a long, thick pole of flesh with a distracting inch of foreskin. But he was already losing his hard-on, sauntering across the stage to some generic power ballad. I actually found him cute, despite the song. He wasn't too muscled and hadn't shaved off his chest hair and pubes the way most of the dancers had.

I looked back towards Raggedy Andy. He was checking out the dancer, but with no smile on his face. The beer in his fist was almost empty, the label torn off and in shreds in the ashtray.

All of a sudden I knew what I had to do. Propelled by a rising sense of urgency, I sat straight up in my chair, my hands on my knees. "Carol, switch seats with me?"

"Why?" she hollered from her end of the table.

"Quick. Before I lose my nerve."

Carol rose from her chair, a metre from Raggedy Andy, and came over to where I sat. I got up and uttered a hushed "Thanks" as I passed her by.

Raggedy Andy noticed the switch as I sat down, but returned his gaze to the bottle in front of him. I must have been drunker than I thought because before I knew it I did something I never do. I leaned in and said hello.

"Hello," he responded with a polite smile.

"I'm sorry to bother you, but my friends and I are conducting a survey," I said. "How you would rate this guy?" I motioned towards the stage.

He looked puzzled. "What do you mean? On a scale of one to ten? A five, maybe?"

"A five? I'd give him a seven. At least he doesn't have shaved lands."

"Shaved what?"

"Shaved lands. You know … down there … He keeps the lawn trim but hasn't buzzed off the bush."

That got a small chuckle from him. "I don't know," he said. "He's not my type. I don't really come to these kinds of places."

"Oh, me neither," I lied. "But it's my friend's birthday." I pointed over to the corner where Izo sat, getting a lap dance from a moustachioed man in athletic shorts. Incredulous, she sat there with a petrified look on her face, plotting her revenge on the friends who had bought it for her. "What about you? What brought you out tonight?"

"My friends thought I needed some cheering up. I think it's doing the opposite." He spoke wryly, as if everything he was saying was meant to be funny.

"I'm Will." I offered my hand.

"James," he said and shook. The exchange pulled his friends' attention from the stage and they began to whisper.

"How about them? Are they enjoying the show?"

"Definitely," he said, glancing at his girlfriends. "You'd think your friends wouldn't be the type, though." We both looked over to Izo, who could no longer stifle her laugh, as the man, now buck naked, swayed about on her lap. His penis, semi-erect, was bobbing up and down in front of her like a paddleball, causing Franny and Carol to double over with laughter at our table.

"They're on a field trip," I joked. "Some kind of archaeological dig. I won't tell you what they found in the bathroom."

That got another chuckle out of him, the sound so great as it fell out of his frown. "So ... James, what is it you do?"

"I'm a medical student. Second year at McGill."

"Are you from Montreal?"

"Why do you ask?" he answered. "Don't I sound like I could be from here?"

"Yes. I didn't mean anything by that. It's just ... I don't know, sometimes you ask silly things when you want to get to know someone."

He smiled. "Halifax. I'm originally from Halifax."

"Halifax. I've never been. What's it like?"

"Different," he shrugged. "Beautiful. Progressive. Unpretentious. I'm sure you'd find it boring."

"Boring? Why do you say that?"

"It's nothing like this."

"Please, do not take this as being representative of what I find exciting," I said. "I've always wanted to visit Halifax. Well, all of Canada. But the farthest I've been is Ottawa, and that was to go to Parliament and the National Gallery on a school trip."

James nodded, and looked again at the stage. "What about you?" I asked. "Besides the strippers, how do you find Montreal?"

"It's great," he said, swallowing a gulp of his diminishing beer. "Montreal is a beautiful place. There are so many things going on, so much to do. I love the different languages, the culture ... But it can be a bit overwhelming at times. I'm happy to be here, but I don't know if I could live here — permanently, I mean — once I graduate."

The dancer finished his song, kissed his fingers, and sent it off to the crowd. Everyone clapped. Izo, relieved her own dance was also over, ran to our cluster of tables and dragged Franny and Carol with her to the bathroom. The space more bare, I now noticed that Angie and Geneviève had progressed in their courtship and the two were kissing, deeply, Angie's hands running up the girl's thighs. The sight of the two of them, as restrained as any two passionate people can be in such a crowded bar, made me anxious and keenly aware of what I too was attempting.

I looked at James and he smiled into his bottle. I noticed it was empty.

"Can I buy you a drink?"

"Um, sure," he said. "Thanks."

I grabbed the waiter and ordered. "So," I said, hoping the purchase allowed me to ask something more personal. "If I may ask, what's got you so blue that you needed cheering up tonight?"

He sighed with amused resignation. "I got dumped," he said, the look on his face more exasperated than sad. "A couple weeks ago. My boyfriend of three years, who moved to Montreal to be with me when I got in to McGill, ended up leaving me before Christmas for a co-worker of his."

"Yeeesh," I offered.

"Yeah. No. I'll be all right," he replied, not permitting any sympathy. "It was for the best anyway."

"What do you mean?" I asked, the question as much a surprise to me as it was to him.

I didn't think James was going to answer at first, but there must have been something trusting about my face because he soon opened up as though we were good friends. "I don't think we were together for the right reasons," he said. "We were too comfortable. We wanted different things. Thanks," he acknowledged as the beer came and I paid for it. James went on to tell me the story of how his boyfriend told him one night that he wanted out, that he'd been sleeping with a co-worker he had now developed feelings for. "He told me he needed to experiment. He needed to be with someone who appreciated him. So he moved out and went to live with him."

James went quiet for a moment, stifling the resentment that had begun to build in his voice. "I wasn't sure he was the right one for me, but when he said he wanted to leave Halifax to be with me in Montreal I thought, wow, okay, I guess this is for real. But in the end I think he wanted an excuse to leave, you know? He wanted to know what it would be like to live in a big, anonymous city. I was his reason to go. Anyways …" He tagged on the last word as if to disregard all he had said before.

I recognized the anger and disappointment in James's face. Like the dancers in the bar, James too was stripping before me, his emotions raw and exposed. The exchange felt intimate, much more so than the action on the stage. I couldn't pretend not to notice the similarities between us, both set adrift by the ones we loved. And although his situation was different from mine, his words echoed everything I had hidden for months. James was handsome. His pain was attractive. There was a beauty in his sadness, unlike my own, a faith that all was not lost. And just below the heartache I could see glimpses of strength, the unapologetic hero who would pick himself up once he was done nursing his wounds and get on with his life, no worse for wear.

"I can't believe I'm telling you this," he said. "We just met. You're going to think I'm crazy."

"No, I don't think you're crazy," I said. "In fact, you sound quite sane — saner than I am, in any case."

He leaned back in his chair and smiled, the blood still swirling in his cheeks. I wanted him so much right then. Wanted him inside, outside, around, and through me. Men as handsome as James are rarely single. And here he was in front of me, reclining in his chair in perilous comfort daring me to catch him.

But I couldn't. What would be the point? All I could aspire to be would be a rebound, a midway point between two great loves. He would work out his frustrations with me and I'd prime him for the next person. That is, unless his old partner came back once he realized the grass isn't greener out there. It's just shaved lands.

Carol and Franny came back from doing lines with Izo in the boys' bathroom. They tapped the girls at our table on the shoulders and they all got up and picked up their coats. "We're leaving, I guess," I told him. "We're going to dance. At Parking. You're welcome to join us if you want."

James smiled and gripped his bottle. "That's nice of you, Will, thanks, but I think I'm going to stay with my friends. You have fun. It was nice meeting you. Thanks for the beer!"

"WERE HIS FRIENDS DYKES?" CAROL wanted to know once we were outside.

"What do you think?" I said. We walked to Parking, Angie and Geneviève holding hands.

"Did you get his number?"

"No."

"Why not?"

"Because he just got dumped."

"So?"

"I don't need to be the rebound guy."

"Will," said Angie. "That's exactly what you need."

PARKING NIGHTCLUB WAS A RIOTOUS mix of men and women. Pill-popping eighteen-year-olds out all week danced alongside middle-aged businessmen who'd be getting up early the next morning. Wanting to avoid a hangover, I switched to drinking water. The girls continued to drink themselves silly — except Angie and Geneviève, who disappeared upon arrival.

I spent the rest of the night hanging out with Carol, Izo, and Franny, and watching the groups of men dancing by the speaker on the main floor. Carol, somewhat inebriated, was telling me about her time in New York. "You really should have come with us, Will," she hollered. "It was so much fun. And you'd have liked the boys! They were so nice and cute. Angie kept turning to me to say how much you'd like this one or that one."

"Yes, she's a regular pimp," I said, not surprised. "If I spent as much time trying to get me laid as she does, perhaps I wouldn't be going home alone again tonight."

Carol squeezed my elbow. "You should've asked that guy for his number!"

"I know, I know," I admitted. The girls were upset I had done nothing about James, but no one was more disappointed than I. Why hadn't I done anything? He was sitting there, right in front me, smiling, laughing at the things I had said. I couldn't remember a time I had felt so confident. Perhaps that was the reason I left things the way I did. My brief confidence had made me believe if this was indeed meant to be, then I would be seeing him again. Right now, though, that felt doubtful. I had considered running back to Adonis to ask James for his number, but that seemed crazy. I'd wait until I ran into him again. "Next time, I promise."

"You need to realize you're a catch," Carol said, drunk serious. I couldn't help but laugh. A little nerdy, she was small and feisty, with short dark hair and thick glasses. She pretended to be so hardcore with her pierced septum and sleeve tattoos, but she was a lightweight in comparison to her friends.

"Thanks, Carol. You're a sweetheart."

ABOUT AN HOUR LATER, STILL glued to the bar, I saw James standing on the other side of the club, hands in pockets, watching the crowd.

I shot straight up. "See you guys later," I said to no one in particular and revolved around the axis of the dance floor. All night I had wondered what I would say if I saw him again, but none of those words came to mind as I pulled up beside him and tapped him on the shoulder. "James?"

"Will," he said, apparently happy to see me.

"This is a nice surprise. I thought you weren't coming."

"Yes, well, the dancers kept getting worse," he said, smirking. "You left at the right time." By the looseness of his speech, I could tell James was drunker than before. The sweat from his brow further curled his hair at its edges.

"Are you here alone?"

"My friends were tired and called it a night, but I didn't feel like going home."

"Can I get you something? A bottle of water?" I didn't wait for an answer. I dragged him up to the bar and ordered two bottles of water. I realized, as I handed his over, that I was more nervous than before. What had happened to the self-assured boy in the strip club who had chatted up a complete stranger? I had spent the last hour regretting not asking him out, and now stood frozen before my next opportunity. I didn't know what to say.

"Have you been to Parking before?"

"Once," he said. "Last summer." James looked up to the ceiling and the open clusters of mirrored lights that burst through the room like shooting stars. "I had forgotten how big and loud it is." He looked back to me. "We have only one gay club in Halifax. It's nothing like this. Just a small dance floor, a smoke machine, and a DJ booth that sits right off the bar. I used to think my hometown was boring, but maybe it's not boring. Maybe it's just, like you said … sane."

What he said sounded ridiculous. "And Montreal is crazy?"

"A little bit. Or maybe a lot. I don't know, you've lived here longer than I have. Doesn't this get to you? The pace? The noise? The way people treat each other?" James placed his hand on my shoulder as he spoke and I realized, from his grip, how drunk he really was. "I've only been here a year and a half and already I'm exhausted."

For support I placed my arm around his waist. "Montreal isn't crazy," I said, smelling his sweat on the collar of his untucked shirt. "Sure, it's got some attitude, but what large city doesn't? I don't think you've been here long enough to see how great it is. Then again," I said, setting up for a laugh, "if you're using Parking and Adonis as reference points then, yes, I can see how you think it might be a little crazy."

I got what I wanted. James smiled, the rose in his cheeks spreading further throughout his face. He put his arm around my shoulders. "Will, you're a cute guy," he said. "What are you doing here?" James's face was serious. I couldn't tell if he was hitting on me or simply asking a question.

"I don't know," I said, flummoxed. "More social anthropology." This time he didn't find what I said funny.

"I couldn't imagine researching this," he said, removing his arm and using it to unscrew the cap from his water bottle. "In scientific research there's always the next question," he went on. "The research is never over. Each question leads to another and then another. I couldn't research this. I'd go insane." James took a swig from his water. I looked at him and saw a puppy, one whose paws were turning from soft pink to hard brown. I then looked across the suffocating dance floor and saw the club as he did: the past, the pain and the next question.

"What time is it?" he asked.

"I don't know," I shrugged. "Must be close to midnight."

James considered this. "I think I should go."

"You're not going now," I said to him in the way a drinking buddy might. "Stay. Keep me company."

"I have to get up early tomorrow," he said, responsibly.

"Can I get your number?" I blurted.

"Sure." James walked over to the bar and asked for a pen and wrote his number on the back of a matchbook.

"It was nice to meet you, James," I said, and leaned in to give him a double-cheek kiss good night. As I approached his face he balked, nervous. I had forgotten how boys from outside Montreal aren't used to kissing goodbye on both cheeks. He hugged me awkwardly, and left.

Once he was gone I realized I didn't want to be here either. It was too loud and hot and packed. I caught sight of the face of a watch on the sweat-slicked arm of the man standing next to me. It was ten after midnight and the club showed no signs of slowing down — the dance floor swelling to capacity. I looked across from where I stood. The girls were still dancing and drinking. I decided not to say good night to anyone. Finding a ten-dollar bill in my pocket, I ducked outside and hailed a cab.

THE NEXT MORNING I COULDN'T remember how James looked. In my memory he was young, soft, beautiful, but when I tried to picture him I drew a blank and thought of the Raggedy Andy doll, a ghost of his image in my head. What I could remember, however, was his voice as he spoke over the loud speakers. I remembered his posture, his boots, his jeans, his dark wavy hair, and the smell of his shirt. I could remember these individual details but not the whole. It was as if I'd woken up from a deep sleep, my arms heavy and full of pins and needles. James's face was hazy and I couldn't make out its profile. It was just out of reach, elusive, and then remade. James's image became replaced by that of Max; solid, clear, and never-ending.

This would never work.

I took the matchbook James had scribbled his phone number on and threw it into the trash. How could this boy from Halifax compete with the one in Montreal who still had my heart? Whose city was my own, and who I still saw in its streets? No, like New York, Halifax was another city I wouldn't be visiting soon. I had thought I was getting better, but I had underestimated Max's power. And when I closed my eyes I could still feel his gravitational pull across time and space, holding me within his orbit.

C
h
a
p
t
e
r

4

I'm amazed that I became a geography teacher. English teacher would've made more sense. Geography was one of the classes I hated most in high school. Maybe it was the teachers I had, or the dull brown textbooks with their lifeless copy that made my brain struggle to stay awake, but up until I began to focus on my studies and prepare for my education degree, I couldn't tell you anything about Canada's boreal forest or where to find Abitibi-Témiscamingue on a map. No, in the beginning, the most important geography lessons I learned were outside the classroom.

For instance, I learned about the city of Regina because that is where Shaun Findley was from. Shaun Findley, whose body was like the Prairies, his chest as flat as Saskatchewan, overlain with rolling wisps of golden hair. He was the first guy I slept with. He was twenty-five and I was eighteen. During the two weeks we saw each other I would sit up in my room at night and flip through my old high school textbooks, reading from chapters on the Prairie provinces: Manitoba, Saskatchewan, Alberta. I'd look at the photos of the flatlands and think of him: rural images of farmers on tractors collecting wheat, beautiful red sunsets bleeding into the unbroken horizon, no mountains for miles.

But Montreal has a mountain — and the west side of Mount Royal glared at me disapprovingly through the large windows of Shaun's Westmount apartment. Shaun lived in a giant yellow concrete monster on Sherbrooke Street West that faced a small park behind which ran a climbing row of expensive houses. The building had a deafening buzzer that would let me in and follow me up the stairs to the second floor. The noise gave me the impression of being buzzed in to visit a prisoner, and I couldn't shake the feeling each time I climbed those stairs that there was indeed something sketchy about the man I was coming to see.

I found it odd that Shaun could afford such a lavish place on a Gap clerk's salary. The apartment was modern and spacious, much nicer than where I lived with my mother, with high ceilings and hardwood floors. It had one bedroom, a large bathroom, a kitchen, and an enormous open living room with one mirrored wall that led to three giant windows he opened when he smoked. It made the apartment cold.

I was at his place one rainy November day after having slept over. Outside, the trees were sad, bare, having lost most of their foliage. Their nakedness allowed me to see through the woods and into the exposed, warmly lit houses that would normally have been hidden from view. On this morning he seemed distant, with the same blank look he'd had the previous night when I met him for a movie. Shaun walked around the apartment in silence, getting dressed, making breakfast, and watering his plants.

After we ate, Shaun's friend François came by to pick up some pot. The three of us hung out in the living room while François rolled his joints, cutting them with tobacco on the hard silver cover of Madonna's *Sex* book. While we waited for him to finish, Shaun told me about Regina, showing me where it was by tracing a map of Canada with his index finger on his living room's plush carpet floor. "Did you know when the city was founded it was treeless?" he asked. "And most of the trees and shrubs were planted by man?" With broad strokes Shaun continued to outline the trajectory of cities he had lived in over the years. "We moved to Calgary when I was sixteen and then I went to Vancouver for college for a couple of years before moving here last June."

"What do you think of Montreal?" I asked.

"It's okay," he offered. "I'm meeting a lot of people, but finding it hard to make good friends … Except for you, François darling."

François smiled. He didn't say much. Every so often he'd rise from his chair, tall and birdlike, and head over to the kitchen to get something, apologizing each time he walked over the country. "Oops … sorry, Canada!" he'd giggle with his Quebec accent, destroying borders with his John Fluevogs. Once he was done rolling, François expertly wet the sides of one of the joints and sparked it up. Almost at once, Shaun rose from where he was sitting next to me and took the joint from François. He inhaled deeply as he walked towards the windows. I didn't smoke; just sat frozen on his living room floor, south of Ontario, and watched the two of them.

"I've decided," said Shaun, taking another toke before passing the joint back to his friend, "that I'm not going to fall in love this year."

"Darling," François exhaled, "I think that's a fabulous idea."

I HAD MET SHAUN THROUGH Angie, one Tuesday night at K.O.X. The weekly party was called Zucchini. G-stringed cowboys in suede chaps and leather Stetsons danced atop speakers to underground house, while bartenders in briefs served two-for-one beers. The club was part of a sprawling complex called Station C, an old post office that had been gutted and revamped into a multi-level discotheque. Outside, the building had kept its initial majesty — concrete walls with stone columns and ornate cornices — while inside, the space had turned into a sexual hotspot. The club housed three very different bars: a small dyke club named Sisters upstairs; a men-only leather dungeon named Katakombs downstairs; and in the centre, where the main entrance opened into a gigantic hall, was K.O.X., a pansexual circus featuring the most outlandish creatures I had ever seen. The place reminded me of a high school gymnasium, what with its court-sized dance floor and rows of wooden bleachers running up to the rafters, but the similarity ended there as the place was still very much a noisy club with six stations for booze and clusters of dim lamps and antique couches at the back. A thick gloss of sexual possibility highlighted everything, from the crowded unisex bathrooms to the drag queens who worked the door. I remember there being an old-fashioned photo booth in one of the far corners of the room and, remarkably, a mid-sized swimming pool that was set up for a couple of weeks one hot July.

I was sitting with Angie on one of the couches, watching the crowd and nursing my beer, when I saw two men catch her eye and walk towards us.

"Quick. Stand up," Angie ordered.

I stood up with her as the two men approached. I had known Angie for three years by then, and it never ceased to surprise me how many gay men she knew. "Hey boys," she sang her greeting, kissing them hello on both cheeks. "Fancy running into you here."

"We're slumming until the baths get hopping," the tall one said, twisting his lips to the amusement of his gorgeous, bespectacled, friend.

Angie sighed. "You guys are lucky. If only we had saunas for women in this city."

"What would be the point, dear?" the tall one responded. "You've already slept with them all."

There was a dark collective chuckle, Angie laughing along. "All right, all right," she said. "Let's not get into who's more whorish, okay?" She turned and placed her hand on my shoulder. "Guys, have you met my friend Will? Will, this is François and Shaun."

"Hello," I said, shaking both of their hands but looking only at Shaun. He was striking; handsome and smart-looking, with dark blond hair and a wide smile.

"Will." He repeated my name over the music and into my ear. "Have we met?"

"No … I don't think so." I knew I would have remembered him.

"Are you from here?"

I looked over to see Angie pulling François aside. "Yes," I said. "Are you?"

"No, I'm from out west," he took a sip from the straw jutting out of his plastic cup. "Regina. I moved here this past summer to go to school. I'm studying political science at Concordia."

"Well, you came to the right place," I smiled. "Quebec is never boring when it comes to politics."

"That's why I wanted to come."

"Do you speak French?" I asked, trying to compete with the club's pounding bass.

"I speak four languages," he answered with pride. "You kind of *need* to if you're serious about getting into politics."

"What other languages do you speak?"

"Italian and German. You?"

"Just English and French …" I couldn't stop myself from staring at Shaun's lips, the divine curves that professed to speak all those languages. "So, how do you know François? Is he also from Regina?" That was a stupid question. Anyone could tell by his name and accent that François was a Quebecer. I wanted to know if they were an item. But before Shaun could answer he was being whisked away. François, excitedly singing along to the song now playing, was dragging his friend to the dance floor. Shaun shrugged and waved as he left. I soon lost sight of the two of them among the crowd and smoke.

We sat back down on the couch.

"Where did you meet those two?"

"At a Visual Arts exhibit at Concordia a couple of months ago," Angie said. "François's a student in the program and had a piece in the show. He knows Carol."

"Are the two of them together?"

"I don't think so. Make it happen, Will."

SOON AFTER, I LOST ANGIE to the dyke bar upstairs. On any other night I would have followed her up, but this time I decided to try and catch another glimpse of my crush. I peeled myself off the couch and went to sit up on the bleachers overlooking the dance floor. I searched among the hundreds of bobbing heads. First I looked for François, as he was the taller one. Nothing. Then I scoured the areas closer to the bar for Shaun. Nada. Maybe they had gone to the baths.

Sitting on these wooden benches reminded me of watching

the boys playing basketball in my neighbourhood park as a teenager. Like most gay kids I wore an invisible marker on the playground, one I couldn't see but the other boys were able to identify. The courts were thick with them and their distracting, developing bodies. As they'd reach for the ball, lunging at hoops, they would bare their bellies and expose the tight coils of hair that curled into their navels. Never picked to play, all I could do was watch from the bench: a silent witness to their masculinity and my own secret attraction. Years later, it's only the location of the playground that's changed. Now it happens after dark in the bars and clubs that line Ste. Catherine Street East. Men with their shirts off still reach for the prize. The girls are the ones we confide everything to; the boys, the ones we want to play with. But everyone here prefers the old games, like tag, the hunt-and-chase game where the rules change the moment the person you've been pursuing is caught.

I had only spoken to Shaun for a moment but his features had been burned into my brain. From where I sat I daydreamed about his body: the rough terrain of stubble that ran across his soft jaw, and the level expanse that dominated his broad chest. Shaun wore thin, round glasses that made him look bookish with tufts of blond chest hair that sprang out from his collar in an open invitation. The thought of him made me feel light and buoyant, the only weight keeping me down the anchor in my pants.

I had almost given up on seeing him again when I ran into him in the bathroom. I noticed that people often congregated in K.O.X. 's bathroom the way they would in the kitchens of house parties. It was the one place in the club you could overhear the bawdy and playful conversations that regulars would routinely throw above the stalls.

I was washing up at the sink when I saw Shaun come up

behind me in the mirror. He placed his hands on my hips. "There you are," he said to my reflection. "I thought you might've left."

I blushed and turned to face him, holding my wet hands up as I moved to the electric dryer. Turning with me, he hopped up onto the lengthy counter of the sink to sit as I dried my hands. "No, still here…. I seem to have lost Angie, though."

"How come you're not dancing?"

"It's okay, but it's not my type of music."

"Me neither," he said. "So … where did we leave off?"

"You were telling me how you know François."

"François, yes. I met François at school," he said, swinging his feet under the sink. "He's a friend … We're taking an elective together. A queer cinema class."

"So," I asked. "What does a political science major do?"

"Well, I'm an anarcho-socialist," he said. "Do you know what that is?"

"No, I don't." Was I supposed to?

"We support the elimination of bourgeois institutions, and the abolition of things like property and the state. Property, or ownership, is a source of great social inequality. We believe that by favouring the collective needs of the community — while still maintaining the rights of the individual — we'll live in a much more utopian society."

"… Uh huh," I acknowledged, trying to follow.

"I'm a separatist, too. The rest of Canada is such a cesspool of privilege and dominance. I identify more with the working class, with the men and women of Quebec who are determined to make their own country. I think it's fabulous."

"Well, that's very interesting," I said, processing it. "I have to admit I've never met an English separatist from the west of Canada before."

"I have my reasons. It's all very complicated." Shaun waved away the topic with his hand. "I can tell you more about it sometime. If you're interested."

"Of course I'm interested," I muttered. Of course I wasn't. The whole thing smacked of pretension, but Shaun looked so smart and confident sitting up on the counter in the fluorescent light. His arrogance was attractive.

"So what do you do? Are you a student?"

"I'm in my first semester at Dawson College. Social Sciences. Not sure what I want to do with it yet."

I looked for a reaction on his face. There was none. "How old are you?" he asked.

"Eighteen," I said, suddenly aware of my reflection in the mirror. How odd, I thought, watching myself in an attempt at flirtation, seeing what Shaun sees.

Shaun jumped down from the sink and grabbed my hand. "Follow me," he said, pulling me towards the dance floor as François had done to him. He held on tight as we wove in and out through the crowds of people. I didn't feel much like dancing, but loved the feel of being led. I felt I would follow him anywhere.

We stopped in a spot near the centre where François was dancing, the cigarette in his hand a prop for his movements. François's brooding face glanced at the both of us but made no acknowledgement we were there. He kept moving to the beat, serious in his pointed shoes. Shaun's dancing was a bit frantic. He was all angles and jolts. The term "anarchic" came to mind. But soon enough he stopped moving altogether. Grabbing both my hands, he pulled me towards his lips.

What can I say except it was bad. Horrible, really. Not like what I had come to expect from watching gay independent films with Angie. I thought it would be soft and generous, full of tenderness with bursts of fireworks. Instead, it was drunken and voracious. Shaun's three-day stubble felt like a scouring pad on my face and neck. All I could do was try and keep up.

Shaun soon pulled away and, grabbing me once more by the hand, took me over to the bleachers. We sat together on the first row, our knees pointed towards each other like two kids at the prom.

"Do you want to get out of here?"

I stared at his jaw. It was red and wet with saliva. I opened my mouth, started with "I …," and then stopped. It had been three years since the night in September when I first began to figure out who I was, and in that time I had done nothing more than read about it. I was almost going to tell him that I had never done this before, that it was all new to me, but that felt stupid to say. "Yes …" I finally said, unsure of where it had come from. "Let's go."

I got up and followed Shaun to the coat check to retrieve our coats. We then headed out the door.

The cab ride to his place was long. We didn't talk, mainly glanced hungrily at each other as we fiddled with our fingers on the upholstery. That night, Shaun took me over the threshold to where my curiosity became carnal, to where I began to learn about how my body could perform and what I am capable of. I finally had a frame of reference for some of the acts, smells and tastes that, until that night, had been beyond my comprehension. Shaun insisted we keep the lights off. I had wanted them on. I wanted to see his body, see mine on top of his; the mingling of two men entangled in that sloppy mess I'd wondered so much about. But in the end it was dull and rudimentary. We jerked each other off, the stamp from the club, a bold letter K, still visible in the dim light on the backs of our hands. The experience was quick, mechanical. Like his kiss, Shaun's touch was rough, with no real thought or care. I would later come to recognize this as bad sex; but, for now, it was only pleasant bumbling, for nothing my hand could do alone could match the explosive power of someone else's skin upon my own.

When it was over I couldn't sleep. I lay in limbo, wide-eyed at what we had done. Shaun fell asleep almost immediately and, for a while, I watched him as he slept, his breath moving in and out as the light began to seep into the room. In the cold light of morning I got a better look at his bedroom. It was a mess, furnished with piles of unwashed socks and university textbooks. Our clothes were strewn in pockets on the floor, on top of shoes and notebooks. A solid bust of Lenin sat fixed on his dresser, a giant poster of the band Nitzer Ebb hung next to the window.

I waited until a respectable hour and then got up, around six, to go home and pick up my stuff before heading to school. My mother wouldn't be worried I hadn't come home, but Angie might. I was supposed to sleep over at her place. It's what I did most nights the two of us went out. I did that so as not to worry my mom. She didn't need to know how late we stayed out, or how drunk I got, or if I got lucky. But I'd never had an opportunity to take advantage of this arrangement until last night. I couldn't wait to tell Angie.

I gathered my clothes and got dressed. I went over to the other side of the bed to rouse Shaun. "Shaun," I whispered. "Shaun," I said again, this time touching his arm. He opened his eyes like a sleepy cat and then closed them again, scrunching up his face in a frown. "I have to go. Thanks for last night." I leaned in to kiss him goodbye but he didn't kiss back. He just moaned and recoiled into the sheets.

ONCE FRANÇOIS HAD LEFT WITH his two grams of pot, Shaun and I went for a coffee before his shift. We walked in silence towards the Metro, and took the train downtown. On the ride in I couldn't get what he had said out of my head. "I've decided that I'm not going to fall in love this year." Who says such a thing? It was obviously a comment meant for me to hear, a message about his lack of intentions. But it was thoughtless. It made me feel awful and sad — awful that I didn't seem to cut it as a lover, and sad that this would have to end so soon.

"Listen, Will," he said over a double cappuccino. "This isn't working. The last two weeks have been nice, but I'm not looking for anything serious. You're cute and all, but I don't want a boyfriend. Besides, western Canadian boys aren't good for you. I'm not saying we can't sleep together every now and again, but I just ... I don't want you to expect anything from me."

I sat in silence as he continued. When I think of it, I was mute the few times we were together. So much was going on inside of me I never knew what to say to him. I almost apologized, almost begged him to reconsider, but I wasn't sure what I wanted anymore. What did I like about Shaun, anyway? His age? His body? His confidence? There wasn't much I liked about him as a person. What I liked was the feeling of being complicit, of having another man beside me that I had permission to touch, the ability to care for. And that was something I wasn't too keen to let go of.

I began to catch nearby strangers glancing in our direction, picking up on parts of Shaun's speech. They could tell what was going on, could read it in my face, hear it in his listless articulation. I felt embarrassed.

Finished, Shaun asked me what I was thinking about.

I was thinking about our conversation in the bathroom and that first disappointing kiss. I was thinking about the dark walls of his bedroom and the clutter on his floor. I was thinking about our tumbling sex, how fast and strange it was, but how powerful and fascinating. I was thinking about how mistaken I was about my feelings for him and how stupid it made me feel.

"Nothing," I said.

ON NIGHTS LIKE THE ONE I met Shaun, when I sat alone on those bleachers, watching the crowd below, I would often wonder about the faces that Angie and I saw out almost every night. I knew nothing about them, or what I did know I knew through third parties. These boys were in the bars as often as I was. I knew them by reputation, but would never nod or acknowledge them in passing. Watching them lined up along the speakers, ordering drinks at the bar, or leaning in to deep conversation, I pondered their private lives; imagined what their own unspoken truths might be. I find another man's silent past to be noble and fascinating. All these men were once children like me, children who felt different. Who emerged out of emotional obscurity to answer the question we had been posed as kids and call it by its name. But by then it was too late. We had already learned how to hide our desire, steal burning glances, and not fall in love.

I can't help but imagine what might have happened if we had grown up on the same playground, lived in the same neighbourhood, attended the same school, gone to the same parties. Would this have begun earlier? Would we have had a real adolescence instead of a delayed one? Would we have been good friends? And then I catch myself thinking about Shaun and François. No. Shaun, François and I would not have been friends as kids. They too would have kept the ball from me.

Chapter

5

I returned from the Christmas break to discover they had moved my things into a new classroom. One of the French teachers, Richard Dalpé, had retired before the holidays and I inherited his old room. It was a corner spot on the second floor with long, thin windows on both sides of the building — much better than the windowless, ground-floor space I had been teaching in. The first day back was a quiet one. With students not starting until the following day, we teachers were expected to use the time to prepare our lessons. I had done most of this work over the holidays and instead used the morning to unpack and settle in.

The room looked empty without the stuff Dalpé had accumulated over the thirty years he had taught here. I had never seen his blackboard as dark and clean as it was now. It had always been covered in translucent clouds of white chalk with row after row of conjugated verbs. Now the only signs it had been used were the crushed bits of chalk in the grooves of the tray. Dalpé had left a couple of things behind — a Larousse dictionary that was missing its cover, a torn poster on the *imparfait* hanging on the wall, and a stack of tattered *L'actualité* magazines. I collected everything and put it all into a box by the door.

I took out my own teaching tools and began to personalize the room. I put up a map of Quebec and one of Canada. And I put up a map of the solar system. I had intended to hang a 3-D mobile in the front of the class, inspiration for their mid-term assignment, but I didn't have time to make it over the break. Instead, I opted for a colourful poster I'd found in the supply shop that showed the orbits of the planets around the sun. The illustration of the sun was huge; orange and angry. And the Earth looked so small compared to it, different from the dry rocks and gas giants circling the star. The Earth gleamed like a marble, the swirling atmosphere making it look like an experiment under glass.

I went down the aisles and straightened the desks, making sure each one was clean and empty. At the back of the room I found a number of books, dog-eared copies of *Agaguk* and *L'Étranger* I too had read in school. I collected them and added them to the box by the door. In so doing, I noticed one slim volume in the bundle of paperbacks. It was a lone copy of *Le Petit Prince* by Antoine de Saint-Exupéry. I had read this book too, but only in the last year and a half. It was Max who had introduced it to me. He couldn't believe I had never read it and lent it to me in the first few weeks we were dating. There was so much to love about this little book. I was touched he wanted to share it with me, with its messages on love and loneliness. We had a good laugh about one of the characters being a geographer who didn't go anywhere, who never explored the world he was mapping. Who sends the Little Prince to Earth.

When Max and I broke up I bought my own copy, in English. I didn't have it in the original French, so instead of chucking it into the box with the rest of the remainders I saved it and put it in my bag.

I MET MAX IN OCTOBER 2004 at a Halloween party in Mile End. I had stumbled in late along with Angie, Carol, and Izo. We had been to a screening of *The Rocky Horror Picture Show* at the Rialto, rice buried deep in our hair. Angie and I had gone as two Transylvanian partygoers, dressed up in matching suits with funny eyewear and pointed party hats.

"Are you one of the Pet Shop Boys?" a handsome man in a plaid shirt asked me out of nowhere. He was dressed as a cowboy, curly blond wig under a cheap straw hat and a flower-shaped gift tag around his right wrist that spelled out "For Harold."

"No," I said, taking a look at what I was wearing. "But I suppose I could be. My friend and I are transvestites from the planet Transsexual, Transylvania. You know, *The Rocky Horror Picture Show*?"

"Of course," the cowboy said. "Were you at a screening?"

I removed my hat and rubbed my scalp to answer his question, grains of rice raining onto the floor. He laughed. "It must have been wild."

"It was," I said, putting the tiny hat back on. I took the tag around his wrist in my hand and looked it over. "For Harold ... The Cowboy from *The Boys in the Band?*"

"Very good," he said, impressed. "Almost no one I know has seen it."

"Well, it's not the most upbeat of films."

"That doesn't mean it can't still be great. Some of the best stories are tragic ones. I think *The Boys in the Band* is my favourite movie. I've seen it a hundred times!"

"Really? A francophone whose favourite film is *Boys in the Band*?" I said with a nod. "I think I like that."

He smiled and took a swig from his beer, a handsome ranch hand taking five. "So, you can tell I'm a francophone?"

"You have a bit of an accent," I said.

"Damn." He looked down. "I was hoping it wasn't noticeable. I've been auditioning in English."

An actor. "It's slight," I said to ease his worry. "Hardly noticeable. Adorable, even." He smiled again and so did I.

Suddenly I felt something under my foot. A grain of rice had made its way down into the sole of my shoe. "Hold on," I said, taking off my sneaker and removing the offending crumb. "God, I am covered in rice."

"Don't worry," he said. "I'm sure they'll all come falling out once you get home and take off your clothes."

I almost lost my balance putting the shoe back on. What the cowboy had said sent a surge throughout my body. He had undressed me in a sentence and it felt as if I had fallen ten feet.

"I'm Max," he said, extending the hand with the gift tag on it.

"Hi, Max," I said, shaking back. "I'm Harold."

IT'S A WONDER MAX AND I had never met before. We knew the same people, hung out at the same places. I might have seen him a hundred times before, on the streets or in bars, but if I had I'd never noticed him. Max didn't stand out the way the others do, the tall and beautiful who trot about the bars like fresh young ponies out of the gate, nor like the worn and muscular apes who swing topless from speaker to speaker. His beauty was so subtle, so unobtrusive, that he blended into his surroundings like a gecko, lithe and colourful yet modest and discreet. Max had short brown hair that was thick yet receding, with deep blue eyes that were as vibrant as Neptune. He was of average height and build, with furry arms and thick fingers. During the two uninterrupted hours we got to know each other I could not stop staring at his hands — the way they held the beer bottle and swept the synthetic hair from his face.

As the party wore down Max asked me if I wanted to leave. We took a cab to his apartment, our hats and accessories off and in bags. We got out a block before his building so he could pick up some milk at the *Couche-Tard*. His street was dark and quiet. It had rained that afternoon so the fallen leaves were clumped together, their earthy mustiness sent airborne by our sneakers. He was telling me about leaving his hometown of Drummondville at eighteen. "My mother died when I was young, and I never got along with my father. He remarried when I was twelve, had two more kids and forgot all about me. When I came out, he freaked. Tried to get me to see a psychologist. Wouldn't leave me alone with my brother or sister. After a while I couldn't take it. I needed to leave, so I saved up some money and left for good. Just packed up one day while they were out and took the bus to Montreal."

I muttered my wide-eyed, sympathetic disbelief: "… Shit!" I had heard this kind of story before, but Max was the first person I had met who had lived it. "I can't imagine what that must have been like. Have you spoken to them since?"

"No," he continued, matter-of-fact as if he had told this story a hundred times. "I haven't spoken to my father in six years. But believe me, it's for the best. I don't need that kind of bullshit in my life." He stopped in front of a red-brick building and took out his keys. "We're here."

Max jiggled the key into the lock, turning it with a loud snap. The door creaked open and he led me upstairs in the dark, the bluster of our feet accompanying us to his second-floor apartment. He then opened the door to his home and took a couple of blind steps to where he knew the lamp was. With a click the room lit up, and I became introduced to the life and colour of his walls.

"Bienvenue," he said, taking off his coat and shoes and throwing his bag on a table nearby. "You can put your stuff on the hook behind the door."

I closed the door and did what I was told. I took off my shoes and left them next to his, wading into the centre of the living room to have a look around.

Max's apartment was larger than mine. He had two more rooms than I did, with a balcony in both the front and back. Across the vacant lot behind his place was a strip club frequented by an east-end biker gang. On future summer nights I would often find myself awakened by the odd noise — the crash of a beer bottle against the pavement or the drunken squeal of a stripper getting into someone's car. Below and to the right of him, the apartments were empty. On freezing mornings Max and I would break into them to turn on their heat because his floor was cold. It was easy to do. Lousy locks were hitched on all of the building's back doors. With little effort one could walk up the spiralling metal staircase onto his back porch and, with a screwdriver, knock the hook off the latch and let oneself in. Not that Max had anything valuable to steal. All he had was a shitty VCR and maybe thirty CDs. He had no couches, either; just two futons that turned into beds when old friends would visit from Drummondville. His television only received three channels (all French) and his VCR was missing several buttons. He had lost his remote control, so in order to watch a video we'd have to take a chopstick out of the kitchen drawer and insert it into the hole where the play button once was. Nothing seemed to work well. There was also a clock over Max's sink that was perpetually 4:37. There were no batteries in it. Max hated the ticking sound so he'd taken them out, but he left the clock on the wall. It became an apt metaphor for how I felt when I was there. Time stood still. Minutes would turn into hours, the lost time replaced by music and sex, and then I would look out the window, surprised to find that morning had arrived.

"So what do you think?" he asked once I had a chance to look around.

"It's nice," I responded, not completely truthful. When Max brought me over this first night I thought I could never spend much time in such a place. I would be surprised, though, to find it would soon become a second home. I would become oblivious to the broken cupboards, the mismatched dinnerware, the faulty washing machine in the middle of the kitchen, and the rotted floor coming up in the bathroom. The space, although falling apart, would be held together by what was happening between us. And despite the piles of dishes and complete disarray of clothes and cassette tapes, I'd find myself at ease.

I took a few more steps into his place and snooped around. I skimmed the titles on his bookshelf, stopped at the fridge to check the magnets, coupons, photos, and flyers that were stuck to it. That's when I noticed a photo of Max as a child stuck somewhere between an electrical bill and a grocery list.

"Is this you?" I asked. He came over. It was a brown-and-orange square photo taken by a dinosaur of a camera on what must have been his fifth or sixth birthday. Youthful likenesses of his parents — his mom still alive and his dad unhardened —

stood behind him as he blew out large bright candles on a tall white cake.

"Yes," he said, close. So close I could feel the heat radiating off him on the back of my neck. "It's one of the only pictures I have of me as a kid." Max smelled wonderful from where he stood. His scent enveloped me, pulling me in like a magnet. Immediately I turned to face him and, pushing into him, tasted the warm spread of his tongue. I felt the corners of Max's mouth widen into a smile as he stepped back, pulling me onto the futon with him.

THE NEXT DAY MY BODY ached, and for weeks thereafter I would continue to be sore, having been subjected to the scrapes, scratches, minor bruises, and cricks that, along with the sleepless nights and fatigue, are welcome symptoms of a new relationship.

Sleeping with Max on that first night made me feel like an outlaw. For here I was, his naked accomplice, taking part in the one thing that had estranged him from his family. It was exactly what I wanted — a conspiracy of two. And as I fumbled around his body, becoming more acquainted with its crooks and corners, I felt the history of desire in both of us. Was that something I could do? Leave everything behind?

Max was right — some of the best stories are tragic ones. Despite being sad, there was something powerful about his story. And in that moment, engaging in this deviant behaviour with him, I felt closer to him than I had to anyone else before.

After Max told me his story, I told him mine. Naked in bed, our legs entwined as we watched the light seep through his bedroom window, I told Max about my mother's cancer diagnosis six years earlier — the little scare that had developed into a nightmare before going off to sit in remission.

I've never known my mom to feel well. She had bad allergies (tissues strewn everywhere, coming out of sleeves and tucked behind pillows) and was a complete hypochondriac, keenly aware that the library's patrons were scattering their germs on the tables, books, and chairs. So I didn't think much of it when she told me she'd found blood in her stool.

"It's probably from hemorrhoids," I had said. For years I had seen the creams in the medicine cabinet, but this was the first time I acknowledged her problem. "I wouldn't worry," I reassured, telling her it would go away in time.

"You're probably right," she had said, but still called to make an appointment with her doctor.

I don't remember how much time passed between that call and the colonoscopy, but it was long enough that when it did happen I had forgotten what had prompted it. I was working on the day of her test. Thankfully, a colleague from the library agreed to pick her up and drive her home. I walked into our apartment that evening, fresh from my shift at the restaurant where Angie and I still worked (by now I was a waiter). I knew my mom was home because the door was unlocked. With a thud I dropped my knapsack onto the floor and headed into the kitchen. The apartment was dark, inadequately lit by the retreating day. Leaving the lights off, I opened the fridge to get something to drink. "Hi, Mom, I'm home," I called to the rest of the apartment. "Where are you?" And that's when I realized she was sitting in the dark, at the dining table next to the kitchen.

"Mom? What's wrong?"

"I had my colonoscopy today …"

I immediately remembered, and the room closed in.

"… They found some growths. They think it might be cancer." Her voice was thick and wet. "I have to go in tomorrow for an MRI."

I stood there, petrified; my mother deep in thought. The only thing moving was her hand as she brought a crumpled tissue to dab her eyes. I had seen tears on my mom before: angry, frustrated ones after a fight that dried up once I apologized; or important, noble ones after the passing of a great aunt. But in the wake of these fresh, messy ones I could see the terror and uncertainty on her face.

"This can't be happening, Will … What are we going to … I mean, what if …" She couldn't complete her thoughts, stopping mid-sentence and starting elsewhere. All I could do was nod and keep eye contact, listening but not showing how frightened I was.

"Don't worry," I said and sat down next to her, pulling up my chair as close as it would go. "It's not — it's going to be fine. Do you know what they have to do?"

"They'll run some tests. Then we'll know whether it's nothing, or if I'll need treatment. But they said if it is cancer there's a chance they'll have to remove part of my colon."

As she spoke, I reached into my coat pocket and retrieved a pack of smokes — not caring that I was outing myself as a smoker. My mother didn't take notice. She sat motionless on the wooden chair, by the fruit bowl, and stared at the floor. I lit one up and immediately felt better. Smelling the mix of sulphur and tobacco, my mom raised her head and reached for the pack now lying on the table. She took one out and expertly lit it, looking at it as she pulled it from her mouth. It must have been twenty years since her last one, and although it was odd for each of us to see the other smoke, it felt like the right thing to do — to sit in the dark and smoke cigarettes.

I asked more questions. She had no answers. After a while I got up to order us food. I turned on the lights to look for the phone number. The light was shocking and exposed our long, puzzled faces. I opened a bottle of wine from under the sink. When the pizza came, we ate what we could and watched TV. My mom's knitting needles and yarn sat in a jumble by her chair. It was the first time I'd seen her so engrossed in television, her chin tight in her palm as she lost herself in the stories before her.

Around 11 p.m. I looked over to find her asleep. I got up, turned off the TV, and, waking her slightly, led her to her room. I pulled back the covers and tucked her in, kissing her forehead.

I then went through the rest of the apartment and closed up. I turned off the lights in the front room. I wrapped the remainder of the pizza in aluminium foil and put it away in the fridge. I found the chicken breast she had taken out of the freezer defrosting in the sink and threw it in the garbage.

I was tired but didn't want to go to bed. Instead I snuck in next to her and watched her sleep for the longest time, listening to the clock in the hall tick forward. She was out, peaceful, floating in a deep slumber. Worry lines and wrinkles danced on her brow; her lips crumpled near the crescent opening of her mouth as the eyes, heavy, twitched in their sockets. I couldn't imagine life without her.

At some point I must have made my way back to my bedroom because I awoke the next morning in my bed and she was gone. A note on the kitchen table told me she had a couple of things to do before her MRI that afternoon. "Don't forget there is pizza in the fridge," it said. "I'll call you when I get home. Love, Mom."

I ate breakfast and futzed around for about an hour before going to work. Angie was off, so I couldn't share my anxiety with her. I spent most of my shift in a blank state, thankful for the lunch rush.

I was midway through my day when my boss called out from behind the counter. "Will, telephone," he said. "It's your mom."

My plates were up but I ran to the phone. "Mom?"

"Hi, Will," she said, her voice pointed but composed. "I'm all right, but I'm still at the hospital. They want to keep me overnight." It seemed my mother had had a slight panic in the MRI and the hospital wanted her to stay for observation. Her blood pressure was dangerously high. She sounded okay but wanted me to bring her some comforts from home. I told her I'd be there as soon as I could.

My boss let me go early and I rushed home, walking as quickly as I could up St. Laurent. Once there I picked up some of my mother's clothes, her toothbrush, crosswords, and hand creams, and made my way via Parc Avenue to the Royal Victoria Hospital.

People milled about the hospital's main hallway. I waded through them to the information desk where a receptionist informed me that, due to overflow, my mother was in the birthing centre. She told me how to get there and I took off to find her.

The Royal Vic is a maze. Different floors lead to different wings with all these twisting hallways and confusing annexes. At one point I had to take an elevator up two flights and then walk down a long corridor to take another elevator to where I needed to go. The odours of bleach and latex soured the halls. The second elevator was small and cramped, built for visiting couples with flowers and stuffed animals. The doors opened to the ring of baby cries and laughing siblings. I could hear the shuffle of feet, the crinkle of flowers wrapped in cellophane. I peered through the doors of these happy scenes to find my mother in one of the rooms, in a bed, sharing the space with three other patients.

"Hey, trooper, how are you feeling?" I swooped in beside her.

"A little tired," she said, shifting in the sheets.

"You had me worried to death. What happened?"

"I feel so silly," she said. "I had a bloody panic attack in the MRI — have you ever seen one of those things? I was fine until I saw it. It's so claustrophobic and noisy, like an airplane. And I suppose I was shaking too much because they put these weighted blankets on my legs and shoulders to keep me from moving. When I came out I was bawling. Oh, Will, I was so embarrassed! And the nurses all looked worried and took my blood pressure. They said it was abnormally high. Well, what do they expect after putting me in that thing? It's like being buried alive!"

"What did the doctor say?"

"Nothing yet. I'm still waiting for the results. They want me to remain overnight for observation. My pressure's still high, but I'm feeling much better. They want to make sure I don't go home and have a heart attack. I'll be out tomorrow morning, though. Thank you for bringing my things."

I placed the bag beside the bed. My mother looked tiny lying there in a thin spread of hospital linens, like a child in a painting smock. "So they haven't told you anything?"

"They're not up here on this floor too often. Something about the hospital being overcrowded. I've only seen my doctor once." I could hear a groan in her voice.

"Can I get you something? Water? Anything?"

"No. Do me a favour, though. Turn off the television. I have a bit of a headache."

I took the remote from beside her bed and zapped the hanging television off. I could better hear the other patients in the room now, coughing and talking in French to their own visitors behind grimy curtains. I stayed until the end of visiting hours. We sat and talked, turned the TV back on, and watched some game shows. She had asked me to bring her knitting and crosswords but didn't touch them while I was there. Around a quarter to eight I looked at the clock on the wall and knew it was time for me to leave. My mom was beginning to fade, her eyes heavy and tired.

"I think I should go," I said, moving to sit on the bed beside her. "Are you going to be all right?"

"Yes, I'll be fine," she said, shifting herself upright and rubbing her eyes. "Thanks for keeping me company, Will. You know how much I love you. I don't know what in the world I'd do without you."

I felt a rush of blood to my chest. There was a sharp finality to my mother's words, like the last thing you say when you're not sure you'll see the other person again. Suddenly I felt as if I was going to lose her. And I felt that I needed to be honest — as if nothing else in the world were more important, and all the guilt and sadness gave way to the things I'd never said, and before I knew it I was opening my mouth and saying, "Mom … I'm gay."

"What?" It wasn't shock. I don't think she had heard me right.

"I'm gay," I said again. I wouldn't be able to say it a third time. "I'm not sure why I'm saying this now. I've known for a while and wanted you to know. I didn't … I'm still the same person. It's just … I've always felt different and now, well, I don't."

My mom looked up to the ceiling and then back down. I could see she was surprised, but above all tired. I kept talking, babbling as I shook. I didn't tell her anything specific, just tried to find the best way to put it into context, but failed. I'd imagined many times how I'd tell her, what I'd say, yet here I was, unprepared and unscripted, sitting on the edge of her hospital bed, tripping on the words as they came out. I was twenty-one now and had known for years. I had put off telling her because I wasn't sure how she'd take it. I had almost told her once. One night she had asked me if Angie and I were dating and I snapped at her. "No, Mom, Angie's not my girlfriend," I had said, prompting an argument about privacy that ended with my mom declaring she would no longer ask me about my personal life. In my room later, I felt defeated. I'd had an opportunity to be honest with her and instead chose to push her away.

I could see in her eyes that she was now processing, putting together places, things, people, comments, phone calls. Water began to gather in my mother's eyes as I stood up. "Mom, don't cry," I said.

"No, it's not that. It's just …" She wiped her eyes. "It's all of this … But it's not what I would have wanted for you, Will. It's such a lonely life."

"Oh," I said, embarrassed and unsure what to say next. I could see a door closing in front of me, and myself too immobile to run through it. "Um, listen, I'm sorry I said anything. This isn't the right moment. We can talk about it another time, if you want. I just … I wanted you to know that I love you, too." I kissed her on the forehead and turned around to pick up my bag. "I'm going to go now, okay? Good night. I'll talk to you tomorrow."

Only once I was back in the elevator did I realize I was crying, my face flushed and wet. I tried not to look at the woman sharing the confined space with me; she, politely, looked straight ahead and held on tight to her purse.

I felt alone as I left the building and entered the night. The sky was open and purple. I could hear the call of a bird — or was it a bat — somewhere over the parking lot as I headed towards the street. I found myself wishing it was me in that room, and not her, because I knew I could handle it. I didn't believe myself when I told her everything would be all right. But I'd believe her. If our roles were reversed and I was the one sitting in that bed and she said to me "Don't worry, Will, everything is going to be all right," I'd believe her. I'd believe her because she is my mom.

I COULDN'T GO HOME, so instead I went to Angie's. Angie was living in her first apartment, located in the McGill Ghetto and five blocks from the hospital. Thankfully, she was home when I rang the doorbell.

"Will." She answered the door in a black apron with a dish-cloth over her shoulder. "What are you doing here?"

"My mom's in the hospital." I said, still in shock. "I just came out to her."

"You gave her a heart attack?"

"No, no," I said. "She had an MRI today and freaked out in the machine. Angie, they think she has cancer."

"Oh my God! Come in, come in," she said, and pulled me into her apartment.

"What is it? What happened?" asked Angie's new girlfriend Holly, coming to see what the noise was about.

"My mother," I said, sitting down at the kitchen table. "They found some growths in her colon and think it might be cancer. She went for tests today and they asked her to stay overnight because her blood pressure was too high."

"Is she going to be okay?"

"I don't know."

"Here," Angie said, pulling a freshly lit cigarette from her mouth and giving it to me. "And so, you *came out* to her?"

"I wasn't thinking." Holly poured me a glass of wine. I noticed the candles on the table. "I'm sorry, am I interrupting a romantic dinner?"

"Don't be silly." Angie lit another cigarette for herself and returned to the stove. "You're joining us."

"Oh, Will," said Holly, sitting down beside me.

 "So what did she say?" asked Angie.

"That's the thing, she said, 'It's a very lonely life ...'"

"... What does that mean?"

"I don't know, I didn't ask."

"And so they think she has cancer?"

"She'll get some results tomorrow."

"Oh, Will, I'm so sorry." It was the only thing Holly could

say. She was such a sweet and empathic girlfriend. I'd miss her when Angie dumped her two weeks later.

I STAYED FOR MOST OF the night. Angie and Holly had rented *Roman Holiday* but fell asleep before it was over. They went to bed around one in the morning and left me with some blankets on the couch. Around 3 a.m., not being able to sleep, I got up and left them a note. I walked home.

Outside the city was still, the occasional noise coming from cars zipping along Parc Avenue. I walked along the dark side of the mountain, passing the trees, the George-Étienne Cartier Monument and the blinking red traffic lights. I thought of my mom asleep in a crowded room on the other side of the hill and lit up another cigarette. The wind took my breath away. "I'm going to have to quit these," I said to no one.

C
h
a
p
t
e
r

7

On Saturday, January 14, two weeks into the new year, my mother turned fifty. Her sister, Mary, came in from Florida to celebrate. I had proposed marking the occasion with a dinner at a fancy restaurant in the Old Port, one my mom had often talked about trying, but in the end it was a home-cooked meal she asked for.

I'm not a good cook. One of the few things I can make is shrimp pasta, which is exactly what it sounds like. That day I went out to the sheltered confines of the Jean-Talon Market, squeezing my way through crowds too tight to be in such a cramped winterized space, to find the freshest ingredients available: tomatoes, garlic, zucchini, onion, and shrimp that I would later toss in lemon and oil. I also picked up a bottle of wine and, for dessert, a dense chocolate cake.

Mom dressed up for dinner, hiding the folds of her neck in a light blue turtleneck over which rested a gold necklace. Her sleeves were bunched up above her elbows and she wore crisp, black slacks. Her hair was pulled back into a tight ponytail of greying streaks. She sat erect at the kitchen table, fidgeting with the rings on her fingers as if they were dials to a combination lock. She looked happy, her face wide and lit with the glow of the wine disappearing before her.

"You didn't tell me how the first week of school went," she said. We were alone in the kitchen, my aunt smoking on the balcony.

"Good," I replied, my back to her and my hands deep in the cold sink checking the shellfish for veins. "We've started on urban sprawl and public transit. I've given them their first assignment — a report on another city's public transportation."

"That sounds like fun," my mother said, getting up to pick up something from the counter and then sitting back down. "Do you need me to look up anything for you? We might have some transit maps at the library."

"No, thanks. I have everything I need." Behind me I began to hear clicks and snaps and, turning, my hands still in the sink, I found her opening up a collection of pill bottles, splitting the tablets into halves and placing them into a plastic pillbox with slots for each day of the week. "What are those pills for?" I asked.

"Cholesterol, high blood pressure, estrogen … I'm getting old, Will. Who knows what shape I'd be in without these."

"I didn't know you still had high blood pressure."

"It's from you," my aunt teased as she rejoined us in the kitchen. Along with my aunt came the pungent waft of American tobacco as she took off her coat and chucked it on the couch. "You know I'm joking. My God, it's cold out," she added, sitting down beside my mother and getting reacquainted with the wine. "I forgot how cold it gets in Montreal."

Sitting side by side you can tell my aunt Mary and my mother are related. Although much heavier, my aunt still shares some facial features with her sister: the same sharp nose and chin, the same fleshy earlobes and thin eyebrows. But her face is much fuller and rounder than my mom's. Sometimes, when I catch my aunt in profile, I get a glimpse of my mother and wonder if this is how she'd look had she never been sick.

"Doesn't everything smell good?" my mom asked her sister.

"I haven't cooked anything yet."

"A woman loves a man who can cook," my aunt began. "You make something special for a woman, Will, and she'll be eating out of the palm of your hand."

I had forgotten how my aunt spoke in cliché. Over the years I had learned to ignore her inane comments, but this one irked me. It made me realize that my mother had never told her sister about me.

"So, Will, when are you going to come visit? Did you know we moved last October and are now five minutes from the water? You'd love it."

"I might come one day. Maybe Mom will come with me?"

"You know how hard I've tried to get your mother to visit," she said, trying to catch my mother's eyes that were too busy concentrating on splitting pills. "Of course, you're both welcome anytime. There's so much to see." Fuelled by wine, my aunt talked about Venice Beach, yapping as my mother struggled with a childproof cap. I dried my hands and took the bottle from her, twisting it open and handing it back.

Once the ingredients were prepared and the water was boiling, it took me no time to put the meal together. Dinner was served with the obligatory *ooh*s and *ahh*s, and when we were done I got up to further sounds of gastronomical appreciation to make the tea and ready the cake.

As the tea was steeping, I presented my mom with her birthday gift. "For me?" she said, greeting the green box with wide eyes. "Dinner was more than enough." She was already opening the box.

My mom had difficulty figuring out what the tickets were for without her reading glasses. "They're to the musical *Cats*," I helped. "A touring production is coming at the end of August. It's a little far off, but they're great seats!"

The surprise registered on her face. "Oh my God," she exclaimed, looking at me, looking at the tickets. She opened her mouth to say my name, but only the first letter made it out. I had knocked the wind out of her. Her eyes began to tear and she turned to her sister and said, with joy, "I'm going to see *Cats*!"

"Oh, Will, that's such a wonderful gift," my aunt said, getting choked up.

"What?" I said, trying to lighten the mood. "It's just a musical."

"It's not just a musical! This is so thoughtful of you. *Cats*! I've always wanted to see it. Are you coming to see it with me?"

"Of course."

"Oh, and we'll go out for dinner beforehand — my treat! Will, this is so generous of you." Her face seized up again and I went over to hug her and give her a kiss.

"My pleasure ... Please stop it," I said, as tissues were being pulled from pockets. "You're freaking me out here."

ONCE WE WERE DONE WITH the cake and coffee, my mother suggested we play Scrabble. That Christmas I had bought her the Deluxe Scrabble board game, but the box had remained unopened under the coffee table since. We broke it out and everyone chose their tiles. Mom shuffled hers around like a pro while I stared blankly at mine. It being her birthday she went first, placing five letters in the centre of the board: RADIO. She counted her points and swung the tray to my aunt.

"Oh, Will, you left your watch here," my mom said, throwing me off.

"I did?" I said, relieved. "Thank God. I was worried I had lost it. Where was it?"

"On the nightstand in your room," my aunt said. Working off the D, she made the word DOG. "I left it on top of your dresser."

"Thanks. I'll get it after." The board now swung to me. I was at a loss for what to put down, my plans thwarted by my aunt's contribution. Feeling the pressure of the clock, I spelled the only word I saw. RANG. Five points. *Shit! Shouldn't I be better at this? I'm a teacher for Chrissakes.*

My mom turned the board back towards her and focused on her letters. I watched as her silver bracelet kept falling up and down the skinny stalk of her left arm. Momentarily distracted, she pushed the band down towards her elbow as if it were a sleeve, nudging it into the pale fleshy part of her arm before smoothing out the freckled wrinkles. After about sixty seconds of contemplation she added five letters to envelop the word I had put down. "'Frangible.' Thirty-four points!"

"Frangible?" I said. "That's not a word! What's it supposed to mean?"

"Are you challenging me, Will?" she asked with a shrewd smile. "If you want to risk losing a turn you can challenge me and look it up."

"Humph ..." I said, trying to peer through her poker face. Mom was a great wordsmith, but could she be bluffing? I declined to challenge her and tried to concentrate on my new letters.

The game continued, the temperature lowered, and my mom rose to turn up the heat. The cat jumped up to take her place.

"Elizabeth, you get down from there!"

Mom won the game, with my aunt coming a close second; a hundred points separated my score from theirs. I declined my mom's offer to be beaten a second time and, packing up the Scrabble board, brought it into my old bedroom to find a place for it.

The space was full, stocked with familiar furniture, but without any of the characteristics of my old room. I found my watch on the dresser next to a bunch of my aunt's things, and put it on my wrist. I opened the closet door to find space for the Scrabble board and was greeted by three brown boxes. They all had "Will" written on them in the cursive lettering that was unmistakably my mother's. Curious, I dragged them out onto my bed.

Inside the first I found my old G.I. Joe comic books and a bunch of worn-out Star Wars figurines. In the second were yellowing term papers and class assignments from Dawson College. And in the third I found piles of folded T-shirts, clothes I had worn some six or seven years earlier. I smiled. I had assumed they had been thrown out or given away. There must have been a dozen of them, each one an old friend I hadn't seen in years.

I sprang from my bed and swung the lamp on my desk over to the full-length mirror. One by one I felt the stretch as I pulled the T-shirts across my body. They were much tighter than I remembered. How did I ever fit into these? I looked funny: lopsided, late twenties, with a little more stuffing around the sides. It is said that it takes seven years for the body to regenerate, for its cells to divide and its tissues to be replaced. I suppose that meant I was now a clone of who I once was seven years before, when I first wore these T-shirts. The man standing in front of the mirror was no longer the same boy who once sat alone in his bedroom at night and dreamed of the world he would live in. No. What remained now was a copy of the original. A replica of the boy my mother had made. Is that why memory becomes fuzzy? Is information lost in the transfer? And did this mean it would take me seven years to get over Max? A whole generation to pass before my cells fully divided so that any memory of him became an echo of what it once was?

The last T-shirt I tried on was my favourite. A two-tone blue, classic ringer T-shirt with a cluster of smiling grapes on it that said "Great Bunch." I had found it in the kids' section of a thrift shop years ago and was ecstatic it fit me. I was now equally surprised to find that it still did, although I'd have to hold in my stomach.

I went into the living room to find my mom and aunt now settled in front of the TV. "You kept my old T-shirts?"

"Did I? I suppose I never got around to giving them away. The church is supposed to come by next week to pick up some stuff. I can …"

"No, no, no, no, no …" I interrupted her. "No. I don't want you to give these away. I want you to hold on to them. Please, promise me you won't get rid of them. I can't bring them home tonight, but will some other time. All right?"

"I promise."

I went back into my room to put the shirts away, feeling as though I had won fifty bucks. Within the room's four closed walls I had the sudden urge to go out. I checked my watch. It was 10:10 p.m. Saturday. The night was still young. But who to call? Not Angie; I hadn't heard from her since she had hooked up with Geneviève the week before. It irritated me that whenever she met someone new she'd disappear.

I kept on the Great Bunch T-shirt and began to pack things up. Mom, taking my cue, got up to rummage through the fridge to offer me some food to take home.

"No. Thanks. I'm going out."

"Oh? Was that in the plans?"

"No, but an old friend is in town tonight and I told him I'd try and drop by the bar if I could." I felt bad lying to my mother. But it was a harmless lie, one that invited less speculation about my motives. She wouldn't understand her son's need to go out by himself so late at night to dance with strangers.

"All right. Have fun. Be safe!"

I kissed her and my aunt good night, and left them with Elizabeth curled up on the footrest by the couch. "I'll call you tomorrow."

SINCE IT WAS EARLY, I decided to walk to the Village. It was brisk out, but I wasn't feeling the cold. I was energized by the tightness of the T-shirt across my chest. Even in its depths winter feels cleansing: its whiteness, its crispness. I sang under my breath as I took side streets and alleys, heading towards La Fontaine Park and descending into the Village.

I decided to go to Parking. It was still early when I arrived, 11 p.m., but some guest DJ was spinning and had an eager crowd dancing before him. I dumped my coat at the coat check, and headed to the bar for a beer. The bartender who served me was about twenty-one and topless, with a taut ribcage that reminded me of the gills of a shark. I could tell he loved his job, his body. Juggling lemon slices, juices, and liquor bottles, he deftly opened and closed fridge doors, twisting off bottle caps while moving to the music. I tried to meet his gaze, but he didn't look back, just placed my change on the counter beside my drink and moved to the next order.

I took my beer and change and climbed the stairs to the railing that overlooked the dance floor. From my perch I watched the shirtless men below as they showed off their gym memberships — wide pecs and ripped abs tucked into tight jeans. I pulled my own T-shirt down an inch and sucked in my gut, suddenly an insecure gay man rolling into his thirties. They don't look so hot, I thought to myself, cupping my beer. Despite the display of skin, of sexual bravado, I found them to be devoid of masculinity. It seemed to have been cinched, plucked and ripped from their bodies, leaving in its place mounds of sculpted flesh that had lost its urgent magnetism. These men didn't look like the men I grew up admiring, the ones I fantasized about. No, these boys looked like mannequins; imitations of what had drawn me here in the first place.

Thirty minutes later — and several rounds about the bar — I noticed a familiar face across from me. He was standing with three friends at the other end of the railing. Vince was someone I had dated many years ago. He was my age and build, but had brown hair and a short reddish beard. We had slept together, twice, but it was so long ago that I no longer thought of him that way.

I went up and surprised him from behind.

"H-hey," he said as he turned around to figure out who I was. "Will!" We hugged hello. "Long time no see. How are you?"

"Good. You?" I felt the stares of his friends as I pulled back from the embrace.

"Great! I started this new job, teaching at FACE School — you know, the one on University? It's so great to finally have a permanent, full-time job." Vince was effortlessly sexy. He had the rugged good looks of a matinee idol paired with the laid-back manner of a stoner, although I don't think he smoked. I could only imagine the crush I'd have had on him were I a teenager in his class. "And how about you? What's been going on?"

"Not much. Still at James Lyng. No longer with Max. And you? Still single?"

"Single?" hissed one of Vince's friends. "God, don't you hate the word?"

"Oh, I'm sorry. Will, these are my friends. Antoine, Charles, and André."

"Hello," I said. The three of them smiled sourly, looking at me as if I were the punchline to a bad joke.

"But yes," Vince answered, "I'm still single."

"Honey, no, you're not single," said Antoine, the tall one, plastic cup in hand as he touched Vince's shoulder. "You're priceless, precious … available! You belong to the world, and the world belongs to you. Don't think in simplistic terms. Single implies you're half a person, incomplete, that something's wrong with you. And there is nothing wrong with you. You are fabulous!"

Everyone chimed in with their affirmations. I had touched upon a sore spot. I knew that, like me, Vince had had a hard time getting over his ex, Eric, who had dumped him several months before I, too, was let go. My question was meant to be harmless. I only wanted the best for Vince.

His three friends continued their diatribe before moving on to more mundane developments within their circle. I didn't have much to add so I kept quiet. Pretty soon my beer went dry. I excused myself, raising the empty bottle as an indication I needed another. Vince winked at me as I left.

Instead of ordering at the bar on our level, I headed down the stairs that led to the basement to check out the club's other room. Downstairs the music was a mix of old alternative and pop remixes. The crowd was decent but nowhere near as large as the one upstairs. This time I bought a beer from an older, larger man in leather chaps.

I soon felt a tug on my bladder and made my way to the bathroom, lining up with three other guys who waited for the privacy of a stall. Once inside, I locked the door behind me and drained the last few beers into the shadowy porcelain. I heard the creaks of wooden doors opening and closing as people entered and left, the muffled voices of people speaking in French, the regular flushes. New Order's *Blue Monday* was playing, blasting every time the bathroom door opened.

As I peed, I began to notice the graffiti drawn on the thick boards of the stall. There were the standard squiggles and scratches: people's initials, unintelligible illustrations, a Zilön tag of a sheathed cock entering a man's mouth. But on the lower rungs I noticed several sentences scribbled in black marker, each quote on a different slab of wood.

"Don't forget what we had," read one. "Meeting you was a blessing and I don't believe in God," read the other. And then there was the third: "I read about it in books, saw it in movies, but you made me feel things I never thought I could feel and I am afraid I'll never have that again."

I read the words a couple of times and became struck by the sentiment. I had stumbled upon the relics of a breakdown, scribbled onto the dark walls of this bathroom stall. What had happened to make this person write this? I thought about how, when I was younger, the bathrooms of K.O.X. and other gay bars had been an amusing social space. But I suppose they were also a refuge. I wondered how often other men, perhaps plagued by drunkenness and despair, retreated to these rank confessionals to release the emotional anguish exacerbated by what was going on outside. Bars had always served as a distraction for me, a place that promised I wouldn't be alone forever. But now I wasn't so sure. When I went out these days I'd renew my skepticism. And as the night wore on, and the drinks diminished, I'd end up thinking about those who'd disappointed me, and those I missed.

I zipped up, flushed the toilet with my shoe, and opened the stall door to exit the washroom. The sentences on the bathroom stall were confronted now with the ones being sung on the dance floor. Céline Dion had replaced New Order on the speakers. She rhymed "you and I" with "meant to fly." I had heard clips of this song used before on television for an airline commercial. It was a simple rhyme, not very interesting and excessively sentimental, but it had attracted a large crowd to the dance floor. The dancing boys were lost in the chorus. The song had triggered an emotional response, either in the form of a past memory or a contemplated future, and they were alight with nostalgia or hope. After a few verses the schmaltz got to me too. It wasn't the lyrics but the melody, the pitch of her voice. Céline could have been singing about anything, but the notes she was hitting were so high. They were happy and sad at the same time, and I couldn't help but be moved by this sappy remix of a love song.

It had been a long time since I had listened to love songs. I felt they belittled what I was going through. I now thought love songs to be beautiful lies. They made common something I felt couldn't be — but *must* be — and then I'd wonder how special these feelings were in the first place if they were as ubiquitous as the music industry would have me believe. I felt angry I could be led so easily to emotion, that a musical formula could manipulate my heart. In my mind I could still see Max's tape player sitting on the floor of his bedroom, playing the songs that still reminded me of him. Coffee brewing over the music, we'd collapse onto his futon and lie there all morning. What was he thinking, lying on top of me, staring at the walls and singing along with those songs? Where was he if not with me?

I finished my beer, ordered two shots of Jack Daniel's and another beer, and then headed back to the top floor of the dance club. Vince was still on the railing when I returned, alone now, staring down at the people below.

"I wondered where you went."

"Did a bit of a whore tour."

Vince laughed. He always laughed at my stupid jokes.

We watched, in silence, as his friends danced below us. Antoine was up on the speaker mouthing the words to a song he thought he knew while below him two young twinks made out with their shirts off, their chests pale and thin as Popsicle sticks. I turned my back to the dance floor and checked out the level we were standing on. There was a bar not too far from us, and three occupied couches that ran beside it. I noticed two boys in their early twenties chatting near the cash. I could tell from their body language they had just met. The brunet was familiar. He worked at one of the coffee shops in the Village, the one patronized by young university students who use one eye to study while the other holds the rest of the room hostage. I had ordered coffee from him several times in the past year but had never had a conversation with him. Once, I ran into him on St. Laurent as I was coming home from work. As we passed each other my eyes caught his but I became too petrified to smile hello and averted my gaze before he had the chance to react to our crossing. Three steps away I cursed myself for not attempting a polite nod. His beauty was intimidating; it made the most basic of public etiquette impossible. As for the other boy, I hadn't seen him before. He was a redhead, a rarity in the city. He was younger, shorter, with lighter skin than the boy he was talking to. The redhead was also beautiful. All men are beautiful at twenty-one.

"God, I feel so fucking old."

"Shut up," Vince moaned. "You're younger than I am."

I had forgotten Vince was several years older than me. The years looked good on him. "No, you know what I mean. I *feel* old. When did everyone else get so young?"

"I know … One of my students came out at eleven. He's fifteen now and has had a boyfriend for two years. Two years! I've never had a boyfriend for two years!"

We watched as Antoine got down from the speaker and, taking his two other friends in tow, disappeared into the crowd.

"Make any New Year's resolutions?" Vince asked.

"Same things as last year, I suppose. Eat better. Exercise. Read more. Expand my vocabulary … Hey, do you know what frangible means?"

"Frangible? I think it means weak, or frail … Why?"

"No reason."

"My resolution for 2006 is to travel more now that I have a regular paycheque and much of the summer off. And read, too. God, it seems as if I never get to read anything that's not part of the curriculum anymore."

There was a moment's pause and then Vince asked, "But Will, how are you doing, really?"

"I'm fine," I lied. My heart was still purple; soft and sore.

"Have you run into Max since?"

"No. I'm dreading it. It's inevitable, though. I'm surprised it hasn't happened yet. What about you? Do you see Eric?"

"Sometimes. He's here tonight." He gestured towards the men below. "With a new boyfriend. It's been a while, but it's still weird, you know?"

"Yeah."

Vince, resting against the railing, looked like a boy about to drop stones off of a bridge. Why hadn't it worked out between us?

I began to feel the effects of alcohol and realized I was moving to the music. "Vince," I said impulsively, "let's get a drink!" I grabbed him by the hand and led him to the bar. I ordered us both a beer and a shot of Jack. When our drinks came, we slammed back the shooters and chased them down with gulps from our bottles.

"Yowza!" said Vince. "That's brutal."

"So," I asked, the fire within me, "you're not dating anyone? No one on the radar?"

"No, not really. You?"

"Who me? I'm dead inside," I joked. "But you know, Vince," I started to say because I was drunk and it felt like the generous thing to do, "you're a really cool guy. Eric doesn't know what he's missing. I'm sorry we don't hang out."

"It'd be nice if we saw each other more."

Vince leaned in close. We touched as we spoke: his palm on my hip, mine on his back. He smelled as I remembered — leather and vanilla. I bought us more drinks and we slandered our ex-boyfriends. Soon we were playing with each other's fingers, and before I knew it we were kissing. I had forgotten how soft and delicate his lips were. Vince's tongue tasted sweet and suddenly it came rushing back to me: the memory of who I was when I had met him.

I asked him to come home with me. We stumbled through

my messy apartment, making out in the dark. I pulled Vince onto my bed and tore off my Great Bunch T-shirt, gleefully remembering what it was like to rip off my clothes and jump into bed with someone. Vince took a look at my belly in the dim light. "Hey, this is new," he laughed.

"Shut up," I laughed back, surprised he had noticed the weight I had put on. I quickly silenced him with my mouth and unbuttoned his shirt, tugging at where it disappeared under his belt. Vince got up for a second and removed his button-down, pulling off the undershirt he wore as well. Time had also changed Vince's body. I noticed he had filled out and that his chest bore a wilder, denser pattern of hair than I remembered. I shifted my body as Vince came back down, moving my arm to let his slip underneath and fit closer into our puzzle. Kissing deeply, my hand rushed for his belt. With one hand I began to undo the buckle and drag his jeans down to his knees exposing his mustard-coloured boxers. I stood up and took off my jeans and socks, and came back down to him in my briefs. I pulled back the band of his underwear and released the head of his penis, a fleshy mound poking out of the elastic waistband. I took the tip of his cock in my mouth, my hands on his hips, grasping at both sides of his underwear as I circled the dome. He trembled as I slid up and down his shaft. With each downward motion my hands pulled the boxers down a little more until they, too, were below his knees and his legs began to kick at them. Stopping him, I grabbed hold of his legs and, lifting them up, removed the remaining clothing from his body.

Vince was beautiful in his nakedness. His colour, his shape, his smell. I felt drunk on his body and, lunging forward, took him all in my mouth. Vince gasped. His sounds got louder and he got harder, hotter, in my mouth. I moved my hands down and began to play with his balls, massaging the muscles beneath before sliding a finger under to circle his cherry.

Suddenly Vince stopped me. He pulled me up to meet his face where he passionately, wildly, began to devour me, tongue pushing its way hard into my mouth and drawing me in as close as I would go. Here he is trying to tell me something, I thought. He is trying to tell me he loves me. But he doesn't *really* love me — we both know that. He thinks he loves me, or wants to love me, or could maybe one day love me. I've felt that myself many times. Sex makes us want to say I love you even though we know it's not true.

Then it was Vince's turn. He reached down into my underwear to grab my cock but was taken aback to find it nowhere near as hard as it should have been, flaccid in my briefs. I sensed his disappointment, felt it in his distracted kiss. Should I say something? I wondered. Explain what was going on? But what excuse could I give him when I didn't know myself?

"I have trouble keeping hard sometimes," I managed to mumble. "I don't know why. Stress maybe ... or maybe it's the booze."

"Don't worry about it," he said, but I did anyway.

Vince shifted his body and, coming up onto his knees, pushed me down onto my back. He was going to give it to me good and fix me with his skill, and that made me feel terrible. Vince wrapped his lips around my flaccid penis and tried to shape it into something upright and rigid. I made a few sounds for him and tried to force my mind to make it harder. I reached for his cock so at least I'd be doing something, but he pushed my hand away. Nothing. I felt his hands on my body, myself inside of his mouth, but nothing.

It soon became clear that Vince's blow job wasn't going anywhere. He conceded, coming up to kiss me. He continued to tug below as I took his cock in my right hand and rushed to push him over the edge. Vince came in quick gasps, collapsing on top of me, his forehead on my shoulder. Underneath his weight I could feel the warmth dripping down my ribs, matting into my chest hair. Vince raised his head to kiss me and reached for my cock one more time. He found it slightly alert. He did his best to get me off, but I had to take it from him. I almost thought I was going to make it a couple of times but I lost it and, collapsing back with a tired hand, I told him it wasn't going to happen.

We didn't discuss it further. Vince sat up, reached over and took five tissues out of the box of Kleenex on my nightstand. He kneeled on the bed, his limp penis hanging victorious between his legs as he wiped himself, and then me. I looked at his penis, flat and deflated like mine, and became envious of its supremacy.

"Do you want to stay the night? What time do you need to get up?" I asked.

"8:30?"

I looked at the clock. It was already 3 a.m. I set the alarm and turned back to join him under the covers. Vince drew me in close and spooned me from behind. He held on tight and then, kissing the dent in my left shoulder, whispered a hushed "Good night."

Chapter 8

In some ways I miss my secret, but the mysterious distraction I had discovered at fifteen stopped being mine the moment I shared it with my mother. Then it became hers. An unspoken truth that would weigh upon her until she was ready to confront it: that she was the mother of a gay man.

That wasn't her only secret. The cancer was, too. My mother hid her illness from the people in her life. She told her sister, and her boss at work — but only when she required a leave of absence. And she told none of her other co-workers, nor her friends. It seemed odd to me that a hypochondriac wouldn't speak publicly about an actual illness. "It's no one's business but our own," she had said when I asked her why she was upset that I had told Angie. "I don't need anyone feeling sorry for me."

Although I didn't understand, I respected her wishes. Even *we* didn't talk about the cancer. To talk about it would be to imagine its consequences, and my mother didn't want that. "Not now, Will." She'd put her hand to her eyes when I tried to discuss the alternative therapies I'd been researching. "I'm tired." It felt equally impossible to continue the conversation I had started in the hospital. Her comments about gay life sat like a boulder in the back of my brain. "It's a very lonely life." What did she know that I didn't? It didn't feel lonely. In fact it felt quite the opposite. There were hundreds of people in the bars and clubs I had been to since Angie had first taken me out, numerous people who seemed happy and very much like me.

I rationalized that it was normal she'd need some time to come around. I, after all, had had years to get used to the idea. She was also battling an illness and we had more pressing matters to deal with: the treatment, the nausea, and the added stress of recovery. But a year later, when she did get better and her cancer went into remission, I had expected that communication could only improve between the two of us and we would be able to talk about anything. Instead we rambled along as if the past year had never happened. We were so elated by her recovery, so desperate for a bit of normalcy in our lives, that neither of us wanted to rock the boat, and I remained quiet about how I lived my life.

Mom knew Montreal had a gay village, but I doubt she knew where it was. I had discovered it long ago with Angie's help. I hadn't needed to ask. One night at work, long before my mother's illness, she showed up with a glossy copy of a gay city guide called *Fugues* and tucked it into my knapsack as I was leaving. At home I devoured it. Its pages burned into me the names and addresses of the bars and restaurants that populated a stretch of Ste. Catherine Street east of Amherst. Almost immediately I was on my bike, calling out to my mom that I was going for a ride.

I soon memorized the Village's geography, its main drag and side streets, swooping up and down the pavement on my ten-speed to study the homes and faces of those I felt were so fortunate to live in the neighbourhood. Up until then Montreal had seemed small to me. I knew nothing beyond the three outposts of my life: home, work, school. Before, the city seemed to fall off east of St. Denis. Now a whole new area had been unearthed, one of lingering glances and vibrant character that, at night, morphed into a riotous fête the scope of which I had never thought possible. On hot summer nights the glass doors that separated the street from the bars were open wide and, too young and petrified to go in, I'd watch as well-dressed men laughed at each other's jokes and drunk people sang karaoke. When it rained, the streets were stripped bare and older men would buy pitchers of beer for the scrawny hustlers drying off inside. Sometimes I'd see the occasional drag queen in heels buying cigarettes from the corner *dépanneur*, or an attractive young couple having a public meltdown on the sidewalk. The concrete action on Ste. Catherine was boisterous and wild, while the homes on Panet and Plessis remained quiet, serenaded by the neon lights of the Molson Brewery down by the river, singing its red and blue lullaby to the men who cruised in the shadows.

Soon after I had acknowledged Angie's gift she told me about the bars she went to, the theme nights and colourful characters she knew from going out as often as she did. And then, once I turned eighteen, she began to take me out with her, introducing me to people who were happy to meet me but who would forget my name five minutes later. A whole world of possibility existed in these dark boxes and, in the beginning, it would spread out and unravel for me in strange and wonderful ways.

But it was all put on hold the year my mother battled cancer.

I didn't leave the house much in 1999. Instead I watched TV, kept my mom company, and learned how to make a few meals. I also learned how to knit. In between her bouts of chemo, my mom kept busy with an afghan she had resolved to make during her convalescence. It was going to be stunning. The yarn she was using was thick and dense, and was a combination of blue, green, white, and black. Often she was forced to put the bundle down, overcome with pain and nausea. That's when I decided to take it up. One day, after she had recovered from a particularly gruesome attack, I asked her to give me a lesson so I could work on the afghan when she wasn't feeling well. My mom was delighted to teach me. It took a while to get the hang of it, and once or twice I had to unravel complete rows to make it right, but pretty soon I was laying down large sections of the blanket, sitting beside her as she lay twisted on the bed.

Angie tried to get me out of the house, but I had no desire to leave. It felt wrong to dance, drink, and flirt with boys when this was happening at home.

But months passed and it was September again. My mom had finished her treatments and all was clear. No more cancer. The two of us let out a giant breath and held each other fiercely as we heard the news. It was over. We had made it to the other side.

I wasted no time getting back out there. I wanted to put the last year behind me, erasing any memory of what we had been through. And so I switched back to full-time at school, and spent as many nights as I could out with Angie and her friends.

"GOD, THAT WAS BORING." ANGIE sat next to me on the wooden steps of one of the Village's buildings, rolling a joint on some club flyer a baby dyke had handed us on the way out of the bar. It was a Thursday, late September 1999, and we had just bowed out of the Village's most popular lesbian night, a party called Girls in the Sky. "What's wrong with Montreal's girls? Why don't they go out anymore?" she whined, intent on her task, crumbling the bulbs of weed into fine grains. "No wonder dyke nights keep fizzling."

I shrugged. "I thought it was fun."

"Please," she said, licking the joint closed. "The music sucked, the crowd sucked." Angie lit the joint and pulled in the smoke with short deep breaths. She exhaled in one long stream. "Everything sucked."

I took the joint from her and took a toke, coughing on the smoke as it spilled from my mouth. I had lost my tolerance, having given up all forms of smoking once my mom had been diagnosed.

Angie and I were sitting in the shadows of a giant maple tree on Plessis, one of the residential streets that cut across the main drag of stores, bars, and clubs. We were only about half a block from the late-night clamour of pedestrians and taxis, but from where we sat it looked empty and quiet. It was fall, and Montreal was having an identity crisis. One moment it was cool, the next warm. I hadn't needed the jacket I had brought so it lay on my lap like a lifeless puppet. We passed the joint back and forth a couple of times, looking at the darkened homes in front of us lit up by yellow street lamps.

"You guys don't know how good you have it," she continued. "There's so much out there for you. So many men, so many parties. There really are no options for women anymore."

"I don't understand," I said, still struggling with the smoke.

"You spoke to, like, three hot girls tonight. That girl Candace gave you her number. And you danced with the other one, the one who wanted you to take her home."

"Ug, no way."

"And I saw some cute guys and — What are you talking about, the music was great! You were dancing!"

"But it's not like it used to be," she griped. "I remember the old Sky, back when it was on St. André. Boy, that was fun. Any night of the week you'd go out and it would be packed. And it was dark and cruise-y too. When I first came out I had such a blast. The old Sky and K2 bar and Kiev … You don't know what you missed." Angie finished off the joint and reached into her knapsack to pull out a pack of cigarettes. "Now it feels like a watered-down version of that," she continued, lighting one. "I don't know, maybe it's me. I mean, isn't that always the case? Everything looks better in hindsight."

"I suppose," I said, staring at the tree in front of us, mesmerized as it swayed in front of the street lamp. Angie may have felt bored, but I was happy the magic hadn't worn off for me yet.

She shifted towards me. "So I know you don't think so, but that Vince guy has the hots for you."

"No, he doesn't … I only just met him. We're friends."

"Friends don't look at each other the way he looked at you tonight."

"Please."

"I know you don't believe me, but he's been hot for you since you met. Every time we're out I see him following you around like a lap dog. It's like the two of you are joined at the hip."

"He's a fun guy. We get along, that's all."

A gust of wind rolled through the street causing a fleet of helicopter seeds to fall from the trees and twirl down to our feet.

"Wow. Don't you love those things?" I smiled and felt the effects of the marijuana — wide tingling in the wrinkles on my face.

There was a silent pause as we considered the sky. It was an open, cloudless night, and the sky was deep and still. "Lots of stars out," Angie remarked. "I'm amazed we can see them in the city."

"Can you make out any constellations?" I asked, adjusting my eyes. With her interest in astrology, I figured Angie must know something about the stars' positions.

"Well, there's part of the Big Dipper over there," she said, pointing to an area to my left. "And over there is Pisces."

"Where," I asked, staring blankly.

"Right there." She pointed as if I could discern from her finger the vast part of the heavens she was talking about.

Everything about the sky and its constellations felt elusive to me. Looking at two, three stars, in a line, I tried to connect the dots and wondered how astrologers learned to draw meaning from them. How clear these stars must have been before the sky became polluted with the artificial glow of city lights.

"I think I'm going to need glasses. Are any of these stars planets?" I asked, not yet a high school teacher. "Can't we see one of them from Earth?"

"Venus, I think," she yawned. "Or maybe it's Mars."

"Well, it's definitely not Pluto," I said, making a joke. "Hey, why do you think they chose to name a planet after a Disney character?"

"That's not who Pluto is named after," Angie scolded me as if she really thought it was what I believed.

"No, I know. It's named after one of the Greek gods."

"One of the Roman gods," she corrected. "Pluto, the God of the Underworld. He's the reason your little helicopters are falling."

"What do you mean?"

"Don't you know the myth of winter?"

"No. How do you know the myth of winter?"

"I learned it in grade six," she said as if I were an idiot. Angie may have dropped out midway through CEGEP, but she was very smart and retained information like a microchip. I was impressed she remembered her Roman mythology.

"Pluto is the God of Hades, the Underworld," she recounted, "and he was struck by Cupid's arrow. It made him fall in love with the next person he saw, which was …" She snapped her fingers a couple of times. "I forget her Roman name, but she was Persephone in Greek mythology. Anyway, he fell in love with Persephone and brought her down to live in the Underworld with him. But her mother … again, Demeter in the Greek story, became so distraught at the disappearance of her daughter that she looked for her the world over, turning the surface of the Earth into a desert wherever she went. Because of her things stopped growing. Now, Jupiter became worried about this and sent Mercury …"

"How do you remember this?" I marvelled.

"… sent Mercury to order Pluto to free Proserpine — that's her Roman name — and he did just that, but first he made her eat some pomegranate seeds so she would have to return to the Underworld for four months of the year because, apparently, if you eat something in the Underworld you can't return permanently to the surface. And that's why nothing grows in the months she is away and everything blooms when she comes back."

"Four months?" I scoffed. "More like five in the Canadian version … But what I don't get is why anyone would name a planet after Satan."

"He's not Satan!" she said, dumbfounded. "He's the Lord of

the Underworld, the place people go when they die — good or bad.... In astrology," she went on, "the powers of Pluto are transformative. They're associated with rebirth and renewal, beginnings as well as endings.... Mind you, the whole Underworld thing does sound kind of creepy, but apparently there are these beautiful Elysian Fields where the virtuous go when they die. And Pluto rules over the entire place. Pluto and Proserpine."

"Still doesn't make sense why they'd name a planet after him. Wasn't there some better Roman god they could have chosen? Why do you think they named it Pluto?"

"Probably because it's at the farthest edge of our solar system," she said. "Because no one's been there. Because it's cold and dark and mysterious, like death."

The wind picked up and rustled the tree in front us, shaking loose more helicopters. Angie sat quiet, contemplating the sky once more. "You know ..." she started, "I've never told anyone else this before, but as a kid, I used to talk to this star."

"What do you mean?"

"There was this bright star that sat by itself in the corner of the sky. I'd sit at the end of my parents' driveway, back when I was growing up in Mississauga, and tell him about my day. Explain to him what was going on at home. I must have been about twelve at the time. I'd walk out of the house, which was such a crappy place of sadness and sickness, you know, with my brother dying. I'd go outside when things got too much and sit on the curb and talk. It's silly, I know. But it made me feel better. When my brother died we moved to Montreal. My parents couldn't stand to live in the same city anymore, let alone the same house. And neither could I. But when we moved the sky was different. When I looked up, I couldn't see him anymore ... And it's silly to say, but I missed him. Isn't that stupid?"

"That's rather sweet actually ... But why was it a *him*?"

"I don't know. He felt like a boy star."

"Well, just because you don't see him anymore doesn't mean he's not up there."

"Or maybe he's gone."

"What do you mean gone?"

"Maybe he died." She lit another cigarette. "He was awfully bright. Supposedly it takes thousands of years for light from a star to reach us. So maybe some of these stars are long dead and we're only now seeing their light. Maybe my star was dead all those years ago and I was talking to his ... what, shadow? Or the opposite of shadow. What's that, then? Light? I don't know. I was friends with a ghost," she laughed.

Both of us went silent.

"How's your mother doing?" Angie asked.

"My mom? Good. Thanks!"

"But, how is she?"

"Well, the surgery wasn't too complicated. They didn't need to restructure her bowel or anything. And she didn't need the radiation. Just a bit of adjuvant chemotherapy or whatever. She lost quite a bit of weight, though, and the doctor wants her to be more active and put back on some muscle. But the prognosis is good. It looks as if they got it all. So she's fine now."

"But, *how* is she?"

"What do you mean?"

"How does she feel?"

"Good, I suppose. She's back at work, part-time. Doing the things she did before this happened. Getting her life back on track."

"I'm so afraid of cancer," Angie said, unaware of the present irony as she held a glowing cigarette between her two fingers.

"Will, I can't believe I've never asked you this before, but what happened to your father? How did he die? I mean, he did die, didn't he?"

"Yes," I said, moving my jacket again from one knee to the other, wringing its slippery polyester in my hands. Angie and I had been friends for years now and I too found it odd we had come this far together and not discussed this. "He died choking on a sandwich. He was at a restaurant or something — some kind of business lunch — and choked on a piece of chicken. I was like two or something at the time so I don't remember much. I don't remember my father at all, really. The memories I have are more of a suit than a man. This brown, thick two-piece suit and blue tie my father used to wear. I remember how it smelled more than anything else: stale with tobacco."

"You never talk about him. I've known you for how many years now, and I find it strange that, given what I know about you, you don't."

"I used to think about him a lot when I was younger. I'd go through my mom's old photos and ask her to tell me stories, but it pained her every time I did. My mom used to tell me how he used to come home from work and she would pass me off to him. I was a very colicky kid and my dad would stay up at night holding and rocking me and then pass me back to her before going to work the next day."

"God, colic is the worst. My niece had it and you should have seen my sister. She was a mess. It must have lasted six weeks."

"I think mine was more like three or four months."

"Holy shit!"

"I know!"

"That's love."

"And," I continued, "when I was born, my pediatrician said I'd be bowlegged. You know, that's when the legs curve outwards. She asked the doctor if she could do anything and he told her it might be possible, if she massaged my legs into place, that over time it would correct itself. So she did just that. She and my dad, when I wasn't crying or screaming — or maybe when I was crying and screaming — they'd sit in front of me, massaging my legs into normalcy. Sometimes I can't get over that. The idea of them standing over me, doing that, for hours."

Angie and I grew quiet. The buzz had begun to wear off and fatigue was setting in. Angie yawned and I rubbed my eyes, but we didn't get up. We sat for a couple more minutes, silent, watching the wind blow the dust and trash around the street in circles. I thought of the selflessness of my mother and father: a man I never knew and the young girl he married. I suppose I really didn't know either of them — who my dad was and who my mom was with him. In many ways I knew Angie a lot better than I would know either of them. I couldn't talk to my mom the way I could with Angie. My mom could never sit on these steps, shooting the breeze, talking about everything and nothing at once, and have a meandering conversation that, for some reason, drew us closer in ways I couldn't understand.

"Sometimes I feel it's my duty to save my mother," I said.

"What?"

"I feel like that's part of the reason I'm here, on this planet," I said. "Or why I'm gay. That, being a gay man, it's my duty to save her."

"Save her from what?"

"From herself. From life. I mean, look at her. There is nothing in this world she wouldn't do for me. Hasn't already done for me. She's cooked for me, cleaned for me, provided for me, fought for me, loved me. Her whole life, or most of it, has been to take care of me. And now that I'm older, well, I want to give something back. I want her to enjoy life, however much of it she has left. I want to see her out more. Living."

"It sounds like guilt."

"It's not guilt," I said, laughing off the suggestion. "It's something more honest than that."

And on that note, Angie got up. "Will, you are the biggest momma's boy I have ever met. How are we ever going to find you a man?"

I laughed as she pulled me up from the steps. Maybe I was still stoned.

Lazily, the two of us walked north to Ste. Catherine and took a cab to her place.

Chapter

9

The alarm went off at 8:30, waking Vince. I had been up for about twenty minutes by then, staring at the walls of my room. I hadn't slept much. I'd tossed and turned most of the night as if at sea, the sheets the violent waves that kept pulling me under. At some point I nodded off and awoke spooning Vince. I had a close-up view of the freckles on his shoulders — ripe spots on a banana peel.

He got up to shower and I brewed some coffee. I offered to make him breakfast when he emerged all fresh and clean. He thanked me, but told me he couldn't stay. I watched him as he collected his things and downed his coffee. We shared a lingering hug on his way out the door.

I returned to the kitchen and refilled my mug. On the windowpane above the sink, frost had formed overnight. The summer sun was long gone, living now in another part of the sky. Its absence touched everything around me: the counter, the floor, the circulating air. I could feel the cold biting my nose, my fingers. But inasmuch as I was in my apartment, hungover and frozen, I was somewhere else entirely. I was back at the bar with Vince amidst the beer and shooters; I was in bed with Max, nestled in the folds of his warm comforter.

The chill in the room snapped me from my reverie, and I moved over to the thermostat to turn up the heat. On the floor in front of me, in the doorway to my bedroom, rested the jeans I had worn the night before. I picked them up and gave them a whiff. They reeked of cigarettes. I checked their pockets before throwing them into the washing machine. Then I went into my bedroom and collected the dirty clothes I could find, including my old T-shirt. I stripped the bed and dumped everything into the drum and started a wash.

I looked outside. It was snowing. Thick wet patches fell heavy from the sky, increasing in number as they accumulated on the tree behind my building. My aunt was returning to Florida today. Would her flight be cancelled? I was glad I didn't have to leave the house, but still thought how great it would be to board a plane today and emerge hours later in the sun and heat. Maybe I should go visit her. Where was Venice, Florida anyway?

I walked to the front of my apartment, to my bookshelf, and took down my Oxford Atlas of the World. It was a Christmas gift given to me by Max. We had often talked about travelling together to parts of the world that neither of us knew much about. Inside the front cover he had inscribed "Where to first?"

I found Florida on page forty-five, a flaccid mass that reminded me too much of the night before, and then located Venice, a small city on its underside by the Gulf of Mexico.

I flipped through the rest of the book, looking at the shapes and borders of various countries. The black interconnected lines of latitude and longitude reminded me of the gift I had given Max on his birthday. Last spring I had come across an old electrocardiogram in a box of keepsakes. When I was a child, my mother — always the hypochondriac — had me tested for a heart murmur. Of course I didn't have one, but the doctor gave me the EKG when we were done. When Max and I began dating I had the idea of framing it and giving it to him as a gift. The printed graph was proof of my heart; the only tangible evidence of its tiny, intricate workings. I figured it belonged to him anyway. In the time we were together it beat only for him. His scent, his touch, sent it racing. His voice, his presence, calmed it down. It rose and fell for him in such a way that the sharp points outlined on the page appeared to be music he had written, even if the EKG had been taken many years before I had met him. When I'd look at it, I'd become mesmerized. This is how my heart looks, I'd think. Nothing more than a thin black line on a red road to somewhere. A map of my heart. And that felt right. It felt like what it should look like. Not the bloody, misshapen organ we had learned about in biology class, but an expression of its function. My life force, my capacity for love, the brain of my heart. And that is what I wanted him to know he had.

"You're giving me your heart?" he had asked, touched.

"You have it already," I had said. "It's just a reminder."

What did Max do with the gift I gave him? Did he throw it away? He was never fully aware of how much it belonged to him in the first place. So where is it now? Somewhere? Nowhere? Lost in the city? Maybe if I stare at these pages long enough I'll find it — in a map of Canada, or Montreal. A map is used to help us locate our position, chart journeys, tell us about a specific place and time. But I feel lost in all of this emotional geography. And it gets worse as I circle the terrain, as contours do, farther and farther away from the peak.

"I'VE ALWAYS WANTED TO GO to Alaska," he said. Max and I were on the 80 bus, hanging on to the handles as we stared at our reflections travelling against the darkening hill of trees and snow. It was mid-February, the sun setting at the prompt hour of 5:26 p.m., and the bus struggled as it climbed up Parc Avenue.

"I don't know," I said. "Don't you get enough of the cold and snow here?"

"But it's bright in Alaska, at least in the summer. And I don't mind the snow and cold as long as it's clear and sunny. You just need to be prepared," Max chided me as he felt the fabric of my thin polyester shell. On this particular day he and I were coming back from an afternoon spent outside in the Old Port and I was chilled to the bone.

"Montreal's winters are horrible," I said. "They weasel their way in at the end of November and punch you in the face on the way out in March. That's five months of cold weather. I'd rather take a trip down south to Mexico, or to Greece. Wouldn't that be nice?" I imagined myself cranking up the heat once we got back to my apartment, placing the ice cubes that were my toes on the surface of the radiator. "I can't wait to get home."

Max smiled and hooked his finger into my jean pocket. Immediately I began to warm up.

More people got on the bus at the next stop, forcing us to move to the back. We ended up hanging above two young women deep in conversation. By the look of it they were both students, chatting away about a teacher they had in common.

"Isn't he the worst?" said one. "He'd better not make that required reading. Already he has us reading useless stuff."

"Have you been up close to him?" said the other. "He doesn't clean his ears."

"Gross!"

"You'd think his wife would give him a hint it's not okay to have crusty ears. That's probably why he doesn't understand a thing I say. I swear, if I have to clarify myself one more time in class I think I am going to have him committed."

Max and I had stopped talking. It felt almost rude to, but I couldn't help overhearing the conversation and wondering if my students talked about me this way. These women spoke way too loudly for such a tight, cramped space. Everyone on the bus respected the commuter's rule of silence, staring into their newspapers or listening to music on their headphones, while these two let everyone know their business. It began to grate on my nerves.

Did it feel loud, though, because these women were English? Despite the large number of anglophones in Montreal it felt rare to overhear English in public. French was all over but I never *heard* it. I was able to tune out the French voices around me and concentrate on a book in the Metro or corrections in a coffee shop. Even French cellphone conversations became part of the white noise, part of the hum of the bus climbing up the mountain. But these two young women, sitting beneath us, having this obnoxious conversation in English, drove me nuts. I rolled my eyes and placed my head on Max's shoulder.

"Oh my God," I said, getting off the bus and into a snow-bank. "Why wouldn't those two girls shut up?"

"The ones below us?"

"Didn't you find them annoying?"

"They were pretty loud."

"I apologize for my people."

We navigated across a series of unplowed streets to the snow-barricaded building where I lived. I opened my apartment door and was greeted by a watery mess on the floor.

"Aw, shit. What happened?"

My fishbowl had fallen from its perch and lay in pieces and puddles on the hardwood floor. My small orange goldfish, Norman, lay immobile on its side.

Max looked around. "I think your shelf collapsed. See, the pegs here are ripped out of the wall."

"Aw, that shelf was here when I moved in." I had been living in this apartment for the past year and a half — since I'd moved out of my mother's — and the space looked much as it had back then. My bedroom had a series of shelves exactly like the ones I had placed my fishbowl on. I'd have to secure them now, too. "Shit … Poor Norman."

The phone rang. "Do you mind getting that, please?" I was already on my knees picking up pieces of glass and feeling mortified to come home to find my pet fish dead on the floor.

"Hello?" I could hear off in the background. "One moment."

Max passed the phone to me. "I think it's your mom."

"Hello?"

"Hi, Will. How are you?"

"Not good. My shelf collapsed and it knocked my fishbowl onto the floor. Now there is glass and water everywhere. Norman is dead. Can I call you later?"

"I'm sorry, Will. Be careful picking up the glass. Listen, I called to see if you felt like coming over for dinner, but it sounds as if you've got your hands full."

"Yes, Max and I just got in and we're going to cook to-night. Unless of course, you'd like to join us?" Had I asked that? Since I had moved out my mother had come over every few months for dinner — but not since I'd started to date Max. I'd been trying to muster the courage to get the two of them to meet, but felt the occasion needed to be perfect. But perhaps the best plan was no plan?

"Thank you, Will, but no, not tonight," she said. "I've already got something on the go. I thought if you were free — But that's fine. Another time."

"Maybe tomorrow?" Max had shown up with a broom and a garbage bag and began to help clean up.

"Okay, have a good night. Call me later if you like."

"Thanks. I will. Bye." I hung up. "Remind me later I have to call my mom," I said to Max, almost an afterthought. He didn't say anything, just looked at me and the mess on the floor.

MAX AND I MADE DINNER that night (shrimp pasta and a salad), and then retired for the evening on the couch. Before bed he remembered something and got up from where we were sitting to surprise me with an item from his knapsack.

"What's this?" I asked, yawning and looking at the video-cassette.

"Remember how you said you wanted to see me act?"

"Get out!" I barked, snatching the cassette from his hand and running to the VCR.

"Don't get too excited," he said as I kneeled in front of the TV and pushed the cartridge into the machine. "It's a tape of me in high school. I came across it the other day while cleaning out my closet." The warped lines running across the screen soon gave way to an old Wendy's commercial. "At least, I think it's on here. I haven't seen it in years."

Max took the remote from me, stopped the tape, and fast-forwarded it. He soon stopped it again, pressed play, and all of a sudden there he was — a youthful likeness of him — located somewhere between the picture on his fridge and the man in the room with me.

"Oh my God! You were so young!" I said, placing my hand over my mouth. The younger Max wore a black coat outfitted with feathers, a large brimmed hat, tights, and knee-high boots. His face was pale, powdered white in high-school-drama-club makeup. "What's this?" I asked.

"*Cyrano de Bergerac.* I played Christian de Neuvillette."

"Oh my God …" I repeated, spellbound. There was Max in front of me, a good ten years younger — thirteen, fourteen. Smoother. Without the stubble and delicate lines now on his face. His voice was the same, but slightly warped in the way an audio recording makes it more effeminate.

"I sound so gay."

"Nonsense. What are you saying there?" I said, trying to follow. It was written in verse and Max was projecting to the back of the room. He spoke with a boisterous voice, pompous and full of emotion.

"Something about wanting to find out the identity of the woman I have fallen in love with …" Max sounded distracted. I looked beside me to see him cringe at his performance.

We watched it for thirty more seconds.

"Okay, can we stop this now? This is horrible."

"No, not yet," I said.

"It was a silly play," he said. "I didn't know what I was doing. I'm much better than this now." Max got up and turned off the TV and removed the tape.

"What are you talking about? You were great."

Max was embarrassed. He placed the tape back into his bag. "No, it was crap. Wait and see. I'll get another part and you'll come see me."

"Come here," I said and pulled him to me. "Talk to me. Tell me ... What's your dream role?"

"My dream role?" he smiled, coming around. Max thought about it as he sat on top of my chest, wrestling with my arms. "I guess that would have to be Cuirette in *Hosanna* ... or Luc in *Les Anciennes Odeurs*. Any male lead in a Michel Tremblay play, really ... Tom in *The Glass Menagerie*. Stanley in *Streetcar*."

"That's a lot of flowers for me to buy," I said.

Max smiled and lowered his head to kiss me, the comforting warmth making me sleepy.

I yawned. "I'm tired."

"It's getting late. Didn't you want to call your mother?"

I looked at the clock on the vcr display. It was 10:30 p.m.

"No, it's nothing important. I'll call her tomorrow."

Max pulled me up and the two of us readied ourselves for bed.

BEFORE NODDING OFF, WE HAD sex. Three-and-a-half months in it had become quick and efficient, but still passionate. Sometimes when Max came up behind me and breathed into my ear, the surface of my skin would ignite and I'd get hard. It was no longer only about what he looked like, or how his body unfurled naked in front of me. It was about his scent, his tongue, his breath. And several months later, when Max would stop going to the gym and put on a couple of pounds, his thickness would do the same. There was something intoxicating about the idea of there being more of him. Extra weight I could tumble around with and love.

Yes, love. I had known something was up. I could feel it happening as we pressed ourselves together, swirling around like snakes. But it was on this night, in bed, thinking of the young

Max in the video and the older one sleeping beside me, that I admitted it to myself. Over the next few weeks I found myself wanting to say the words, but I couldn't. Instead I would sigh. He'd ask what was up and I'd smile and say, "Nothing." I'd sit on top of the words to make sure they didn't come out. In fact, I felt like telling him all the time, but I knew that I shouldn't. He wasn't ready. I wasn't ready. And besides, it would change things. When you tell someone you love them over and over again does it not diminish the meaning of those words?

This was indeed a first. Nothing with Shaun or Vince or any other of the other men I had fallen for had come anywhere close to it. I had read somewhere that the first time you fall in love your brain creates a pathway, one with a juicy dose of dopamine at the end. It's like walking in a tall field of grass. Your first time through you leave an imprint, a trail of parted blades that bend straight at the ground. It leaves a mark so the next time you find yourself before it you know how to get to the other side. And then you do it, again and again. Even if the payout is no longer as great as it once was. In essence, it too becomes kind of like a map — a worn-down blueprint of memories we spend the rest of our lives retracing. And here I was, wading into love's tall blades for the first time.

C
h
a
p
t
e
r
10

How it ended is a blur. From what I can remember, we didn't argue and I didn't protest. He kept talking and I listened. For how long, I don't know. It happened so fast that before I knew it I was back on my bike, riding up Parc Avenue as if I had never got off in the first place. It would only be once I got home, within the safe enclosed walls of my apartment, that emotion seeped out of me. I felt duped, embarrassed. Was this a joke? How could this be happening? Bit by bit the world was crumbling, the sky falling, and I sat silent in my apartment, afraid that if I moved I would hasten its erosion.

HE HAD CALLED ME AT home. It was a Saturday afternoon in late September and I had spent most of the day marking assignments.

"Can you come and meet me?" the voice said, grave and troubled.

"Max? Is everything okay?"

He let out an uncomfortable sigh. "No, not really."

I stood up from my chair. "What's the matter?"

"Just … Can you come and meet me? I can't talk about this over the phone."

"Where are you?"

"Outside Place des Arts Metro, on Bleury."

"I'll be right there."

I HOPPED ON MY BIKE and sped down Parc Avenue towards the subway station, fighting for space with cabbies and pedestrians and sailing through street lights. What could be so important that he couldn't tell me over the phone? It had been a couple of days since I had heard from him, which wasn't peculiar. I had been busy with corrections and figured he had been overwhelmed with work or had been pulling extra hours with his acting coach. But something else was up.

Max was where he said he'd be when I arrived, standing outside the Metro doors. I got off my bike and walked towards him, leaning in for a kiss. Only he didn't kiss back. Instead Max recoiled from my touch.

"What's wrong?"

"I can't do this anymore."

"… What? What can't you do?"

"*This*." He began to lead me away from the subway doors, my bike in tow, as people jumped off the 80 bus and into the underground. "I don't want this anymore. I need to be alone."

Was I hearing this right? "You … Are you breaking up with me?" I asked, confused, walking with him through the parking lot on the corner and into the shadowy storefronts on Mayor Street. A noisy truck tried to wrangle its way into a loading dock to our left — an elephant backing up. "Is there someone else?"

"I haven't been ... unfaithful," Max chose his words. "And I don't want to be. Will, this hasn't been working for me for some time. I'm sorry, but I don't think we're meant for each other."

I stopped walking, dropped the bicycle and backed myself up, much like the truck, onto a stoop outside one of the closed boutiques, feeling first to make sure the ground was below me.

"I don't understand ... Don't you love me?"

Max paused for a second, mouth open. "That's the thing ... I'm not *in* love with you. I don't know if I ever was. I might have thought so. But that's not to say I don't still care for you, or didn't enjoy the time we spent together. I'm sorry, Will, but I need to be honest about how I feel."

I opened my mouth to say something, but no words came out. A shield had gone up, and now I'd only be able to listen to and record his explanations so that I could sift through them later by myself. I soberly took in everything he had to say, listening as his words swirled about in front of me, petrified to let them sink in but knowing I could do nothing to stop their relentless attack on everything I once believed in.

"Things have become stale between us," he went on. "And I want more, something different. When we first met I thought you were nice, but you weren't the typical guy I'd go for. I thought I'd give it a try, see where it would go — and we had fun. But this ... is no longer enough, I'm afraid."

Max had a look of utter calm on his face, one of clarity and purpose. I stared at the shapes of his soft features, the contours I was being told I could no longer touch. They felt so far away, these perfect lines; and one by one I could feel them detaching themselves from me.

I WAS PARALYZED FOR A week. I called in sick and stared at walls. I ordered in junk food and sat in hell. I replayed in my mind everything that had gone down in those final moments, wondering if I could have done anything to prevent it. Maybe I should have fought to keep him, but what could I have said in the face of all that? Nothing Max had said made any sense, and with each day it was becoming painfully clear that I had been in the dark about everything.

Mom could tell something was up. I lied and told her it was nothing, that I was feeling under the weather. With Angie, all I could do was cry. She'd try and reason with me, remind me of the things that had once annoyed me about Max (his messiness, his chronic tardiness, the way he clicked his teeth), but these habits now all seemed trivial. I could hear what she was saying, remembered how exasperated I had felt at times, but my current state had erased and rewritten his character flaws and turned them into poetic mannerisms for me to mourn. They reminded me of the things I *did* love about him: his sense of humour, his undeniable talent, his killer smile.

In the stillness of my apartment the only things that moved were the hands of the clock in the hallway, reluctantly dragging me with them into the future. I couldn't believe it was over. And I continued to sit by myself and do the math, but no matter how I added everything up the answer was always zero.

AFTER ABOUT TEN DAYS, I finally left the house. Angie and some of her friends had been invited to a private party being held on top of the Olympic Stadium. Priape, the city's gay sex shop, had turned thirty, and its owners were throwing a bash on the tower's top-floor observatory. Everyone had been invited: local celebrities, community activists, gay politicians, and staff members of the Village's bars and clubs. "You can't miss this," Angie ordered over the phone. "Everyone who's anyone is going to be there. There's going to be booze, boys, amazing food. I don't want to have to spend the rest of the year saying, 'You really should have been there.'"

When it seemed she still hadn't convinced me, she added, "Also ... I'm going to be wearing a dress."

"What?" I spat into the phone.

Angie explained how the event was going to be fancy, and how she had made a bet with her new girlfriend, Stephanie, to see who would be the one to show up in a dress. Angie had lost. I had seen Angie in a dress on all of two occasions, and both times had been a treat. For the first time in almost two weeks I could feel a smile on my face.

I wasn't so sure, though, in my state, that the best place to be was at a sex shop party with gobs of gay men on the prowl, but the prospect of seeing Angie as a fem again was way too appealing. Besides, it was time to get out of the apartment. Over the past week the air in my place had begun to feel stale. I had sat around in my sadness like damp clothes and now my body had begun to ache.

I didn't spend too much time making myself look present-able. I showered and shaved, and took out of the back of my closet an old suit jacket my father used to wear. It was a grey tweed herringbone blazer with suede patches at the elbow. In all these years I had never tried to replace it, dragging it out each time I was invited to a fancy event (which was rare). The jacket smelled old and musty, but it made me feel sharp and stylish. I wondered if it made me look like my dad.

I met Angie at her place. She greeted me at the door in a bathrobe and makeup. "Excuse me, Miss," I said to her painted face, "is your son home?"

"Very funny," she laughed and pulled me inside. Angie was alone in her apartment, constructing her feminine persona in the bathroom mirror to Siouxsie and the Banshees. I marvelled at her skill. "Well, my older sister used to enlist me to get her ready for her dates," she explained, finishing up on her eyes. "She was such a whore ... I suppose I learned a thing or two. Can you pass me the lipstick?"

I took the lipstick off the top of the toilet tank and handed it to her, watching her spread the colour across her lips. It felt odd watching Angie do this, yet it still seemed so natural. I had known Angie for years and had always found her handsome in her boyishness. Why should I be surprised to find her beautiful in her femininity?

"There. How do I look?" she said, stepping back from the mirror and presenting herself to me.

"Gorgeous," I said, drinking her in. "Izo is going to crap her pants. Now, where's the dress?"

We went into her room. Angie removed her bathrobe and stepped into her gown, a beige thrift-store cocktail dress. I zipped her up. Angie then pulled her hair up and back, setting the length with gem-encrusted clips. Finally, she took out a plunging set of earrings and fastened one to each lobe.

"Shall we take a picture for your mom?" I asked once the look was complete.

"Are you kidding? The last time she saw me in a dress she pestered me for weeks about how I should dress like this all the time."

"You look beautiful. But you should grab a coat," I said, staring at her bare arms. It was the beginning of October and the day had been very cold. "It's chilly out there." Angie grabbed a jacket from her closet and draped it over her arm. She checked herself in the mirror one last time, smoothing out her dress and picking up her keys and purse. "Let's go."

We rode the subway in our finest, got off at the Pie-IX Station and followed the signs for the stadium. Located in the east end, far from the downtown skyscrapers, Montreal's Olympic Stadium is massive. The building is made up of two parts: an enormous oval arena that resembles a flying saucer, and a 500-foot tower slanted above it like a scorpion's tail. I had only been to the stadium a couple times in my life — once as a child for an Expos baseball game and then later, with Angie, for a circuit party — but I had never before travelled up the building's long spine to the observation deck.

A bit lost on the ground floor, we caught sight of some familiar faces and followed them to the funicular at the base of the tower. The cable car operator waited a couple of minutes for more people to arrive before shutting the door and cranking the lever. We felt a sudden lurch, and then slowly began our ascent to the top. The funicular had a glass wall. As we climbed, higher and higher, we watched the city drift further and further away. Houses and people got smaller as we approached our destination. "Holy shit," Angie gasped and grabbed my hand. I too was mesmerized but said nothing, just stared outside at the disappearing ground.

The lift came to a queasy halt and the doors opened to a party in full swing. Down-tempo house played under a rumble of male voices, while tuxedoed waiters delivered trays of tempura shrimp and stuffed mushrooms. Most people were well dressed, in jackets and ties, with the odd gym boy in dark denim and a designer T-shirt. There were also a couple of drag queens and several scantily clad men who I assumed were the entertainment. Angie and I checked our overcoats and then ran over to look out the windows by the bar.

"Would you look at that?" Angie said, pointing to the cluster of downtown buildings in the distance. "We're so freaking high." Below us cars sped up and down the street like matchbox toys. I felt a chill being this far away, atop this forlorn outpost. Angie grabbed my hand and pulled me with her. "Come. Let's go find the girls."

Angie's friends were by another bar at the back of the room. It took us a while to wade through the crowd to get to them. There were loud screams as the girls realized who was walking towards them.

"I don't fucking believe it," said Izo, a little disturbed.

"I don't clean up too bad, now, do I?"

"Not bad at all," said Stephanie, Angie's girlfriend of one month, swinging in to examine the outcome of their bet up close.

"You're looking sharp too, fella," said Carol, feeling the fabric of my jacket. "How are you doing?"

"We're not talking about it," Angie said.

"That's right," I agreed, taking two drinks from a passing waiter and handing one to Angie.

"All right then," said Carol, raising her cocktail in a toast. "To not talking about it!"

Everybody drank.

IT WAS GOING TO BE a great party. As I stood at the edge of our group, by the shrimp platter, I watched the scene evolve. I was amazed at the number of people invited; all active in the gay community, all people I didn't know. Angie, unsurprisingly, knew many of them, people who came up to her and did a double take at the feminine drag she was pulling off. Every few minutes one of two cable cars dropped off another dozen people who made their way into the crowd, laughing, clinking glasses, kissing each other hello.

I downed the remainder of my martini (my third in thirty minutes) and turned towards the bar to order another.

"Excuse-moi," said a man in a pinstriped jacket as he sidled in next to me.

"Pas de problème," I responded.

"Oh, you're English," he replied, picking up on my accent. "I can never tell. I'm so bad at spotting other Anglos. Great party, huh?" The man ordered a gin and tonic. "My name's Peter."

"Will." I shook his hand.

"Nice to meet you, Will." I took a moment to give him a once-over. Peter was about my age, handsome, and a bit huskier and taller than I. He wore black wing-tipped shoes, and his smile was wide and genuine. He took a sip of his drink and turned to face the crowd with me. I reached for some shrimp.

"So, what brings you here?"

"What do you mean?" I said, ripping a few tails from my mouth.

"What's your connection to the store?"

"Oh, my friend," I said and pointed to Angie who was feeding her girlfriend from a chicken skewer, "got some tickets and invited a bunch of us. I've been to Priape before, I'm just not … connected — is that the word? — to the store or anything …"

"What do you do?"

"I'm a geography teacher."

"Elementary?"

"High school."

There was an uncomfortable pause as Peter waited for me to share more. I didn't have the energy, but then, not wanting to appear impolite, I asked him, "What about you? What's your 'connection' to this event?"

"One of the store's managers is my roommate."

I nodded.

"That, and I run a discussion group for gay youth. They invited some of our administrators."

Another awkward pause. "What do you discuss?" I finally asked.

"Well, it's a coming-out group. But kids are coming out earlier and earlier these days, and more with the support of their parents. So sometimes we just talk about what's going on in their lives, their boyfriends or girlfriends, their concerns, safe sex, that kind of stuff. So much has changed since I came out twelve years ago. Boy, was I petrified. I can remember sneaking out to use a pay phone to call a gay help line in case my parents picked up the receiver ... Nowadays we get the parents dropping their kids off at the meetings, or calling to ask about our services."

"Huh."

"That's not to say everyone has it easy," he continued. "Oh no, some kids have it hard. But the group is more of a social group nowadays, for those who are too young or don't want to go to the bars."

"Bars," I repeated. I didn't feel like making small talk with this man, but I didn't want to be rude. I was hoping he'd get the hint and leave me alone.

"What about you?" he asked. "What was your coming out like?"

"... What?" I asked, taken aback, almost choking on my shrimp.

"You? When you came out to your friends and family, what was it like?"

I stood before Peter speechless, surprised he had asked such an intimate question. It was as if he had asked me if I'd ever been in love. "Don't you think that's awfully personal?" I answered, somehow. "I don't even know you and you're asking me about one of the most … vulnerable times in my life."

"Oh, I'm sorry," he said, putting his drink down on the bar. "I didn't mean to offend you. I was just trying to make conversation."

"Well, that's not something I share with just anyone," I said, feeling the emotion begin to swirl. "Not everyone wants to be as forthcoming as the people in your discussion group. But then again," I said, talking more to myself than to him, "why do I make these things out to be romantic when in reality they're nothing more than tedious anecdotes about myself? What more is to be said? We all come out. It can either be a good experience, or a bad one. There are no new ways of doing it. But somehow we stupidly believe that by sharing this information it can bring two people closer together."

I stopped and stood there, not able to look Peter in the eye. Peter began once more to offer me his sincerest apologies, this time in his facilitator's voice. I felt an immediate tug of sadness and suddenly became afraid I was going to cry right there in front of him, by the shrimp platter. "No, I'm the one who's sorry," I said. "Will you excuse me?"

I put my cocktail down on the bar and headed towards the washroom, through the swarms of people that had arrived during our conversation. I couldn't walk in a straight line and had to snake my way through the crowd, trying to avoid the bodies but bumping into them as I went along. This party was almost all men so the line for the bathroom was long. I decided to leave, but went over to the coat check to find an even longer line there.

Thankfully, now away from Peter, I began to feel composed. The crowd, though, was still too much to handle. I looked for an isolated spot to retreat to and that's when I noticed the staircase to my left. Several people were climbing it, and I fell in behind them and followed them up to the observation deck's second floor.

Immediately I felt a change. There were fewer people here and the air was fresher. I could breathe again. I walked over to the window and sat down by its ledge.

The view was incredible. Night was falling and in its wake the city was lighting up, little pinpricks that would burn brighter as the sun disappeared. Slowly I watched as downtown turned into a towering cake, its fierce candles lit by floors of 24-hour fluorescents. I found something reassuring about the glow of those solid buildings and the busy searchlight above Place Ville Marie that threw its luminous arm around the city.

From downtown I looked north to where Mount Royal sat, higher and mightier than any of the city's tallest skyscrapers. The mountain remained dark, save for the white light of the cross perched on top. At its feet knelt the Plateau and the rows of three-storey homes that made up my neighbourhood. There was no way I could see my apartment building from here. All I could make out was a blur of street lamps that danced around my eyes as I tried to focus. I found the two tall chimneys of the factory near Laurier Park, and then the dome of the Portuguese church not far from where Angie's parents lived. From there I could triangulate where my apartment — cold, dark, and empty — must be.

From there I figured out where Mom lived. The three-storey building I grew up in, southeast from the one I lived in now. One of those lights must be hers, I thought. The living room, lit up by her yellow lamp and the TV tube. She'd be sitting there, in her chair, having left her nightly message on my answering machine and getting up once more to make some tea before sitting down with Elizabeth to watch whatever was on.

And then I searched for Max's place. I looked over to the edge of the Village, to the lighted section of Hochelaga-Maisonneuve where his apartment was. I could clearly make out the old penitentiary on Fullum, standing firm among the neighbourhood's crumbling homes. Max lived several blocks from there and I wondered which clusters of street lights were his. There were too many of them, too far away, and bleeding one into the other for me to make them out. But I knew his home was there, somewhere, held in place by the concrete and trees that surrounded it. And there, in the blur of light, was who I had been not two weeks prior. A part of me still lives there, I thought. A part of me still floats outside his window, looking for a way to get back in.

Thinking about who I had been with Max was like looking through a scrapbook of nights spent in his building. It involved all of the senses. When I closed my eyes I could still smell him as he slept: the stale scent of his pillow and the dryness of his hair. I could taste the sweat on his skin and body, the harsh remnants of his cologne, and the sweetness of his tongue. I could see his face, looking directly into me, and remembered the looks we exchanged — waterfalls and roller coasters. And there were the sounds too, the white noise of his breath and the moans from when he told me to go deeper. I could feel Max beside me, his heat, and the softness of his body that my fingers circled as if it were my own, tracing along his limbs as if they were a city map. But none of these moments held any shape. They were gaseous, intangible, memories of the real thing.

If I were a better geography teacher would I be able to locate what I'm looking for? Would I be able to find it out there? Teaching in front of a classroom I have often wondered about the men who came before me, the pioneers who mapped out the great expanse of this country before turning it into backyards and alleyways. How hungry they must have been to discover what lay beyond the borders of the unknown. If I had a better grasp of that knowledge, and maybe some pioneer spirit, would I be able to figure out where I went wrong? Make sure the same thing never happened again?

I heard a sharp squeal of laughter. More people had ascended to the second floor, and suddenly I was in the room again. My face was flushed, my eyes damp. Looking down at the city had haunted me. And now each nook and cranny, each store and restaurant, would soon come to remind me of him, and people, cars, buses, and traffic would all hum his song. There are so many people alive in this city, I thought, looking out, and I used to think we were the only ones.

Another chill ran through me. I could feel the cold coming through the window, the wind twisting around the tower and rattling the glass. The sky began to move and all of a sudden I saw snow. That can't be snow, I thought. It's the beginning of October! But then, it wouldn't be long before winter was here, the snow coming to blanket any memories I had of him and us.

Suddenly, I needed to speak to him. Right away. I shot upright and quickly looked for a pay phone but there were none on the floor. I ran down the flight of stairs to find one, unoccupied, by the bathroom. I put my quarter in and dialled. The phone rang and rang. After about seven rings his answering machine picked up. Not leaving a message, I hung up the receiver and, no longer caring what anyone thought, shoved my way to the front of the coat-check line.

The cable car was sitting there, and once I had my jacket in hand I ran to the car as the operator was about to close the door. As we began our descent I stared eagerly at the ground, anxious to reach the bottom. The car couldn't keep up with the speed of my mind, and by the time we reached the ground floor I was dizzy. As the doors opened, I bolted from the lift, tripping on a step and falling as people called after me to see if I was okay. I waved my hand and mumbled something as I regained my composure and proceeded to find the door to outside.

If it had been snow, it had turned to rain by the time it reached the ground, tiny wet drops disappearing into my over-coat. I made my way to the Metro and took the subway to the Village. I looked for Max in every possible shop, restaurant, and bar on the strip, but he was nowhere to be found.

I then began the path to his house and the cluster of street lights I had tried to discern from above. As I entered his neigh-bourhood, I could see the Olympic Tower in the distance, the party still going, playing hide and seek with the build-ings I passed on the way to his home. I felt spooked by these streets, hated by them and their shops as they looked at me with distaste and judgment, threatening to tell and making it abundantly clear how unwelcome I was. I had once been on such good terms with these corners and sidewalks. I had wit-nessed the seasons fill them with puddles, leaves, trash, and snow, and tonight they stood in silent disapproval of who I was and what I was doing.

I approached his street and circled his building to spot a dim light on in his kitchen. What should I do?

I kept walking to find another pay phone and found one in the lobby of the strip club behind his house. I walked in to the smell of beer and smoke. The DJ was calling another dancer to the stage, while a couple of hard-looking men wearing leather vests and faded tattoos passed by. I called and the phone kept ringing — barely audible under the roar of the rock number on the speakers. I hung up the phone and left the club.

The wind outside had picked up, shooting cold raindrops onto my face. I returned to the back of his building to stare once more at the faded light in his kitchen. Was he home and not answering? Was anyone else there? I couldn't decide what the right thing to do was, but I couldn't imagine walking home not knowing if he was there. Desperately, I plucked up the courage to climb the fire escape up to his back balcony. The wet metal was cold on my skin as I pulled myself up the dark stairs. Once on his balcony, I snuck towards the window and peered inside.

No one was home. A soft light was on in the living room, reflecting off the walls and making the apartment glow a rich red. Two extra chairs had been pulled up to the tiny table in his kitchen, its surface strewn with empty Corona bottles and a full ashtray. I tried to discern how the space had changed in the last two weeks and was relieved to find it hadn't. How simple it would be, I thought, to unhinge his lock and walk into this place once more — to see it again from the inside. But the thought frightened me, and I became afraid of getting caught.

So I left. I walked home, having the conversation I wanted to have with him by myself, speaking aloud to the rain. "So, what were you up to tonight?" I asked, cold and delirious. "Well, I was at this party, 500 feet above the city, looking down, and all I could think of was you." My voice grew louder and my sentences swifter as I walked home, my jacket soaking wet. "I miss you, Max. Don't you miss me?"

When I got home I peeled off my sodden clothes and left them in a pile on the floor. I slid into the cold bedsheets. "No, I'm going to wait for him to call," I said, one last thing to myself out loud. "And he will. Once he realizes what a huge mistake he made. And who knows. Maybe by then, I'll have moved on."

But Max never did call.

Chapter 11

In a city as small as ours, I thought I'd run into him. It'd be sheer coincidence, of course. I'd be out somewhere, with friends, at the movies or at a club, and I would get this sense of gathering doom, the way animals can pick up on an approaching storm. I would feel a sudden panic, my ears would burn, and then I would turn around to see him standing behind me. He'd smile. I'd swallow. We'd say hello, pick up from where we'd left off, and this moment I had been anticipating, dreading for months, would be over and everything would be right again.

But it didn't happen like that. In fact, in the three months after we split, after that sad day in the fur district on Mayor Street, I had no news of him. There were no sightings from Angie, no word from our mutual acquaintances, and I never ran into any of his friends. It was as if he had vanished. The first month was the hardest. Every time I walked into a club or patrolled the Village, I felt anxious. I braced myself for a surprise meeting on the street, leaving the house impeccably dressed, and I'd keep checking over my shoulder, scrutinizing the corners of the city to see if I recognized him amid the architecture, but in those three months that meeting never happened.

I PLACED THE ATLAS BACK on the shelf and returned to the kitchen. The snow had relented and the sun was coming out. I poured myself a bowl of cereal and sat down at the table. Crunching away, I looked at the empty seat across from me and thought of the mornings Max had sat in it. What had happened to him in the last three months? Was he at his own kitchen table, having breakfast with someone else? Was that why I never saw him out anymore?

The thought of Max with another man made me feel heartbroken and a little crazy, but it was the not knowing that was worse. I knew it was possible I'd have to wait another three months — maybe longer — before I found out what he had been up to. That prospect seemed much too much to bear.

Before I knew it I had leapt from my chair and reached for the phone. I dialled the seven familiar digits that lead to his voice, feeling as if I'd always remember the numbers, forever know the pattern my hand traced on the keypad. The phone rang like jolts from a power drill. Over each buzz I thought about the last time we had spoken, how it had been about sadness and silence. Before I could decide whether or not to leave a message, he answered.

"Allo?"

"Max. Hi, Max. It's Will."

"Will." He sounded surprised. "Hi. How are you?"

"Good. Did I wake you?"

"No. I got up a little while ago," he said. I pictured him in his pyjamas, plopping cubes of sugar into his morning coffee. "It's nice to hear from you."

"Yes," I said, taking a breath. "It's been too long."

The conversation was quick, lasting about three minutes. During that time we spoke about my students and his acting, about the January weather and the recent snow. It was great to hear his warm voice again. It possessed a gentle kindness — was flirtatious almost; or was that wishful thinking? At some point, though, I felt all of this was too much and needed to get off the phone. "We should do something sometime," I threw out there. Max agreed, and we settled on Thursday. We chose a place and a time and said our goodbyes.

I hung up the phone to my cold empty apartment, to the half-eaten bowl of cereal and the desperate moments of not five minutes ago. I couldn't believe how simple this was. With one phone call Max was in my life again.

THE REST OF THE DAY, and the four that followed, ran painfully slowly. When Thursday came I was relieved the wait was over.

That morning, as I walked the ten blocks to the Metro, I felt elated. The day was starting off cold, but bright and glorious. If you've experienced Montreal in the winter then you'll know about the light. Montreal's sky glows a brilliant blue in winter — much like the waters of the Caribbean. It's clean, open, and clear. The vibrant blue makes the trees stand out, their branches spikes of inverted bronchioles. When I look at them, I feel as if they breathe the same way I do — ice momentarily seizing our lungs before being chased away by the warmth of our cores. The sun might not do much to keep us warm, but at least it's there. Cold and dazzling. Not even at a 45-degree angle at this time in the morning, it struggled to make its way into the sky, round and blinding. The sun shone so bright that it threw the longest of shadows, including mine, far onto the frozen pavement, infiltrating the ice and reflecting into the heavens. This is why we live here, I think. Why we brave the cold.

The day went by fast. Two of my classes presented their first assignments of the semester — reports on public transit systems. Most of my students had chosen sprawling meccas like Chicago, New York, Paris and Hong Kong. Only one chose another Canadian city. Sarah was new to Montreal and presented her hometown of Halifax. It may have been a small system, but she did a great job outlining the changes over the years from horses to streetcars to trolley buses. She also had interesting anecdotes about the city's ferries and shared with us her favourite bus line — the six — that went down a street called Quinpool.

Sarah's descriptions of Halifax made me think of James. I'd thought about him several times since the night we'd met two weeks ago. I still felt bad for not calling, for getting rid of his number. Listening to Sarah's presentation conjured him up now before me; his ruddy face, his thick curls. It gave me what felt like a privileged view of his city. I felt I could see it as he might — its history, its street life. It felt oddly intimate to know how a person might get around his hometown.

If I'd called James we might be dating now, I thought once class was over. As appealing as that prospect was, it wasn't exactly want I wanted. I had what I wanted: a date with Max. If I had called James, I might not have called Max. But would that have been so bad? No, I thought, it's best I got rid of his number. James deserves someone normal — not someone like me, still hung up on an old boyfriend. I would've wasted his time.

MAX AND I HAD AGREED to meet for coffee at one of the nicer places in the Village, a café-bistro that served a variety of cakes and pastries. I had arrived early and chosen a table near the back. Max was late as usual. I sat in a frayed leather chair facing the door and, refusing the commanding advances of the waitress, flipped through a dog-eared copy of *Fugues* that someone had left behind on the table. I had already seen this issue but skimmed through it anyway, catching glimpses of the photos and ads. The publication had changed much since Angie had stuffed it into my backpack those many years ago. It was slicker now, with ads for cars, condos, and vacation spots. Sex ads still clogged the back, along with the personals and club photos from the drunken nights out. I never recognized anyone in these photos anymore. The faces were of much younger men, hanging off of each other as if it were their last day at camp.

I closed the publication and looked around the room. The café was filled with couples: men and women on same-sex dates, old friends catching up over coffee. I felt nervous sitting there alone, but before I could obsess any further Max walked in, removing his tuque and gloves as he approached the table. I stood to greet him.

"I'm sorry I'm late," he said, shivering. Max's cheeks were red. I felt how cold they were as we kissed hello on both cheeks, the sides of my smooth jaws rubbing against the careless blond bristles on his face. Such a common gesture for former lovers.

"It's good to see you," I said, sitting down.

"It's good to see you, too," he said with a smile. Max looked the same. The understated, scrappy boy I fell in love with. He unwound the layers from his body, unveiling brown cords and a light blue T-shirt. He grabbed a napkin from the next table over to wipe his nose from the cold. The waitress, seeing my company had arrived, came to get our orders. We spent the next few minutes, our first together in months, scanning the menu and conversing with the waitress about the layers of chocolate on their various cakes.

"I didn't know if I should call," I said, once she had taken our order. "I figured it had been a while and I hadn't seen or heard from you. I was wondering how you were."

"I'm glad you called. Things have been good," he said. He told me how he was busy, still at the restaurant but now a manager, looking for roles and catching the odd play. I told him I saw Michel Tremblay's *Albertine, en cinq temps* in December at the National Theatre School. "Isn't it devastating?" he said, alight. "I wish I had known, I would have loved to see it again." I had debating calling Max back when I had found out the play was being presented. Instead, I went to the show alone hoping to run into him but knowing it wasn't likely. Standing in line with my ticket, and then sitting in the theatre as the lights went down, I felt as if I were doing something with Max. It was as if he had gone to the lobby to pick up a program and I was waiting for him to return.

"The production was good," I said. "It's a little hard to suspend your disbelief, though, when you've got five students in their twenties playing Albertine at different times in her life. Still, it was powerful. It was incredible to see her argue and plead and reason with herself. If only we could do that," I continued. "Talk to our younger selves and tell them what to expect."

Max grinned and, reaching over the table, grasped my right wrist. I looked down at his slender fingers, the supple blue veins underneath the soft back of his hand. "It's good to see you again, Will," he said.

"Yes, it is," I replied.

MAX AND I TALKED FOR another hour at least. It felt great to have him sitting across from me, sharing what was going on in his life. It was effortless, much as I had remembered it always being. We spoke about work, movies, music, and friends, but neither of us brought up the weighty topics of sex or dating. As much as I had wanted to know if he was seeing someone, I wasn't sure I could handle it if he was.

We finished our coffee and cake and then sat at our table drinking water out of tall glasses with the tallied cheque sitting unturned on top of a saucer. "Il faut que j'aille à la toilette," Max said at one point and got up to go to the washroom.

With him gone I could sit alone with my feelings. I felt excited, nervous and frightened to be with Max again, but I realized I wasn't at all closer to what I wanted. I wanted *him*. Those lips, those hands all over me. He had said he was happy to see me, but did he mean it in the same way I did?

Returning from the washroom, Max sat back down and took another sip from his water. Our waitress came by to fill up our glasses one more time, leaving the pitcher of water on our table as she left.

"So, are you seeing anyone?" I spat out, not looking at him as I asked.

Max took a moment to answer. "No," he said. "You?"

I looked up and thought about the misfires: James, Vince. "No … No one."

Max smiled and my insides began to thaw. "Do you want to grab a drink somewhere else?" I asked. "Or do you have to get up early tomorrow?" It was a Thursday evening, about a quarter to ten and a work night for me, but I didn't want to go home.

"No, I don't have to get up early," Max said, twirling the handle of his spoon.

"Then let's get out of here."

Max and I bundled up, paid the bill and walked outside. It was milder out now, the wind having died down. We walked for a bit, aimless in the snow. "Why don't we grab a drink at my place?" he suggested, and the two of us wordlessly turned up the street in the direction of his apartment. The streets along the route were empty, freshly plowed; the buildings frozen, quiet and forgiving, some of them alight with wilted strings of coloured Christmas lights.

Max opened the front door to his building and we climbed the musty stairs to his second-floor apartment. He shuffled for his keys in the dark. I heard them dangling and, for a second, had the unpleasant thought of him bringing someone else here, turning the key in the lock for a stranger behind him.

As Max opened the door to his apartment I was greeted by the familiar smells of old books and heating. He flicked on the lights and suddenly we were inside.

Max's apartment had changed, but not much. He had the same furniture, although he had moved a futon and a bookcase over to the other side of the room. A couple of strange lamps now sat on either side of his television, and several new posters decorated his walls. But it was the same place. The same ratty old floors, the same kitchen table and dishes in the sink. The same broken washing machine in the back jostled out of its place next to the dryer.

Taking off my boots I excused myself and headed to the washroom, thrilled to once again pee in his toilet. Upon flushing, I used the masking sound of the rushing water to obscure the clatter of rummaging through his medicine cabinet. I looked for any new clues to his life but found none. My old toothbrush was gone along with any other sign I had once been here. I found only matchbooks and incense sticks, half-empty bottles of cologne, and the familiar scent of deodorant and glycerine soap bars.

When I came out of the bathroom I noticed Max had lit several candles and was sifting through his tape collection for something to play. He found a mix tape I recognized and popped it in.

"What do you want to drink?"

"What do you have?"

Max took some vodka out of the freezer and mixed it with some juice and Perrier for fizz and brought the concoction over to where I was sitting. My eyes were drawn to a colourful bag from a trinket shop on Laurier that gave its merchandise in bright blue bags with a childlike rainbow drawn in what was meant to resemble crayon. "What's in there?" I asked, sipping from the punch.

Max went over to get the bag and brought out a martini shaker he had bought for a friend's birthday, and a bubble bath he had picked up for himself. Max screwed off the cap and held it up to me. "Smell."

It smelled like lavender, and his body, and the baths we had taken together. I smiled at Max across the nozzle of the bottle, and then stopped. I took a sip from my cocktail. "I've missed you," I said. It seemed almost impossible to say. I watched as it floated between us for a second as I waited for Max's reply.

"... I've missed you, too," he finally said.

We live in the unspoken, Max and I. I realized this as I sat on his couch, struggling with what to say next. There were so many things I wanted to tell him: how I still felt about him, how angry I had been when he left. I wanted him to know how important he had been in my life. And I wanted to ask him how he felt about me. After this time apart had he changed his mind?

But I was scared of the answers and couldn't say anything more than "I've missed you." And Max took my lead. He agreed with me. He always dittoed my feelings whenever I had the courage to express them. But he was never the first to speak up. I had forgotten how much that used to frustrate me. I used to think it had something to do with him being an actor. That emotions, responses, were merely a learned behaviour and he was reading me, like so many times on stage, in an effort to understand how to interact with my character.

I was happy to be sitting here, having Max tell me what I wanted to hear, but it was coupled with doubt over his sincerity. So we sat, quiet on his futon, and said nothing for a couple of moments.

Impulsively, I reached out to kiss Max on the lips. It was a timid peck to test out boundaries, soft and gentle. But I could feel Max kissing back, a little more confident, deeper and a moment longer, lips further apart. I kissed him again, and he kissed back. Kiss on top of kiss, it escalated until we were pushing one into the other, devouring each other in a fit of pent-up passion.

Pulling off his clothes I led him, with my mouth, down onto his back, horizontal on the floor, our faces pressed together in one masticating slobber as our limbs flew about in a clash of skin and bone. I tore at his jeans, ripped off his briefs, and grabbed his buttocks as I bit down into his neck. Max gasped, his familiar pink flesh now exposed on his living room floor. Looming over him, I pulled his hips further towards my knees, his furry legs bent at an angle across my left shoulder. I spread his cheeks below me, and slid my hand between them to find his soft, warm centre. We kissed as I rubbed at it, waking it up. I pulled off my remaining clothing to become as bare as he was, lying prostrate on the shabby carpet of his apartment floor.

I pressed my naked body down onto his and felt my own cock, rigid and strong, pushing up against his left thigh. I felt a moment of relief as I looked down to find my penis as alert and impressive as I had remembered it. It felt harder than ever and I had the overwhelming urge to split him with it. I threw Max's legs over my shoulders and began to grind into him, folding his body in two as I pushed towards him. Innocently, I thrust at him in a whole manner of different positions, teasing him as my mouth and tongue become reacquainted with the corners of his body. I worked Max over hard on the carpet, window shades open and out to the dark world, until he was red and slick with sweat. I felt flushed and warm too, my body electric.

At some point I was in him, pumping away. He was on top of me, under me, to the side of me. I pulled out of him and pushed back in, churning away as his hot body responded to me. We fucked, harder and harder, and my knees began to get raw from the carpet on his floor. We got up and moved over to his bed where we approached climax. Slamming into each other, our breath rising and falling, I felt it, the point of no return. "I'm going to come," I muttered into the creases in his forehead and within moments spilled into him, white ropes disappearing into his dark centre.

I shuddered and, withdrawing my cock, moved to finish him off only to find he too had come, a dark mess on the sheets. Exhausted, we collapsed into puddles on his bed.

I LAUGHED, OUT OF BREATH, and stared at the ceiling. It was the only sound I could make: a breathless guffaw. I looked over to Max and he too said nothing. He breathed heavily as he reached across the bed for a towel. I felt as if I should say something, but I wanted him to be the first to speak. I wanted him to tell me what he was thinking. But he got up wordlessly and headed over to the bathroom where I heard the tap open and close as he cleaned himself up.

In the coldness that followed I realized that we'd just had unsafe sex. For the first time in our relationship I had come inside of him. What had possessed me to do that? And why didn't he stop me? I was sure I posed no risk to him. I had had an HIV test right after we broke up and my dalliance with Vince was as safe as can be. But what about Max?

No, I'm sure I'm fine, I reasoned. But still, I had never been this careless before. Why this time?

I wondered if perhaps a part of me, however small, might have thought the risk was worth it. That because of my feelings for him, I was willing to take on every sexual risk he had taken in his life as my own. But if so, that was stupid. Maybe that's one of the reasons people still seroconvert in this day and age, I thought. Maybe it's not the promiscuous ones at risk anymore, but the ones desperate for love.

Max came back into the room and went to his dresser. He opened it to look for his PJ bottoms. "Do you want to spend the night?" he asked, his back to me.

"No, I have to go home," I said, and began to collect my clothes in the next room. "Work tomorrow."

We kissed goodbye on the lips and hugged. I walked down his crooked staircase and into the snowy trees and street lights. I looked back at his home, his building, and had a sudden vision of it condemned — all boarded up, planks of plywood covering the windows and doors. I saw a squat, an empty ghost of a building, and I got sad. Thinking about his apartment as a gutted cave, where nobody lived anymore.

It was almost 1 a.m. by the time I got home. I tried not to think about my carelessness, about what we had done, and went straight to bed where I had heavy dreams; exhausting ones I couldn't remember the next morning.

C
h
a
p
t
e
r
12

I woke up startled and confused. My body was sore in a way it could only be from sex. The muscles pulled, the knees red; the results of pushing and pulling and twisting around another person's body in a fit of indulgence. My face felt tight and raw, and in the mirror I became reacquainted with the battle scars of lovemaking — superficial bruises and red scrapes up and down the nape of my neck. The mere caress of my hand against the battered skin sent shivers down my spine, the lingering aftershocks of a powerful explosion. Immediately hard, I took my cock from my briefs and thought about the sex the night before. It took no time to get me off, one or two minutes, and soon I was back in my own body, catching my breath and cleaning up the puddles pooling at the edge of the sink.

Is it our history together that makes this so intense? I wondered. This proximity to him and the powerful memories it evokes that made this climax, and the one last night, so overwhelming? It was comforting to think this erotic knowledge of Max was information I had not lost, but merely forgotten, and that suddenly its brilliance was at my fingertips again.

Yet, in the coldness that followed, in the long empty drip, there was the worry that something wasn't right, an unwelcome warning of the dangers of unsafe sex and the things left unspoken. I knew if Max and I were to pick up where we had left off I would need to be more careful — about everything.

Embarrassed about the state of my body, I called in sick to work. I ate breakfast, read the paper, and went back to bed for a couple of hours. I awoke again, shortly before noon, and figured I'd take advantage of the unexpected day off. Perhaps I would go to the museum, or go shopping? A part of me wanted to call Max and see what he was up to. But that would be too quick, I thought. Best let this thing take its time.

EMERGING FROM THE SHOWER, EXAMINING once more the booty marks in the mirror, I heard the phone ring. Thinking it might be Max — but knowing it wasn't — I ran nude from the bathroom to answer it.

I readied my sick voice, in case it was the school. "Hullo?"

"Will? Hi, it's James!"

"James?" I spat out, the frog in my throat gone. "James from Adonis, James?"

"Yes, that's the one," he laughed.

How did he get my number? I was the one who had taken his and thrown it away. "Wow," I said, puzzled and dripping on the cold tile of my kitchen. "I'm sorry if I sound surprised, but I didn't think I'd be hearing from you."

"Yes, well, I'm sorry about that. I was so drunk the night

we met I couldn't find your number anywhere in my pockets. I guess I must have lost it. And then I was worried I had given you the wrong number, or it was illegible or something."

"Yes," I found myself saying, "I had trouble making out the numbers."

"My handwriting isn't good on the best of days," he joked. "So anyway, I went back to Adonis the last two Thursdays to look for you."

"Oh God!" I said, oddly touched. "Back to that place? I'm so sorry."

"I know, right? I went alone because my girlfriends couldn't make it. You weren't there, but then last night I saw this girl I remembered from the night I met you. The one who got the lap dance?"

"Izo."

"Right, Izo! And I went up to her and told her how I had lost your number. And lucky me, one of her friends had it … How've you been?"

Great, I thought. I just reconnected with the man I love. We had hot sex last night and I performed beautifully. "Not too bad," was what I said. "Been busy with work. My mom turned fifty and we celebrated. Not much else new." I was beginning to feel cold, but the phone's cord was nowhere within reach of the bathroom. Instead, I reached for a yellow dishtowel hanging off the stove and began to dry myself at the kitchen table.

"Fifty!" James exclaimed. "That's quite big deal."

"My aunt came in from Florida. It was nice."

"I'm surprised to find you home," he said. "I was a little embarrassed to call and thought I'd be leaving a message on your machine. Are you sick? You sounded like you might be sick when you answered."

"Oh, no. I had a dentist appointment this morning," I

answered without thinking. "Still a bit sore. What about you?" I asked. "What's new?"

"Not much. Getting back into school. Looking for a reason to procrastinate," he said, being coy. "Will, I was wondering — if you weren't doing anything tonight — maybe we could go for a coffee or a drink or something?"

"Tonight?" I said, reaching for an excuse. "I can't tonight. I'm having dinner with my mother. We're prolonging the celebration. You only turn fifty once, right?" What the hell was wrong with me? Hadn't I once wanted him so badly? "Maybe some other time?"

"Sure, are you free this weekend?"

"I'm not sure what the weekend is going to be like. Listen, James, why don't I call you tomorrow?"

"Okay," James relented, a little disappointed. "Will, I wanted to apologize for being so drunk the night you met me." He sighed. "It's … It's not like me to behave like that."

I didn't know what he was talking about. His behaviour had been fine. Sure, he had drunk a lot, but I remembered him to be articulate and sincere. I was the one who was a mess, and his apology made me feel like a jerk for not calling. "James, please don't apologize."

"No, I felt so embarrassed, like shit the next day. Anyway, you seem like a very nice guy. I was in a bad place that night and you looked out for me. I hope I didn't screw things up. I'd like a chance to get to know you better."

I started to feel uncomfortable. "No, no worries," I said, itching to get off the phone. "Listen James, let's talk tomorrow, okay?"

"Sure," he said. "Here, let me give you my number. Clearly this time." I wrote it down in my notebook as James gave it to me over the phone.

I ENDED UP NOT LEAVING the apartment. Instead, I tried to lose myself in *Sabrina*, an old Audrey Hepburn movie I found flipping through the channels. James's call had left me distracted, and what had begun as a morning of possibility was now turning into a day of detention. I felt confined by the sudden intrusion and all of my lies.

I hated lying, and felt bad that I had invented plans with my mother to get out of going for a simple coffee with James. But, I thought once the movie was over, if I did go to her place for dinner, then, technically, I wasn't lying.

I called up my mother to see if I could snag an invite, but there was no answer. I tried the library and the person who answered told me she wasn't working. Where could she be?

Around 4 p.m., bored and listless, I hid my hickeys under a high-collared shirt and, grabbing my keys and coat, walked the twelve blocks to her house. Outside, the city was melting. It was a rare, mild day. On the street, dark water bled out in trickles from the snowbanks and evaporated on the sidewalks. The sky was blue, bright, and I greeted it with my jacket open. The fresh air had me feeling optimistic. I thought of our city thawing, and I thought about Max.

When I got to her building I let myself in. I hadn't lived here in two-and-a-half years but the place still felt familiar. Outside, the facade looked the same — grey and cold but with some new features. Satellite dishes now hung from two of the balconies and a bright orange bedsheet had been raised indoors to cover one new tenant's windows. And the tree, the one with the single branch of leaves in front of our building, was long gone. Cut down the same week we got Elizabeth.

I climbed the steps in the centre hallway, two at a time, and let myself into the apartment. "Mom?" I called at the doorway.

"Will!" she replied, her voice busy in the kitchen. "What a surprise! How nice …"

Elizabeth came over to see me, stretching out her two front paws on the ground in some sort of greeting. I grazed the hairs on the back of her head as she leaned into my fingers, purring. I took off my shoes and went into the kitchen.

"What are you doing here?" The TV was on and Mom was watching *Oprah*, taking things in and out of the fridge and cupboards.

"I was in the neighbourhood and thought I'd drop by. Want a guest for dinner?"

"Of course," she said, excited yet perplexed. I gave her a hug and in my arms I could feel her stress, her indecision over what to make for dinner. "I don't know what I have. I was going to heat up some stew, but I know how much you like that." She pulled away to check the freezer.

"Whatever's fine, Mom," I said, cheerful. "Don't worry about me."

"What are you doing out of school so early?"

"Ped day," I said.

"And your face, it's so red," she said, turning around.

"Oh," I said. "Sunburn from the snow. Did you see how sunny it was out today?"

"Well, there is some moisturizer in the cabinet if you want to put some on."

"Thanks," I said, and did just that, settling in front of the TV to apply the cream.

Mom pulled out a pasta sauce from the freezer to heat up. "Do you need any help?" I called from the living room, already transfixed by the television. Oprah had on some former child star whose life had spiraled into porn and alcohol.

"No, I'm fine. You relax."

Mom prepped the meal and listened to the TV as I watched it, my feet up on the hassock. We spoke over commercials, questions she'd been meaning to ask. Things like "Can you come shopping with me on Sunday?" and "I was thinking of repainting the kitchen. Which colour is best?" In return I told her that Sunday would work, and an olive green might be nice. In fact I told her anything that changed or brightened up the apartment would be welcome. Since I had left home, the only update my mother had made was to replace our ratty old couch once the cushions had given way.

Oprah soon ended and the supper-hour newscast came on. "NASA today launched the New Horizons spacecraft," one of the top stories began, the American anchor speaking over a shot of a rocket lifting into the air. "The vessel is on a ten-year reconnaissance mission to explore the planet Pluto and beyond."

"Will," said my mother, "would you mind ..."

I quickly shushed her. "Sorry. I want to see this."

The mission's principal investigator spoke next. The man wore a grey blazer and a light brown moustache. He spoke of Pluto being the only planet in our solar system left to be photographed and studied up close. "This mission could rewrite everything we know about the planets in our system," he said to a shot of the spacecraft being manipulated by scientists in white suits and masks. The vessel was the size and shape of a grand piano, shimmering in what looked like gold foil — gift-wrapping, almost — with its satellite dish busting out on top like a bow. "Pluto is a planetary embryo, an object that's only partially formed as a large planet. It stopped developing at a stage of planetary formation that the Earth went through, that all the larger planets went through. By visiting it we hope to get a better idea of how solar systems and planets are built out of clouds of gas and dust."

The satellite's trajectory was shown as a computer simulation, flying past our system's celestial bodies as it moved towards the misfit planet. The newscaster's voice returned, explaining that scientists have no idea what the surface of Pluto looks like and that some have speculated we could see craters, geysers, or patches of frost. The simulation ended on a low-resolution image of the spinning yellow and black sphere. "New Horizons is the fastest spacecraft ever launched," the voice began to wrap up, "travelling through space at nearly 35,000 mph. But it still has a long way to go. Pluto is located three billion miles from the sun, and it will take New Horizons almost ten years to get there. The spaceship is scheduled to arrive in July of 2015."

"Cool," I mumbled to myself. I pictured the tiny vessel leaving Earth's orbit and moving slowly, for ten years, across the black image we know and think of as our solar system. How strange and impossible this must all seem from above, I thought. How comical and insignificant in comparison to the rest of the universe. And what a lonely mission this must be for New Horizons. This man-made object will go farther and deeper into the unknown than any of us ever will. And it's not coming back.

"Sorry, Mom," I said, standing up. "You were saying?"

"I was going to ask if you'd mind setting the table."

I went to the kitchen and got out the plates and cutlery and set places for us. "Hey, where were you earlier?" I asked, remembering how she had not been home when I had called. "I tried to reach you like five times today."

"I was at the library downtown," she said, draining the noodles. "I had to take part in this special training. They're bringing in ten new computer terminals to our branch that operate on a new system, and I still have trouble understanding the one we work with. By June, our catalogue is supposed to be completely online. And the young ones, the ones right out of school working at the library, they are taking to this like fish to water. My brain is too old to learn these kinds of things."

I hated it when she spoke like this. It was the same way she talked when I tried to explain to her how to program the VCR. "I'm sure it will be like most of the other things you had to learn," I said. "You'll get the hang of it."

"I don't know, Will," she said, more stubborn than usual. "It doesn't feel like my world anymore."

"You're only fifty!" I laughed. She didn't think it was funny.

I wish my mother didn't give up on things so easily. It's as if she convinces herself she can't do something before she tries. Even if I tell her she can, and take my time trying to show her, she gets flustered and walks away. And then I get impatient and start speaking to her as if she were a child. It's not one of our finer moments. I don't know why I act this way when I do. I guess I wish she could be more modern, more self-sufficient. How cool would it be to have a mother who could teach *me* something about computers? How about one who left me behind to go visit the islands of Greece? One who had a companion, a lover, who took her out night after night? A mother I didn't have to hide hickeys from? Who I could talk to about Max?

I wanted to tell my mother about Max — about the one thing on my mind, hidden in my collar but blatant on my sore, red face — but I didn't feel like getting into an argument. Mom knew who Max was and what he was to me, but it ended there. I knew she didn't care for him. As far as I knew she wasn't aware we had broken up. I had never told her.

As Mom dished out the plates I turned off the television and looked for some music to play as we ate. She only had a handful of CDs, twelve maybe, and I sifted through them looking for the least obtrusive. I settled on Ella Fitzgerald.

"Looks good," I said, sitting down.

"Thank you ... Do you want some wine?"

"Sure," I said, getting up to get the corkscrew while Mom retrieved the bottle.

"So, if you're already feeling old at fifty," I said, sitting back down and opening the bottle, "have you thought about early retirement?" I was only half teasing her. I did want my mother to enjoy the second half of her life as much as possible.

She scoffed. "What would I do with an early retirement? I'd be lost."

"I don't think you'd be lost," I said, pouring the wine. "You could take up a hobby, those Chinese cooking classes you were talking about, for example. Plus you could read all of those books in your room. Or volunteer."

"No, I'm afraid I won't be able to retire for some time, Will. I'll be needing the income."

I hadn't thought of that. I guess I had assumed money was okay, and she had been amassing a nest egg for her retirement. I wasn't doing it for myself, but she surely must have been. Mom and I never discussed financial matters. I had no idea how much she made, or if she was entitled to benefits or a pension. The thought of her working into old age bothered me. "What would you do? If you could retire early?"

"I don't know. Your aunt Mary keeps talking about moving me to Florida. She says there are a lot of snowbirds down there."

"That could be fun! But what would I do?" I asked jokingly. I liked the idea of Mom moving to Florida only because it might make her happier. In Quebec it seemed as if winter lasted forever. She had also been in the same cramped apartment for over twenty years and I liked the comic thought of her living in some sort of sunny retirement community, playing shuffle-board with the likes of my aunt and uncle. But my mom didn't smile back at what I had said. "Mom? What's wrong? I was only joking."

My mom made another face. And then a third. She quickly got up, silverware clanging as her knees hit the table, and ran towards the bathroom. I was up with her too, food still in my mouth as I followed her. Mom slammed the bathroom door behind her and I could hear the contents of her stomach emptying out into the toilet, the lurches of her body speaking through her as she hurled three times into the bowl.

"Mom, are you all right?" I yelled, panic-stricken, through the door. I didn't know what to do.

It took a couple of moments for her to respond. It sounded as if she had just come up for air. "No. I'm okay," she said. I heard the flush. I heard my mom get up from the floor and wash her face and hands.

After the longest minute, Ella's raucous tune swinging the whole time, Mom opened the door. She looked pale. "I'm fine," she said, closing the door behind her. "I felt a bit nauseous today. I thought it had passed." I caught a sour whiff of sickness. "Do me a favour and get me some water, will you?"

I went to get her a glass of water and brought it to her over on the couch where she was now sitting. "I don't think I can eat anymore. Maybe I'll have some toast or tea later. Do me a favour, Will. Can you please clean up in the kitchen? I don't think I can look at food right now."

"Are you all right?" I asked, still worried.

"Yes, I'm fine," she said. "I'm probably getting the flu or something. Maybe it was something I picked up from work. You know how it is there. You shouldn't be getting too close to me, either. I think I'm going to lie down for a bit."

"I'll get you a cold compress," I said and wet a face cloth to place on her forehead.

Coming back from the bathroom, I turned off the music that had been blaring throughout the whole ordeal. I found I couldn't eat either, with the thought of the red sauce and red wine swimming in the bottom of the toilet bowl. I put everything into the trash, did the dishes, and brought the garbage down to the curb. Elizabeth was curled up next to my mom when I got back. I made tea and toast. The two of us watched television.

I LEFT HER APARTMENT THAT night with a bad feeling. I hoped it was indeed the flu she had and that she'd be okay.

Outside, the temperature had dropped and I was greeted by falling snow in clumps so big they shattered into pieces as they hit my outer layer. When I got home there was a message on my machine. "Will, it's Angie," the voice said, rather pissed. "Geneviève and I broke up. Apparently she's been seeing this girl Amy the whole time and I feel like shit. Anyway, where are you? It's 2006 — get a bloody cellphone already! I want to get blitzed tonight, but at a straight bar. I'm done with lesbians. Call me when you get this."

It's not even been two weeks, I thought as I erased the message. I picked up the phone to call her, but stopped myself. I didn't feel like talking to Angie. It had been a rough day and, as divided as I felt, I needed to keep the last piece for me.

I placed the receiver back on the base. Angie would be fine. She was a big girl — stronger than I was, anyway. Besides, Geneviève was one in a line of many she had fallen in love with over the last few years. She'd get over it soon, and before I knew it I'd be hearing how much in love she was with someone else.

I turned the ringer off my phone and went to bed.

Chapter

13

The next evening I met up with Angie for drinks. It was mild out. Large snowbanks sat at every street corner, while the sidewalks remained exposed and clear except for the rubble of jagged rocks my sneakers kicked around as I walked to meet her. The two of us met up at Drugstore, a bar in the Village. Angie was already there when I arrived, sitting at a table, talking to her friend Karen who worked there as a waitress. Karen saw me walk through the door and smiled as I approached. "Hello," I said and kissed her on both cheeks. "How you doing, tiger?" I asked Angie.

"Miserable ..." she trailed off.

"Can I get you anything?" Karen asked, doing her job.

"Sure. One of those." I pointed to Angie's quarter-filled pint on the table.

"Make that two," Angie ordered, gulping the rest of hers down.

Karen took off to retrieve our drinks. I removed both of my jackets and my sweater and placed them on the seat next to me. "So what did you do today?"

"Nothing," Angie grumbled. "Spent the day in bed with a hangover. Thankfully, the beer is helping with my convalescence." She played with her pack of smokes, lighting one as we waited for our pints. "Want one?" she asked, catching me eyeballing the cigarette. I nodded, and she handed over the pack. I lit one up as Karen returned with our drinks.

"Are you hungry?" I asked, once Karen had gone. "Do you want to grab a bite later?"

"I don't have much of an appetite. I'd rather just drink."

Inside my mind I rolled my eyes.

On my way to the bar I had decided I wasn't going to enable Angie in her self-pity. I may have felt sorry for her, but I also felt impatience. We'd had these conversations many times over the years and each time, after it was over, nothing I said made any difference.

"So, I got my mom tickets to *Cats* for her birthday," I said, changing topic. "You were right. She was ecstatic!"

"Was she?" Angie brightened for a moment, proud. "When's it coming?"

"The end of August. I was hoping she'd want to take a friend from work but she wants me to go with her. I can't get out of this, can I?"

"You're a disgrace to your people, Will," she said, inhaling.

"Hey, why don't you go with her?"

Angie cocked her head and, exhaling, looked at me as if I were an idiot. "You've got to be the one to take your mother, Will. That's the gift!!"

"Yah, I know."

She smirked, settling into the cushioned bench. "So she was

ecstatic, was she?"

"Very ... I made her cry."

"Really? I make my mom cry all the time. Not genuine tears, mind you. Crocodile ones. 'Oh, Angie, why can't you be more like your sister?' Apparently I frustrate her to no end. But the feeling is mutual." She pointedly ashed into the ashtray.

"Is she still on your case about going back to school?"

"Yes. She can't stand that I'm thirty and still work in bars and restaurants. She'd rather I'd be a doctor or a lawyer or something. I think she'd even rather I was a housewife. Everything would be fine as long as I was married and had children. You don't see her giving my brother or sister any grief."

"Well, I don't think that'll change," I said. "She'll probably be eighty and still find something to disapprove of."

"God, could you imagine?" She laughed. "I should tell both of my parents if they continue to act like this I'm going to put them in a home."

I knew she was trying to be funny, but I wondered if a part of her meant what she said. "Is that something you would do? Put your parents in a home?"

"I don't know," she answered, her tone turning from silly to serious as she considered her response. "Maybe. If they got very old and I couldn't take care of them. But I don't think it'll be my job. They have Carmen for that. Or Tony. They're the ones with families, children, suburban homes. We could never live together. We'd kill each other."

"... What about Marco?" I asked about her long-deceased brother. "Did your parents get along with him?"

"Well, yes," she said, her face alight with his memory. "Everyone got along with Marco. I don't know if it was because he was so easygoing or if we were easy on him because he was sick. But I remember him being thoughtful and gentle. Sometimes I wonder if he might have been gay."

"Really?"

"There's no way to know. He was so young when he died. But looking back I feel as if I could see it in his eyes. Wouldn't that have been something? Two of us in the family."

"Two of you to put them in a home," I teased.

"No, he was a good kid. He'd have taken care of our folks."

There was a moment's pause. "Well, I don't have a brother or sister to ship my mom off to. It's just the two of us. And I'm gay, which makes it less likely I'll have a family, children, or a suburban home, for that matter. God, she and I are in it for the long haul, aren't we?"

"Is there no one else who could help you take care of your mom?"

"Well, there's my mom's sister, but she's older and lives in Florida with her husband. I can't see my mom living there anyway. We talked about it the other night, what she'd like to do when she retires. I think she'll probably work until *she's* eighty," I chuckled, picturing it. "And there I'll be. Dropping her off and picking her up at the library at fifty-seven."

I must have been staring at the table, because Angie tried to pry up my gaze with her eyes. "Is that something you want?"

I wasn't sure how to answer. I've always known I'd be the one to care for my mother in her old age. But I never before thought of the options large families like Angie's had when it came to caring for family members. She was lucky. When her brother had died she'd had many people around which, I'm sure, was comforting. When the time came, I'd have no one to share the emotional load with. The thought of caring for my mother in her old age petrified me. It reminded me of the days of her cancer scare when I was, in essence, still a child and felt power-less to deal with it. "No, I could never put her in a home."

"How's she doing? Is she well?"

I told Angie about the night before. How my mother had frightened me by rushing from the kitchen table to throw up in the bathroom. Angie was as concerned as I was. I reassured her that I'd be taking her to get checked out as soon as possible.

Suddenly, the door to the bar swung open and in came a gang of young women and men, already ripped and falling over each other, jacking up the noise level of the bar. I turned back to Angie and shrugged.

"Will, do you ever wonder why your mother never remarried? I mean, she doesn't date, does she?"

"No," I chuckled. "She's fifty!"

"Fifty is *not* old!"

"There was this one guy I remember when I was about eight," I said. "He was a regular at the library. I have memories of being babysat by my aunt when my mom went out on a couple of dates with him. My aunt lived in Montreal at the time and I remember sleeping over at her place once or twice. But it was only a couple of times. I never saw the guy and my mom never spoke of him. Since then, there's been no one. I'm not sure why."

"You never asked?"

"You know we don't have that kind of relationship," I reminded her. "It would be … weird to talk about that."

Angie said nothing and looked at her glass, a wrinkle of disapproval in her face.

"What?"

"Well, you know …" She shifted in her seat. "How can you expect your mom to ask you about your life if you don't show an interest in hers?"

"What are you talking about?"

"You complain about how your mom isn't interested in your

personal life. But you don't tell her about it. Maybe if you did then you could have that kind of relationship with her."

"You're one to talk," I said, my back up. "You hardly see your parents. You screen their calls. You keep them at arm's length."

"Well, that's my choice," she said, picking up on the ire in my voice and relaxing her tone. "You didn't have the same upbringing as I did, didn't have other siblings you always had to live up to, didn't have to deal with the death of your younger brother and the stress it brought upon the family. I love my parents, Will. But I don't have the patience to deal with them the way you do with your mom. We've just been through so much shit. I need distance for my own sanity."

I calmed down. Angie's switch in tone had made me feel better. She had always been such a good friend. I hated it when she made us out to be different.

"But you know," I said, unsure if I should continue, "you're lucky to have such a large family. Sometimes I wish I wasn't as close to my mom as I am."

"Come on."

"No, it's true. Sometimes I wish I could be lost in a family of five or six, or be the black sheep and cut myself off. That way I wouldn't feel as if I owed anybody anything. I wouldn't have to worry about losing anyone. It's stupid I know, and I know I don't really *mean* it. I love my mom, and I'm lucky to have her in my life. I guess … I know she relies on me and … that … frightens me."

We sat between sentences, Angie nodding.

"I often wondered how Max did it," I said, unexpectedly. With the mere mention of his name, Angie's face soured. I hadn't uttered it in her presence in a long time, and it elicited the same reaction from her that it's got since the day he dumped me. Despite her frown, I continued, looking down at my glass.

"He was the gay son, the eldest, with two siblings, a father and stepmother; and then one day he walked out the door because they couldn't reconcile what they expected of him with the way he wanted to live his life." Angie remained silent, refusing to spar. "I remember I used to find that so incredibly sexy, so romantic. Turning your back on eighteen years in order to become the man you were meant to be."

I then blurted out, "I saw him the other night."

"Max?" She looked at me, surprise on her face. I hadn't heard her say his name in months. I remembered how it used to obliterate me every time she, or anyone else, said it, dropping it into a sentence like a bomb that destroyed everything around it.

"We slept together. Wednesday."

"What?! Are you insane?!"

"No."

"Are you back together?"

"I don't know," I said, hesitant to jinx anything, but too content not to be optimistic. "Maybe."

"Are you sure this is a good idea?"

"What? Sleeping together? What's wrong with that? We've missed each other. And it's comfortable."

"Have you forgotten the last four months? Do you really want to put yourself through all that again? Just as you were beginning to get over him he calls and you come running."

"No, I called him …" I said, and immediately regretted it.

"You called him! Will! Why did you do that? I thought we agreed …"

"No, but …"

"You're torturing yourself."

"This doesn't feel like torture."

"You keep forgetting how it was. How you used to tell me you thought *you* should leave *him*."

"I didn't know what I wanted then, or how good I had it."

"Jesus," she said, and lit another cigarette. "You know, I wish he had been a total prick. Really gave it to you good in the end, so you'd hate him. It would have been the nicest thing he could have done. Instead he had to be honest about his *feelings*. 'Honest' my ass! I tell you, if he had been a royal prick and you found out he had cheated on you, or if he had turned cold or abusive, I doubt we'd be here." She ashed into the tray again. "I think it's messed you up, Will. It's those last moments that have altered how you see your relationship."

"Oh yes, how could I forget, your 'How Relationships End' theory," I spat out, turning a few heads. Angie often spoke of this ridiculous theory she had that no matter how great or special the relationship was, it was only how it ended that mattered. "When it's over," she would say, "all you're left with is the ending. That's how we remember each other. It determines whether or not we'll be friends. You can't tell me the way things are left have no bearing on how you view what's come before." Angie was a fervent believer in this and I'd often see it manifested in her behaviour, how she spoke — or didn't speak — of past relationships.

"It's true, Will," Angie said. "You're stuck where it ended. Max was honest with you, told you how he felt, and what did you do? You sat there and said nothing. You didn't yell, didn't scream, didn't cry. You didn't fight for him. In fact, you didn't react at all. You ran home and felt sorry for yourself. So I don't understand why you expect things to be different. Maybe if you had spoken up and got some things off your chest you wouldn't have lost the last four months of your life. Maybe you would've allowed yourself to date other people ..."

"I've dated other people ..."

"... and not be here in the same spot, ready to go through it again. You need to get angry over this, Will. You never did. And I can see it inside you. That's why you're still in this place. That's why it's unfinished."

"That's bullshit," I said, blind with emotion. "And you're one to talk! You've been going on and on about Geneviève. You were only dating her for, what? Two weeks? What grief can you know after two weeks? So what if she hooked up with someone else. Why would you think you were exclusive after such a short time?" As I spoke, I could hear the rowdy crowd of drinkers quieting down, noticing our spat. "You think you know everything. I swear, Angie, you need a reality check on these 'relationships' you're having. You've got the memory of a goldfish!"

"What are you talking about?" she said, folding her arms and recoiling into her seat.

"Come on, Angie, you fall for one girl after the other, each time acting like this is the first time you've felt this way. Then suddenly it's over, you cry in your milk for a couple of days and then — bam — slide right into the next relationship. It's going to be the same with Geneviève, you'll see. I try to be a good friend, to support you in your time of need, yet you can't offer me the same courtesy."

"I am trying to help you," Angie said, emotionless. "You don't want to hear it."

Livid, I grabbed my layers of outerwear and stood up. "What do you know, anyway? You may have dated all those girls, but I don't think you've ever been in love. You just think you have."

I left the bar in a huff, my sweater and two jackets in hand.

OUTSIDE I PUT ON BOTH coats and wiped my face. My eyes were wet but I couldn't remember crying. Angie had got me so angry; I couldn't recall the last time I had raised my voice and stamped out on someone.

I walked to clear my head, and stop myself from shaking. I walked four or five blocks east and found myself in front of Stud, a men-only leather bar at the edge of the Village. Knowing Angie wouldn't look for me here, I ducked inside.

Stud was dark and warm and smelled of artificial smoke. I had only been to the place once or twice before, but never alone. The men of Stud were like the men of most leather bars. They were larger, furrier, and wore black or leather. They were also older, greyer, with shaved heads and full facial hair. I had rarely come here because I thought the bar was for men older than me, but as I walked in this night I realized I was a lot closer in age to these men than I had thought.

I sat down at the bar and ordered a beer from a beefy man in an open vest and trucker's cap. He tore off the twist-cap with his left paw, winking at me as he placed the bottle down and took my cash. The bar he stood behind was rectangular, and sat in the centre of a room off the dance floor. I could see the dance floor from where I sat — empty at this hour, with coloured spotlights thrown now and again inside a vacant square. Donna Summer was playing, but there was no one there to enjoy her. It was too early. Everyone was still in this section. About fifteen men, most of them bearded, either sat around the bar or circled it, heading for the lotto machines at my right or to find a new place to stand and watch each other. It seemed as if most of these men were acquainted with each other and knew the bartender. The bartender kept busy, interacting with the men on the four sides of the bar who flirted with him and stared at each other. I felt nervous sitting alone among these men with their visible appetites. It made me think of the first few times I had gone out alone, frightened someone was going to pounce on me, worried no one wanted to.

The taste of beer calmed me. It made me feel at ease and better about what had happened. I was embarrassed about the scene I had made in Drugstore, but I felt glad I had stood up to Angie. Angie often spoke to me as if I were a kid, as if she knew better. And perhaps she did, but that didn't change the way I felt. I wish I could have been more articulate, could have calmly told her why Max was so important to me, why I couldn't let go; but then, I wasn't so sure myself.

I got the attention of the bartender, who swooped back with a round grin on his burly face, and asked him for a pen I could borrow. "Here you go, darlin'," he said, taking one from a cluster in a cup by the register.

I grabbed a napkin from a pile on the counter and proceeded to write. *Angie*, I wrote like a child in class. *As much as I love you, we are not the same person. I wish I could be as strong and as confident as you, but I'm not. And whether they are right or wrong, these are my decisions to make. You're my closest friend in the world and ...*

"Yeesh!" I said aloud, drawing black lines through the paragraph and flipping over the napkin. Such sentimental nonsense.

Instead of continuing, I began to doodle on the other side of the napkin. I drew a tree and then a fox. I drew a small dark circle with a bunch of rings around it. "Max," I then wrote. Just his name. The tip of my pen a blinking cursor.

I hopped up from my seat and headed over to the pay phone by the door to call him, crumpling up the napkin and stuffing it into my front right pocket, absentmindedly sticking the pen in too. Max wasn't home so I hung up. I then tried my line, calling in to retrieve any new messages. There were none, just the cold electronic voice of the answering service.

I stayed at Stud for two more beers. A couple of walks around the bar and a sorry game of pool later, I decided to move on. I finished my drink, checked my messages one last time, and left the bar to find boys to dance with.

I WAS AT PARKING FOR five minutes before I saw him.

Even in a club as full as this one, I was able to make out the back of Max's head, and his frame, from where I stood. No word for four months and now twice in one week? It's fate, I thought. It was as if I had called out for him, and the universe had answered.

Before I could think about what I might say I took off, skirting the dance floor and coming up behind him.

"Max."

"Will," he said, turning and giving me a kiss on both cheeks. "How are you?"

"Good, thanks!" I looked at the tall boy he was with, smoking and checking me up and down. "I called you tonight," I said, "but you weren't home. I didn't leave a message." This? This is what I had to say?

"Yes, well … Will, this is Bruno. Bruno, je te présente Will."

"Bonjour," I smiled, nervous. I shook the strange, beautiful man's hand but did not kiss him hello. Bruno was much taller and, from the looks of it, younger than I. He was thin and handsome, with dark eyes and olive skin. He smoked as he stood there, inhaling often and in quick puffs as if the halo of smoke in the bar wasn't enough.

"What are you guys up to?" I asked.

"Having a drink. We went to see a restored print of *The Shining* tonight."

I remembered all the times Max had tried to get me to watch the film with him. "Cool," I said. "Is it worth seeing?"

"I thought you didn't like horror films."

"Well, I don't. Not as a genre. But, like you used to say, it's not your typical horror film. I regret not watching it with you."

Max smiled. "Well, you should check it out then."

"Yeah, I'll check it out," I stumbled. "Maybe I'll go tomorrow. I don't have anything to do tomorrow. Maybe I'll check it out tomorrow. Thanks!" I took a big sip from my beer. These were not my words. My words remained unwritten, on a napkin hiding in one of my pockets. "Well, I'm supposed to meet a friend here," I said. "I'll see you later, maybe? It was nice to meet you, Bruno." Bruno nodded in my direction as I left their corner of the bar and retreated downstairs to the club's lower level.

PART OF THE FEAR I used to have about running into Max in a bar was the idea of seeing him on a date or chatting up some guy. I used to wonder if I'd be prepared to intercept that man. Cockblock Max and try to go home with the other guy so they wouldn't leave together. Ridiculous. There was nothing I could do. This Bruno seemed bred to take Max away, to lull and seduce him with his height and masculinity. I thought he had said he wasn't seeing anybody.

Down in Parking's underbelly I erased the thought with a shot of Jack, chasing it with more beer. It was much darker here than upstairs — almost as dark as Stud — and I felt an odd sense of comfort being able to hide in the shadows. Trying to disappear completely, I pulled the bar stool I had been sitting on farther into the corner.

The dance floor across from me was packed with shirtless men and smelled sharply of perspiration and poppers. In its centre, three sweaty beauties took turns making out with each other, their sloppy mouths trying to extinguish the fires between them. Although I found their behaviour crass, I admired their lack of inhibitions. What must it be like to let go like that?

Through the smoke and wall of flesh I caught sight of an

older man standing on the other side of the dance floor, staring at these men. He was much older than me, maybe in his late sixties, and was admiring the salivating triad with a barefaced look of awe and desire. The man had bad posture and his features were long, but what was most remarkable about him was his dress. The man sported a big black baseball cap and an ironic T-shirt too small for his body. He stood there, alone, almost as if he were waiting for someone to stop and introduce himself.

I started to wonder when he came out. Was it late in life? Was that why he was here now, dressed like a twenty year-old? Or was he attempting to turn back the clock and relive the glory days when his beauty burned a hole in other men's minds? How long had he been coming here? I wondered. And had he ever left the bar?

I tried not to judge him but couldn't help thinking I didn't want to be here at his age. Despite the number of places Angie and I go to on any given night, there are many places we won't go. Places for those who never left. We'd often see them on the way to our destination, long faces sitting in windows, drinking beer and watching the street. Sometimes, Angie and I would try to imagine ourselves as an old couple and joke about the kind of old folks' home we'd be put in: easy listening versions of house music tracks being piped through the halls, drag queen nurses handing out pills before afternoon tea dances.

But in all seriousness, what will old age look like for us?

I enjoy going out, but I can imagine a day when I won't want to be here anymore. When it will have served its purpose. For this might be one hell of a party, but one day the party will be over and by then, I hope, I will have left with somebody. Could that somebody have been James? I didn't have to be here. I could be having a coffee or a drink with him right now. I looked at my watch. It was way after midnight. There must have been a point during the night when he realized I wouldn't be calling. Perhaps he had tried to call me too, hung up on my answering machine the way I had done with Max.

God, I'm so silly, I thought. What am I doing here in the basement of this bar, hiding from Max and his date, when I could be out on a real date with someone who is genuinely interested in me?

NOT THIRTY MINUTES LATER, I was surprised to find Max, alone, come up beside me.

"Find your friend?"

"No," I said. I couldn't fake looking out onto the dance floor. "I'm not sure if he's coming anymore."

"Are you okay?" he asked, unsure.

"Yes, I'm fine ..." I said. "Great."

"Listen, I'm leaving. But let's do something again soon. Maybe this week?"

I looked at Max and felt sad and angry — sad I wasn't leaving with him and angry for not being able to tell him. "Yes," I said heavily. "I'd like that."

"See you." Max kissed me full on the lips, prying my hesitant mouth open for a second.

"Goodbye!"

I felt like following him, to see if Bruno was leaving too. But if he was, it wasn't an image I wanted to have in my head.

THEN AND THERE I DECIDED to stop drinking for the night and, pushing aside my bottle, went to dance. I didn't stop. I kept dancing. Song after song, even if I didn't know the tune. I ran a marathon on the floor, step after step, sprinting through the sweat. I pushed thoughts of Max, Bruno, James, and Angie from my mind and thought of nothing but the beat and the wild smell of the men around me. I danced until I lost track of time, until the place thinned out, and I wondered how many minutes I had left before the lights sent me home.

At some point I saw him. I wasn't sure right away if it was him, standing by the bar where I had left my bottle, but then I met his gaze and it came back to me — the dark curls on his head, the colour in his cheeks. It was James, standing tall, long pale arms hanging from a yellow-and-white ringer tee. His face betrayed no emotion, blank as an empty page as he pulled the bottle of beer in his right hand up to his lips.

I stopped dancing and went up to him. "James."

"Hi, Will."

"Listen, I'm sorry I didn't call," I tried to explain. "I wish I had a good excuse, but I don't. I … Well, remember how you told me about your ex? I have one of those too. And it hasn't made things easy for me."

"Oh, I see," he said, softening. "That's good to know. I wasn't sure if I was more upset at you for not calling or at myself for caring so much. I thought it was something I did." This time, James was not the slightest bit drunk. I could tell in his voice he wasn't angry. Frustrated, perhaps. He sounded like a man who had long ago learned to tolerate the chronic lateness of an old friend.

"Yes, I truly am sorry. I'm not sure why I'm even here tonight. I suppose I needed to blow off some steam."

"Well, I was about to leave," he said, draining the last few drops from his bottle. "Do you want to walk out with me?"

We grabbed our coats and left the bar, walking up Amherst and along La Fontaine Park, my ears ringing from the club's mighty speakers. James walked briskly, with his bare hands stuffed into the pockets of his blue winter jacket. He was several inches taller than I, and much of that length seemed to be located in his quickly moving legs. I struggled to keep up.

"Hey, it's not *that* cold out."

"Sorry," he sang, cutting his pace in half. "I have a habit of walking fast. It's not like I'm trying to get away from you or anything ..."

It was late. Besides the slow titter of waking birds, our voices were the only sounds along this quiet stretch of street, the large stone homes dark on our left, the bare frozen trees lined up on our right. At this hour hardly any cars passed and no one was in sight. James took a pack of Chiclets from his pocket and offered me some, looking down at my feet as he chomped away. "You're wearing sneakers," he noticed, returning the gum with a rattle to his coat pocket. "Your feet must be cold."

"I'm okay," I said. "I think I warmed them up sufficiently on the dance floor. I haven't danced like that in a long time."

"You looked good out there," James said. "I can't dance, no matter how hard I try. Perhaps you've got some moves to teach me."

"Please."

"You were dancing for quite a while before you noticed me. I was trying to decide whether or not to go up to you."

"I'm glad I saw you when I did."

"Were you out with friends tonight?" he asked.

"No. I was out earlier with my friend Angie. But we had this big fight and I needed to get away and clear my head."

"What was the fight about?"

"My ex," I felt sheepish admitting. "I know she's got my best interests at heart. She just doesn't have that bedside manner I'm sure you student doctors have. She could learn a thing or two about empathy."

"You want to tell me what happened?"

I struggled. "… I'm not sure I want to say." I hoped he could understand my reluctance. "Sorry," I explained. "I appreciated you being honest with me about what you were going through the night we met, it's just … I'm so lost. I wouldn't know where to begin." Oddly, I felt as if I were letting him down.

"Okay, let's talk about something else then," he said. "Tell me, Will, what's your beef with the world?"

"My beef with the world?"

"Yes. It's my new lunchtime poll. A bit like your stripper survey. If you had to pick one, right now, what would be your biggest grievance? Quick, before you think too much."

I was usually slow to answer this type of existential question, but this time the answer rolled easily off of my tongue. "That things end."

James's smile turned into a question mark. "What do you mean?"

I was as confused by my answer as he was. "People, experiences, all leave you," I said, noticing the violet glow conspiring behind the trees, "and you're left to wonder what's left of them that's real. You feel their absence in a way you could never imagine before — like a piece of you has been torn off. Sometimes I feel like it'd be much easier to live in the past, or in memories. Take a single moment and freeze it in amber. These days I feel like I have no control over the present. Time keeps pushing the world forward when all I want it to do is stop."

"Well, that's an answer," said James, surprised, taking both hands out from his pockets and squeezing the top of my right shoulder. "But it's so pessimistic! Can't you look at it another way? What about all the exciting moments to come? The potential of the future?"

"That's less reliable than I'd like," I said. "Don't you ever feel like you want something to stop? To stay put? Why does everything have to change all the time? Why can't some things stay the way they are? Just one thing. Can I not have one thing that is permanent in my life? One thing I don't have to worry about losing?"

"Nothing is permanent," James chuckled and placed his hands back into his pockets. "What do they say? The only things you can count on in life are death and taxes."

"Well, that's depressing," I said. "What about you?" I asked. "What's your beef with the world?"

"Nothing so profound. Right now, my beef would be with bullshit."

"Bullshit?"

"Yes, bullshit. Excuses. The ones we give each other, the ones we make for ourselves. You wouldn't believe the amount of bullshit you hear training to be a physician. Patients lie to me, lie to themselves, all the time, and I don't see what purpose it serves."

"It must serve some purpose," I said. "Maybe people lie because they can't handle the truth."

"I know it's not always easy to tell the truth. But it's not going to get you anywhere, not in the long run."

"Are you talking about your ex?"

"My ex, and other men I've dated. Men can be such cowards. I'm tired of everybody being so scared all the time. I wish people took more chances. We only get one turn on this silly little planet."

For the first time in the last few hours I thought of the argument that had begun the evening, and what Angie had accused me of — not speaking up with Max or my mother. I hadn't realized how complicit I was in inaction. How silence was its own form of bullshit. "But how can you be so sure of what you want?"

I asked. "It must be so great to feel so certain all the time."

"Don't get me wrong," he said, "I'm guilty of this too. God knows I haven't been the most honest with myself in relationships. But I'm trying.

"It's weird, and I know I'm generalizing," he went on to say when it was clear I had nothing in reply, "but do you ever feel like a part of you might be frozen?"

"I don't know. I hope not."

"Well, I do. I worry about that. Sometimes I think gay men have been hot-wired for self-sabotage. That we're prone to give up too easily."

I couldn't stop staring at my shoes. "And why do you suppose that is?"

"Not sure … Perhaps deep down many of us hold this unconscious belief we don't deserve to be happy, since we've made our families' lives, and society, miserable." The thought made him snicker. "Sometimes I think the only way any of us can have a lasting relationship is to keep deciding not to destroy it."

I looked up from my feet that were now beginning to feel the cold. The colour of the sky was changing, and with it we were no longer alone. Birds had begun to wake each other up, calling out across the park we were now leaving.

"I think you're the one being pessimistic now."

"You're right," he said. "And I guess that's why it's my beef with the world."

Pretty soon we stopped in front of a six-plex with worn balconies that reminded me of where I had grown up and where my mother still lived. "This is where I live," he said, pointing up. I wasn't sure what I wanted to do.

"Invite me up?"

"I can't," he said, disappointed. "It's late, and I have to get up early."

"Bullshit?"

"No. Not bullshit. I'm not the one who didn't call, remember?"

I didn't want to go home.

"Another time, perhaps?" he suggested. "Do you still have my number?"

"No," I hated to admit. "I don't think so."

"Will you call me this time if I give it to you?"

"Of course I'll call."

"Do you have a pen?"

I began to shake my head, but then remembered the pen I had stolen from the bar. "Wait!" I said and took out the pen from my right pocket along with the torn napkin, folding it over so he could write on a blank patch.

James wrote down his number again.

"Good night," he said, leaning into me. I obliged, kissing him back on the steps of his apartment building. "I was right," he said as he pulled back. "You do have some moves."

"So do you."

It should have ended there but I couldn't pry my face from his. The kiss kept on going, around and around, until it was no longer just a kiss. Soon my hands were grabbing at him through his jeans and invading his backside as I took hold of his soft bottom. I felt equal passion from him. Sweetness and intensity as he pulled me close in the cold. Wait, shouldn't you stop? Why are you doing this, I asked myself? What is it you really want? I searched for the clarity James had so recently described, the honesty he looked for in other men, but all I could find that I could call truthful was my immediate desire for the man in front of me. For him to hold me, to take me inside and make love to me.

I began to reach for his buckle, to expose him right there on the steps of his building, but he stopped me. "What? Are you crazy?" James said, pulling away from the kiss with a goofy grin on his face. "It's freaking cold outside!"

I took a step back and wiped my mouth, the taste of him on my lips. In the quiet that followed I could hear how still his block was, the sun now announcing its arrival in a glow in the distance. James panted and looked at me with surprise and desire. He looked younger in this softness. "Tomorrow?" he said. "Can I see you tomorrow?"

"I can't tomorrow," I said, stooping to tie one of my shoe-laces that had come undone. "But I'll call you this week and we'll set something up."

"You'd better, Will," he said, daring me. "Don't destroy this."

James gave me one more kiss and disappeared into his building. As I left, I looked up and wondered which of these six apartments was his, which row of bricks he quietly slept behind.

On the walk home I wondered what I had got myself into. He's too young, I thought. And I'm so full of bullshit.

I threw out the napkin and his number on the way home.

Chapter

14

Saloon hasn't changed much since the morning after Max and I first slept together. Though I've been to the restaurant dozens of times before and since, the place still reminds me of that original morning. I remember how clear and sunny the day was, and how we took our time to walk to the restaurant. I also remember how surprised we were to find it full once we got there, and how we had to wait for twenty minutes at the bar for a table. To pass the time, Max and I ordered mimosas (he had never had one) and we ran into someone he had gone to school with (a girl whose name he'd forgotten). Max had French toast; I had eggs Benedict.

Because of these memories, I had refused to come to Saloon in the months we were apart. But sitting here with him now, almost five months after we had broken up, it looked as I remembered. The place was covered in shades of brown: everything from the dark walls, to the leather seats and booths, to the oversized analog clock that hung in the centre of the room. I did, however, notice three new mini-chandeliers glimmering over the bar. "Are those new?" I asked once we had ordered.

"I don't know," Max said, turning around.

It was mid-February, and Max and I had been out together five times since I had run into him at Parking. In that time there had been no mention of the tall and mysterious Bruno. I had hoped he'd been a figment of my imagination, but I knew Bruno was most probably a casual friend or, at the dreadful most, some one-shot trick Max had picked up. No matter. I was the one seeing Max on a semi-regular basis. I hadn't heard from James in all this time, either. It had been about three weeks since I had left him, breathless, on his doorstep. And as much as we had enjoyed kissing, I figured he too must have realized it made no sense for us to take it further.

On this particular evening Max and I had gone to a movie after work and were having a late dinner. It was only upon waking that morning did I realize it was Valentine's Day. I tried not to concentrate too much on that fact as we found ourselves sitting next to amorous couples at the cinema and restaurant. It was also a school night and, although there had been no talk of me staying over, I'd brought an overnight bag as always.

Max and I continued to have sex each time we saw each other. It was always the same. No matter what the plans were, at the end of the night I'd follow him back to his place where we proceeded to rip each other's clothes off. Max would close the door behind him and immediately my tongue would be at his neck, his pants on the floor. One time we didn't even make it up the stairs. I pulled him down on the steps to his apartment and blew him in the hallway. It was rougher than it had ever been, forceful and urgent. And the wilder the sex, the better it was. It continued to be unsafe too, with both of us taking turns on top. Oddly, the initial slip-up gave us permission to continue. I'd fucked him so I didn't protest when it was my turn. I would have sounded like a hypocrite to demand a condom. But truth be told, I wanted to be reckless. I wanted to show Max that I could be impetuous and desirable. More desirable than Bruno, or any other boy he might be thinking about.

The mornings after, however, were awkward. The two of us would awaken like hungover frat boys who had passed out on each other. We'd separate, stir, and keep our distance. We'd try our hardest not to show any latent interest. There were no tugs, no grabs, no caresses, and I kept having to pull my hand back from out of the air as it flew behind him, eager to land somewhere on his body. I wanted so desperately to reach out and draw him near, to pull him close in a moment that wasn't a prelude to sex, but I couldn't. If it happened, he'd have to be the one to instigate it.

We had made it to the restaurant before the snow. All week, the city had been pummelled by inches of powder, and outside another storm was beginning to blow — thick patches of driven snow falling much harder than the soft spheres of spinning light from the restaurant's mirror ball.

It was late.

I felt the approaching workday and yawned. Max caught me glancing up at the clock above our heads. "What time is it?" he asked.

"Ten … That reminds me. Do you have a quarter? I have to make a phone call." I began to dig into my pockets.

"Do you need to call her now?" Max asked with mild irritation. "Can't you call her tomorrow?"

"No, I told her I'd call her tonight. Things have been … tense recently," I said, leaving it at that. I soon found a quarter in my pocket and got up from the table as the waiter brought Max's water and my Pepsi.

"Our food will be here soon," he said, as if I were a child. "If it comes I'm not waiting for you."

"Two seconds," I said, excusing myself.

THE PHONE RANG.

"Hello?"

"Mom."

"Will."

"Hi, how are you?"

"Good, and you?"

"Good. I'm having dinner with Max," I said, hesitating. It felt like an odd thing to admit. I hadn't mentioned Max's name to my mother in months. "We went to see a movie tonight and now we're having a bite to eat. What about you, what are you up to?"

"Oh, watching television."

"How are you feeling?"

"Good, thank you."

"No nausea?" I asked.

"No nausea. I told you, it was only those few times," she replied. "I'm fine."

My mother had confessed to me several days after her bout of sickness that it had not been the first time she had thrown up in the last month. In fact she had thrown up three times since the beginning of the New Year. I flipped when I found out she had kept it from me. "What were you thinking?" I had yelled at her when she brought it up, more frightened than angry. "I thought it was the flu and that it'd go away," she stammered, still not convinced it was more than that. My mom said she didn't need to see a doctor, but I insisted she did, reminding her of how her doctor had told us to let him know if anything out-of-the-ordinary happened. Usually it took months to see this doctor, but somehow I was able to schedule an appointment within two weeks. We were now waiting for her results.

"Listen, I can't talk too long because my food's coming, but I wanted to let you know I took off work so I can take you to your appointment on Tuesday."

"Will, you don't have to do that. I'll be fine on my own."

"I know I don't *have* to, but I'm going to. They've already arranged a substitute."

"How's school?"

"Good. Nothing much new to report there."

"We're getting a snowstorm tonight. I hope you're prepared."

"It's already coming down like crazy over here. You should look out your window."

"Oh my goodness," she exclaimed, and I pictured her at her window, looking out into the white speckled darkness. "It's beautiful, isn't it? You be careful."

"I will. Good night, Mom. Call you tomorrow."

"Good night, Will."

I hung up the phone and headed upstairs to rejoin Max.

I RETURNED TO FIND MAX flipping through a script he had pulled from his bag.

"What's that you got?"

"A script for a play I'm in," he said, still sour.

"You didn't tell me you're in a play."

He told me the title. It wasn't something I had heard of. "I got the part this week," he said. "It's a small role, but I'm also the understudy for the lead so I have to learn that part too."

I took a sip from my Pepsi. "That must be a lot of lines. Kind of tough, though, if you never get to say them."

"It'd be worse to miss an opportunity," he said, and kept reading.

I shrugged and left him to his work; rummaged through my bag to see if I had anything I could entertain myself with. Just a couple of assignments I had yet to grade. I plopped my bag back down on the floor and slid it under my seat.

I watched Max's lower lip move as he went over the words on the bound pages in front of him. I used to love watching him learn his lines. I had only been in one play in my life, in high school, and was awful. I couldn't remember my lines, wasn't connected to the drama of the scene. On one of our first dates I asked Max what his trick was. He explained to me how he'd first read the script over and over, to the point where the words began to come out automatically. And then he'd memorize his cues, the things that prompted him to say the things he is supposed to say. He told me that as an actor it's not enough to know your cues, you have to know *what* the person you are in the scene with is saying, *what* they are getting at. "When you understand what the play is about," he had said, "what your character's motivations are and what the other characters are feeling, you become that character. All that begins with repetition. Once you repeat something enough times you begin to learn from it, and your response becomes automatic." His studied explanation had made him that much more attractive to me.

I always supported Max and his art, but did he really have to do this now? I couldn't imagine what he was sore about. About me calling my mother? It had been months since he had had anything to do with her, nor had I brought her up to him in the recent time we'd spent together. I had learned long ago not to talk to Max about my mother. It was like talking about him with

Angie — who I still hadn't heard from since our fight three weeks ago. I hadn't called her because I wasn't sure what to say. I needed some time away from her. Also, I knew she wouldn't approve of me continuing to see Max.

Our food came and Max put away his script. We ate the first few bites of our dinner in silence. A sudden gust of wind became audible in the dining room, and we both looked towards the window to see a white squall rattle the glass. "Would you look at that," Max said, both of us mesmerized by the great waves of snow hitting the frame and the already-blanketed sidewalk. This winter had been relentless. Already we had had a record amount of snowfall for the year, with at least another month on the way. All winter the sky had looked like a battleground, with the collateral damage piled up into corners of the street like torn white rubble.

"It doesn't seem to end does it?"

Being sheltered inside one of our old haunts while a storm began to blow outside should have made me feel warm and protected. On any other night I might have found this romantic, Max here beside me. But, instead, on this Valentine's Day, the room felt cold and my Pepsi looked sad.

IN THE TIME WE WERE together, Max met my mother only once.

I had tried to find the perfect occasion to get the two of them in the same room, but every time I invited my mother over, mentioning Max would be there, she graciously thanked me and declined, saying she was either too busy or not feeling up to it. As for Max, he didn't seem to care one way or another whether he met my mom, but I could tell her refusals had begun to get on his nerves. "Remember, I'm doing this for you," he had said to me once I'd orchestrated a meeting, "but only because it's important to you. You know how much patience I have with disapproving parents!"

I finally got my mother to accept an invitation, this one from Angie, for a dinner at her house. It was my birthday, the middle of July, and Angie had offered to host — the real present of course was her agreeing to act as a buffer. This time I didn't mention to my mom that Max would be there, nor did I let on to Max that we'd be ambushing my mother. Angie was the only one I had informed of my plan. She agreed it was time for the two of them to meet and was happy to be a familiar face that could deflect any anxiety. She could also hold my head together if it felt like exploding.

On the night of the dinner, Max and I arrived first. On our way in we were greeted by Angie's new roommate, Brenda, who was a blur rushing out the door. "Good luck," she called back as the door slammed behind her. Max and I looked at each other. I could tell despite whatever he had said about meeting my mom, he too was nervous.

We walked through the apartment, down the hallway, to the square kitchen at the back of her place. It was mid-July and the room was warm, heated no doubt by the three pots seething on the stove. Angie had two fans going — one on the countertop, the other on the floor — with the screen door wide open to pull out the heat.

"There he is. The birthday boy." Angie rushed over to give me a big hug and kiss, also kissing Max hello as he handed over the wine and cake he had tried to hide from me.

I walked over to the stove to admire what was on the menu. "Looks great," I observed, peering into the pots. "What are you cooking?"

"Don't touch," she said, pulling my hand away from where it was about to pick up a wooden spoon. Angie wasn't the most confident chef. She had learned some skills from the restaurants she had worked in over the years, but her dishes were still hit-or-miss. "It's a mushroom risotto. It needs more time, and I have to watch it like a hawk. Sit down. Have some wine."

Max was already at the counter, looking through Angie's drawers for a corkscrew. The two of us had been to Angie's many times before — for poker games, dinners, drunken night-caps — and I loved it each time Max acted familiar in her apart-ment. Like opening a window or getting something out of the fridge without asking. It was more thrilling than when he treated my place as his own.

The doorbell soon rang and we all knew who it was. "Will, why don't you get that," Angie suggested, her hands hovering over pots and pans. I watched as Max twirled about the kitchen, trying to figure out where to stand.

"I'll be right back," I said, and walked to the front of the apartment.

I opened up the door to see my mother, all smiles, dressed up in a colourful blue blouse and sporting large sunglasses. "Hello," she sang as she walked in with her bags. "Happy birthday!"

"Thanks, Mom," I said and hugged her, not able to feel any-thing. Behind me I heard the creaks of the hallway's wooden floor as my friends approached. "Come in, come in," I said.

"Hello, Mrs. Ambrose," Angie said, appearing from the hallway with Max behind her.

"Hello, Angela!" My mother removed her sunglasses and hugged her hello. Pulling back from the embrace she smiled at the strange man standing behind Angie.

"Mom, this is Max," I said.

Even though I hadn't used the term boyfriend to describe Max to my mother, she knew who he was. His name wasn't unfamiliar; I must have said it to her a hundred times. He was often over when she called, was a crucial element to many of my anecdotes. He was also very often the person I was leaving her house to meet. I looked into her face for a sign of recognition.

My mom looked at the ground and then up at Max and shook his hand. "Hello," she smiled.

"Nice to meet you," Max said, almost as confident and loud as if he were onstage.

"Yes. You, too." My mother smiled again and turned around to rummage through the bags she had brought with her. "I brought you something, Angela."

"Mrs. Ambrose, you shouldn't have!"

"Well, you were nice enough to invite us for dinner." My mom pulled out a small square glass vase with a cluster of three bamboo shoots in its centre. "Here you go. It's supposed to bring you good luck."

"I can always use more of that. Thanks, Mrs. Ambrose," Angie said, admiring it. "I know exactly where it'll go. Would you like some wine?"

"Yes, please," my mom said, and took out a bottle of white from one of her bags. "I brought this. But can I please use your washroom first?"

"Sure," I said and silently led my mom down the hall towards the bathroom. Her smile seemed a little forced as she closed the door behind her.

I REJOINED MY FRIENDS, WHO were now back in the kitchen, standing in front of the stove, speechless. My mother was in the house!

"It's way too quiet in here," Angie said to the soft roars of the fans. "Will someone please put on some music?"

"With pleasure." Max left the kitchen and walked into the

adjoining room to where the stereo was. He was still gone when my mom came out from the washroom. "Here you go," I said, and handed her a glass of wine.

"Smells good." My mom sat down at the end of the table. "What are we having?"

Angie hesitated. "A bunch of things ... I got inspired at the Italian grocer down the street."

"So many nice shops in the neighbourhood," my mom commented. "Every time I come to Little Italy, I realize I don't come here often enough."

Music soon started up from the next room; an instrumental jazz track that was all wonky and brassy. "That's quite the music collection you have," Max said, returning to the room. "Everything from early jazz to industrial metal."

"Most of that's Brenda's."

"Do you not live here alone, Angela?" my mother asked.

"No, I have a roommate. Brenda. You just missed her."

"It's such a nice place. So much bigger than your last apartment."

"Would you like a tour?"

My mom said she would and Angie, lowering the heat on the elements and giving us stirring instructions, took my mother on a tour.

"Thank you for doing this," I whispered to Max once the two of them were out of earshot.

"Will," he started, confused. "You did tell your mom I'd be here, right? I mean, she does know about us?"

"Yes, of course I told her you'd be here," I lied. "I mean, I didn't come out and tell her about *you* and *me*. She just knows. She's not stupid. Just ... give her a chance, okay? This is the first time she's met someone I'm dating."

Max was staring at me, a disappointed look on his face.

"I know," I said, grabbing his hand. "I love you for doing this … You still love me, don't you?"

"… Yes."

"Promise?"

"I promise."

Angie and my mom walked back into the room, and I quickly let go of Max's hand and returned to stirring. "And this, of course, is the kitchen and dining area. It's not much to look at, but it's practical."

"It's lovely. And the neighbourhood's terrific. I'd love to live this close to the Market."

"Where do you live, Mrs. Ambrose?" Max asked.

I noticed my mother didn't look at him when she answered. "I live in the Plateau, on Hôtel-de-Ville," she said. "It's nice, but nothing like up here. Will, we should come up here sometime and have Angela show us around."

"We could totally do that, Mrs. Ambrose," Angie jumped in. She quickly turned around to pick up the bottle of wine and made sure everyone's glass was full.

THANKFULLY, WE HAD COPIOUS AMOUNTS of wine and the dinner was soon ready. Angie could sense how pained things were becoming and turned up the temperature on her dishes. The risotto came out a tad overcooked, but the mini gourmet pizzas she had made were delicious, as were the steamed green beans and arugula salad she had thrown together.

We plowed through dinner, talking mostly about food preparation and Angie's recent time in Vancouver. Max and I had already heard about the trip, but my mother hadn't. None of us had been to Vancouver so Angie spared no detail and spoke lingeringly of the immense mountains, the drug-addled

Downtown East Side, and the hip and trendy Commercial Drive where she'd stayed. I was more than happy to let her lead the conversation. It meant Max and I could sit back and react, not struggle to come up with subjects to discuss at the table. Though he had heard some of these stories before, Max would ask Angie a question or make some observation about what she was saying. Each time he did I'd watch my mother's face as she sat beside me, looking for an air of interest or curiosity in her eyes, but found none.

After dinner, Angie brought out the vanilla cake Max had picked up and set it in the middle of the table with forks and plates. Max took out some packages of multicoloured candles and placed twenty-eight of them on the dessert. He quickly lit them and the three of them sang to me a hearty "Happy Birthday."

I blew out the candles and made a wish.

"Do you want to cut the first piece?" Max asked, handing me the knife.

I sliced into the creamy white frosting and cut the first piece, placing it on a plate before handing it to Max. He in turn placed it in front of my mother.

"Oh, no, thank you," she said as it arrived. "I'm stuffed."

"Are you sure?" Max teased. "It's really good."

"No, thank you. Maybe I'll take some with me when I go. But I'd love some more water, Angela, if you don't mind."

"Of course." Angie got up to refresh my mom's glass, while Max sat back down to eat his piece of cake. When Angie returned to the table she placed a small box in front of me.

"You didn't have to get me a gift," I said, picking up the box.

"It's nothing," she said as I opened it. "It's a bookmark. I picked it up at a craft sale the other day." The bookmark was large and gaudy, and made of purple beads woven into navy blue fabric. "Just a little bit of me to put into one of your text-books at work. You can use it this fall and now mark exactly how far your students are *not* progressing in class."

I smiled and laughed at such a sweet, silly gift. "Thanks."

My mom, then, got up and pulled up one of her bags to the table. She took out a square green box wrapped in a yellow bow. I opened up the box and found inside a shiny black leather shoulder bag. It was gorgeous; compact and square, with a smooth body and thin front flap.

"Mom," I marvelled. "This is beautiful. It must have cost a fortune."

"Well, I remember you saying how you wanted a nice leather bag to carry your books in. I figured you could use this."

"I will. I'll have to lock it in my desk or something, but I will. Thank you."

She grabbed the bag from me. "And inside," she demonstrated, "is a cream you can use to moisturize the leather and a spray to protect it from the rain and snow."

I thanked her a second time and leaned over the table to give her a kiss.

Max then rose from the table. "My turn," he said and then headed out of the room. Immediately, I felt anxious. What had he got me? Since we had arrived with only the cake and a bottle of wine I had assumed Max would be giving me his present later, perhaps back at my place. What would I now be forced to open in front of my mother?

Max came back into the room with a large wicker basket decorated by a giant green bow. He placed it down in front of me.

"Wow, what's this?" I asked, looking at the basket as if it were wired with explosives.

"It's a collection of bath stuff," he said as I went through it. Wrapped inside were a large, plush green towel, a bath pillow and several vials of Epsom salts. I also found a scrub brush, a face cloth, some hand moisturizer and body wash. "I figure once classes begin you'll be needing this stuff to unwind."

I didn't know how to react. I was embarrassed by such a gift. It was so intimate, so sentimental, that I felt naked in front of my mother. And it wasn't just I who was naked; Max was, too. I could picture my mom envisioning the two of us together, soaping each other up in the bath.

"Thanks," I said to Max in a daze, and got up. Instead of kissing him I gave him a brisk hug over the plates as if we were cousins and not lovers.

Almost on cue, Angie got up from the table to begin clearing.

"Angela, let me help you.".

"No, Mrs. Ambrose. You're a guest at my place," she said. "Please sit down."

Max and I were up and clearing regardless. My mom looked at us from where she sat. "Well, I think I should be getting home," she said, looking at her watch. "It's getting late."

"I'll call you a cab."

Max hung out in the back of the kitchen while Angie and I followed my mom to the front of the apartment to wait for her cab. We set her up with her stuff, making sure she hadn't forgotten anything. The cab soon pulled up in front of the building and honked its horn. "Thanks so much for the delicious meal," my mom said one more time. She kissed us both. "And say goodbye to your friend for me."

And then she was out the door.

MAX AND I DIDN'T TALK about it until we were alone, in our own cab, heading back to my place.

"That was strange, huh?"

Max said nothing and stared out the window.

"It could've been a lot worse. She just needs some time to get used to you."

Max turned towards me. "Did you not like my gift or something?"

"What?! Of course I liked your gift."

"Well, that was weird. I mean, your face. You'd have thought I'd taken a shit in the basket and gave it to you."

"What?! No, I loved it. It was great."

"Well, you seemed disappointed."

"No. I may have been a bit embarrassed, though. It felt a little private, personal. All that bath stuff. I don't want to put those kind of pictures in my mom's head."

"What kind of pictures?"

"You know. You and me. Together. Naked."

He huffed. "Well, that's what we do, Will. It's not *all* we do, but it's a part of what we do. You know, I'm not asking you to share with your mom the intimate details of our sex life, but I don't see how me giving you bath salts forces her to think about us having sex."

"Like I said, it's personal. It involves my body and you … taking care of it."

"This is fucking ridiculous," he said, annoyed. "We're in a relationship, Will. And if you want your mom to get used to the idea, you have to stop worrying about presenting us as something we're not."

I didn't say anything, just looked out the window at the passing lights.

"God, she couldn't even look me in the eye," he said, unleashing his anger. "And she's totally hoping you'll end up with Angie. She *loves* her!" He calmed down a bit. "And what's the deal with your mom calling her *Angela*? Doesn't she hate that? I'd hate it if anyone called me Maxime ... not that I think your mom would *ever* say my name."

Suddenly, I felt afraid of Max. Not afraid he'd become violent; rather that he could get so angry with me over something I'd done (or not done). I had never before heard him like this.

I let him speak his fractured thoughts as we rode home, not responding. This was the first time he and I had fought, although I wasn't sure I could call it a fight since it takes at least two people to have one.

"I'm sorry, Max," I said as we approached home. "I appreciate you trying, I do. I'll do my best to try harder with her, I promise."

"Your mother doesn't have to like me, Will," he said as we pulled up to the curb. "But you do."

AFTER OUR DINNER AT SALOON, Max and I found a cab in the storm and rode to his place. Once inside, we washed up and climbed into bed but did not have sex. I soon fell asleep and was awakened several hours later by the muffled rumble of a snowplow on Max's street. The truck's rotating lights threw a muted yellow about the room in circles, two or three times until it moved out of the window frame. I looked over at Max. He was out cold, lying next to me, head collapsed blissfully onto his pillow. At one point during the night he had cuddled me, absent-mindedly I think, before turning around moments later.

We're not together anymore, I thought. Our bodies are just familiar.

I got up from the bed to go to the bathroom. The apartment was cold and dark and smelled of the crackling radiators. I peed with the door open and the light off, and didn't flush. Out of the bathroom, I moved over to his rumbling fridge to get a glass of water. The plow was on the street behind his apartment now. I could hear its two smaller siblings, the sidewalk plows, jutting alongside. I took my cup to the window and watched the snow fall into the backyard. Standing there, I remembered the night not five months ago when I'd stood on the other side of this glass, peering in to the life I had been freshly exiled from. Inasmuch as I remembered the pain of that moment, I wondered if it had not been as bad as I thought. For I was back here, on the other side of this window, and life did not seem to be any better.

"What am I doing?" I whispered to my reflection.

I thought of how I had messed things up with James, my fight with Angie, and all the unsafe sex I was having with Max. And I thought of my mother, by herself, lying under this same big storm as me. When will I learn my lesson? I thought to myself. Like all those lines in Max's script? How many times do I have to go through this before I can learn?

Outside the night felt dangerous, the trembling sky covered in absorbent flakes of ice and snow. The farthest figures I could make out in the distance were the blurred lights of the tobacco plant four blocks away. I couldn't wait for spring, to be able to see the mountain from where I stood; or be on top of it, above the buildings of downtown, standing as tall as if I were one of them and looking down onto the city with absolute clarity. But the island felt dead or dying, its heart frozen underneath Mount Royal and its icy limbs, its bridges, lifelessly reaching out to the north and south shores, in desperation to hold on.

I finished up the water, placed the cup in the sink beside the dirty spoons and dishes and got back into bed. The streets were clearer now and Max's body had shifted so he was facing the wall. I settled down with my back to him and grabbed the edge of my pillow as I sank my head into it and tried to sleep.

Chapter

15

Which is the greater love? The one we are born into? Or the one we discover?

For the longest time I have been consumed by the disappearance of love. What happens when it's gone. I used to think that Max leaving me was the end of my world. That in its wake I would remain a ruined person. Someone so alone, so bitter, that everything in my path would disgust me. Instead, I find myself more petrified to lose my mother. A law of nature I understand, but one that has been maliciously hastened by an active cancer.

It came back. Just like that. In her colon. And her pelvis. It took only a moment for her body to turn on her again, bringing back the malignancy with a vengeance. Some rogue, vulgar element had found a way to hide within her tissues, to rebuild itself and then tear everything around it down, ripping through the bowel and spilling out into her liver and abdomen. All of this despite regular checkups and medication. It felt like a terrible, cruel joke.

I went with my mother to her results that Tuesday. Stage Three, the oncologist told us. Recurrence. The silent wait, the provisional prayer, was over. "Remission is sometimes only temporary," the doctor had warned us years ago, and I hadn't forgotten. And in remission we had waited, for seven long years, helpless and afraid this could happen again.

The second time around everything came about so quickly. Three weeks from symptom to diagnosis. And in a city where newspapers editorialize about long waiting lists and the failing quality of public health care, it was frightening to see my mom pushed to the front of the line, to see the doctors work hard to get her the earliest possible appointments because the clock was ticking and every moment counted.

Mom kept it together in the doctor's office, but back home she'd cry. I walked in on her one afternoon in her bedroom, checking her blood pressure, a smudged tear on the mound of her left cheek. Her blood pressure was high, 160 over 110, and she was worried.

"I don't know why this is so high," she said, ripping the Velcro strap from her arm. "I've got to keep it down."

"Well, it's understandable that it's high," I said, hoping to sound logical yet optimistic. More than anything I wanted to steer her away from further anxiety. "You're stressed. Anyone going through what you're going through would be."

"I thought they got it all, Will."

"They thought they did, too."

I sat down on the bed next to her and watched her fiddle with the apparatus, removing it from her arm and shoving it back into the box.

"What am I going to tell people?"

"Whatever you want to tell them."

"I didn't tell many people the first time," she said, sniffling into her sleeve. "Some people at work could tell something was up, but I never said. I'm sure they thought it was breast or ovarian cancer or something like that. But no, it's got to be this godawful one!" My mom made a small fist and slammed it down onto the bedspread. "I wish I did have breast cancer. It's nicer. We could do a walk, raise funds for research, I could meet other women with it. But this one feels so goddamn ugly."

"Well, that's silly," I said, trying to sound bright and, at the same time, together. "All cancer is ugly. It's never nice. Never think that."

"Still." She patted down the creases of her pants. "No one talks about this type of thing. I mean, what happens if I'm going to need one of those … bags? What am I going to do then?"

I didn't know what to say. None of our situation's prospects were encouraging. "Stage Three" meant surgery and chemo and radiation. "High-grade" meant urgent. It meant deep incisions, reconstructions, and a long recovery. And they don't fully know everything until they're inside.

Mom sighed and began to twist the rings on her fingers. I noticed they no longer sat as snugly as they once had. I grabbed and held her hand and, in doing so, looked at it as if for the first time. The tangled wrinkles, the blemishes, the liver spots were telltale marks of an overworked life that had provided so much for me. How withered these hands were — kept busy and tired by raising a child alone. I didn't understand how a part of her could be killing her. This woman who bore me, whose cells begot my own.

Staring at her fingers I started to cry. I don't think I had cried real tears in front of my mother before, but now, gazing at her frail hands, I couldn't hold back and broke down in her lap.

"Shh," she hushed, suddenly apart from her own problems. My mom pulled me close into her embrace and, resting my head under her chin, cradled me. I sobbed for a moment — swiftly reassured in her devoted arms. And soon I pulled myself together and sat back up straight, holding her hand. Through her rings I could feel her pulse, the vascular invasion of her body, and the two of us sat on the edge of her bed in silence, listening to the clock in the hall tick forward, my hand in hers as we breathed.

I HAVE OFTEN WONDERED WHAT my mother was like as a young woman. The only ideas I have come from old photographs; black-and-white crumpled snapshots of the girl she once was. In them, despite the outdated fashions and inflated hairstyles, my mother looks no different from any of the girls I hang out with. Girls like Angie. All you needed to do was pull back her hair, put her in jeans and a tank top, and she could've been hitting the dance floor with the rest of us. I find myself wondering too — if she were my age and not my mother — if we'd be friends. Would we be close, living outside the bonds of family? I'd like to think so. I'd like to think a part of me would recognize in her — a stranger on the street — an extraordinary person so loving and selfless that the two of us would become lifelong friends.

I wonder what happened to the girl in those pictures. The one unmarred by cancer, by duty, by a child. She is so beautiful in them; unblemished. But time has changed her the way it changes everyone. Carving and shaping the hell out of our bodies, weighing down our shoulders, furrowing our brows.

These pictures contain the building blocks of her motherhood and I stare at them fascinated, tracing the smooth roundness of her young face with my eyes. In them I can see the love she will have for me, a love deeper than anything I have ever felt from a man. And that scares me. Frightens me that I can do all of those things I do to men, press my body up against theirs in a variety of different ways, but no matter how hard I try I can't seem to get them to stay inside. I can't make them love me. And with my mother there is no effort. It's just there. As constant and infinite as the universe.

THE DAY AFTER MY MOTHER and I found out, I called Angie; our fight was immediately forgotten. In fact, the moment I told her she hung up the phone and hailed a cab to my place. We sat on the couch for a couple of hours — the TV on mute the whole time — and spoke not of Max or Geneviève, but of my mom and Angie's brother. About life and death and dying. I wanted to be optimistic, but I felt the need to ask difficult questions. About how she dealt with everything, and what she wished she'd known going in.

"I don't know," she sighed, thinking back. "I mean, we knew what was coming. There was no way it wasn't going to happen. But we avoided talking about it nonetheless. We were waiting for a miracle, for something to save the day. But as the weeks begin to pass you realize time is running out and no amount of hope or prayer is going to make anyone stay … And that's the honest truth. Whether we like it or not, people are taken from us. I don't think there was anything I could have known going into it that would have made it easier …

"I'd say make sure she knows you love her," she went on, filling up the silence her words had created. "But she already knows that … There was a time, near the end, when I kept telling Marco how much I loved him. But that soon became too much. It was too emotional, and, after a while, I don't think he knew what to do with those words anymore. It was like I was being selfish, because I was the one who was going to live and I couldn't do it without him knowing how I felt." She took a big breath. "I don't know how that made him feel … Still, sometimes, though, I wonder if I told him enough."

I'd never heard such doubt and regret in Angie's voice. In emotion, I had only ever heard her angry; sadness and remorse seemed to be reserved for people like me, or her other friends. Not her. No, Angie was the tough one, the confident one. But after almost fourteen years I was starting to see cracks in her armour, and as sad as this was it comforted me to know that she could feel as helpless and scared as I did.

"I guess if I were to give you some advice," she continued, "it'd be to spend as much time with her as you can. Ask her everything you want to know. One thing I wish I had been more aware of back then was the passage of time. Near the end, Marco and I didn't talk about important stuff. I don't know why. Perhaps it felt too intense to talk about anything meaningful with a person when they're dying — not that your mom is dying, Will. Let's be clear here. She could still make it through fine. But when you come face to face with mortality, it's easier to pretend it's not happening. So you carry on as normal. And suddenly it's too late and you're left with all the things you never asked."

I was flushed at this point. Cold and red and wet with fear. I was glad Angie was the only one around to see. "What would you have asked him?"

"I wanted to know if he was scared. I wanted to know if he felt he had had a good life. And if I was a good sister to him. I wanted to ask him if I could do anything to, you know, honour his memory. But I couldn't ask any of that. That would have been too hard ... God, what I wouldn't give to talk to him again."

Angie stuck around for the rest of the day and then slept over. The next day she came with me to visit my mom. It felt great to be her friend again. Angie made me feel sane. She was also another person my mother could talk to. When it was just the two of us, my mother and I would sometimes stare at each other, not knowing what to say or do. Having Angie around forced us to discuss other things and to not delve too much into worry and despair. I can't count the number of times I felt relieved to have another face to *look* at, one not lined with fear or anxiety. Angie was also kind enough to accompany my mother to some of her appointments. I had already taken off many days from work and had to be selective about future ones.

I could understand now why my mother hadn't told her co-workers about her illness. I didn't want to tell anyone either. I didn't want to have to explain to colleagues why I had been missing work, nor endure their own personal accounts of the people they knew living with cancer. I thought about it enough on my own and wanted to be left alone.

Thankfully, teaching was somewhat of a distraction. I had assigned my students their mid-term project and gave them a lot of class time to work on it. We were continuing our study of cities and I had given them the assignment of terraforming — choosing a planet and establishing their own colony. I was surprised that quite a few of them chose Pluto, and I told them what I knew about the New Horizons spacecraft and its current mission to explore the planet. Everyone's desks were filled with the building blocks of these fictional settlements — construction paper, pipe cleaners, Styrofoam balls. One student, Joseph, had a terrific hand and had drawn a beautiful city map, its life and detail outlined in varying shades of grey pencil. I asked him if I could look at it and he handed it over to me. He was halfway done and had sketched various city services on different parts of the paper. He had drawn a different animal to represent each of the services. There was a rabbit in the city garden, a fish swimming through the hydroelectric dam, a cheetah taking the rapid transit line. Joseph had also drawn a raven for the cemetery — the bird standing serious on top of a cracked tombstone. We hadn't discussed it in class, but yes, the settlers would need a place to bury their dead, a place far away from the gardens, from the waterways. It was basic urban planning; a fact of life.

Most days I'd sit at my desk at the front of class and watch the tops of their heads as they busied themselves with the work. I'd stare at the clock at the back of the room, counting the minutes until the day was over. I'd look at the watch my mom had given me too, now firmly affixed to my wrist. The days couldn't go fast enough. But though I wanted each workday to be over, I was aware of what the passage of time meant and how with each day we got closer to the surgery, closer to the unknown.

"MOM, CAN I ASK A question?"

I was sitting on the floor of our living room, going through the tattered sleeves of the old records she had stored under the sound system. It was another day, a happier one. We had been encouraged by the quick response of the doctor and his team, their coherent plans, the early surgery date. And her sister had agreed to come in to help with her convalescence, something that would allow both of us to heal faster. All that was left to do was wait.

"Of course you can," she answered, turning around from

where she stood by the stove, waiting for the kettle to boil.

"Why did you never remarry?"

"Me? Remarry?" she howled, surprised. "Oh, I don't know, Will. Life throws certain things your way. I suppose I never met another man as wonderful as your father." The kettle started to whistle and she turned back towards the stove. "What an odd question," she said, almost to herself, pouring the hot water into her ceramic mug. "What on Earth possessed you to ask that?"

"No reason," I said, fingering a dog-eared copy of *Jesus Christ Superstar*. I had been too nervous to look her in the face. "I just find it a little bit strange that I don't know much about your personal life ... Do you have the soundtrack to *Cats*?"

"No, I don't think so," she said, uneasy, returning to her crossword puzzle at the kitchen table with her cup. "Why do you want the soundtrack?"

I was going through my mom's old vinyl as a distraction, so I had something to hold on to while I asked her questions. "I was thinking, if we're going to see it this summer, I should bone up on it first."

"Well, who knows how I'll be feeling by then. But I'm sure they have it on CD at the library," she said. "I'll have a look the next time I'm there, although I don't know when that will be." My mom's tone turned cautious. "Is there something particular you'd like to know?"

"Hmm ... I don't know," I said, thinking. "... Was there anyone else? Someone from the library, maybe?" I had to look at her now. It felt too rude not to. "I seem to remember you going out on a couple of dates once."

"Yes, there was," she said timidly, looking into the cup as she stirred it with her spoon. "His name was Robert. He was a grad student I saw two or three times a week in the stacks.

Sometimes I helped him with his research. He caught me off-guard one afternoon — asked me out — and I said no. He was too young. But he persisted and, I suppose, eventually won me over. He was charming and awfully funny. We went out a couple of times, to dinner and to a play, but that was it. It ended soon after … Honestly, it was all too strange."

"What was strange about it?"

"I don't know," she said, shifting. "Dating again, I suppose. It felt odd to be dating again. It felt … wrong. I just …" The next thing appeared hard for her to say. "I loved your father so, Will. It took me a long, long time to get over him. I know you didn't know him, or you don't remember him much. But he was a wonderful man."

"… Do you still miss him?"

"Yes … but not as much as I once did. It was a long time ago … Sometimes, though, I'll remember something we did together, or come across something that reminds me of him. And when I look at you, Will. Sometimes, I can see him when I look at you."

"Really? How?"

"The way you come in from a day at work to have dinner here and you collapse on the couch. Your father used to do that all the time. Also, the way you look when you're helping me in the kitchen, sleeves rolled up, chopping vegetables. And your eyes. You have your father's eyes."

Elation. Joy. My eyes grew wide as I stared off into space, picturing my father performing the actions my mother had described. But then, instead of my father's face, I saw my own. My twenty-eight-year-old face in the brown suit I had always pictured him wearing.

"Your father was a great man, Will. I tried to get back out there," she said, almost apologizing, "but though I was no longer with him I still felt ... in love with him. I don't know if that makes any sense."

It made perfect sense. "Mom, Max and I aren't together anymore," I said, matter-of-fact.

"Oh," she said with genuine concern. "You're not? What happened?"

"It didn't work out. I don't think we were meant for each other."

"I'm sorry to hear that, Will," she said with sincerity. "When did this happen?"

"Several months ago," I said, standing up and moving to sit across from her. "Recently it looked like we might be reconciling, but I don't think that'll happen now." Max and I hadn't spoken since the morning after our Valentine's dinner, when I had zipped up my jackets in a hurry and run out the door, late for work. He had called me twice, but I hadn't returned his messages — and wouldn't. Not until I knew what I wanted to say.

"Oh, Will, I'm so sorry," she repeated, the words hanging between us. "I remember what that was like," she continued. "Hearing sad songs on the radio, seeing things that remind you of the other person. When your father died, I was lost for a long time. You were only two years old and didn't know what was going on, but I was a complete mess. It's difficult when things are brought to an end when you aren't ready for them to be over."

A sudden pall fell over my mom's face, triggered perhaps by thoughts of her own mortality. I reached across the table and grabbed her hand. I grabbed it because it was still there. And I kissed the inside of her palm.

"Are you okay?" I asked.

"I think so. I'm in capable hands. I trust my doctor. I have you ... Are you okay?"

"I'm all over the place … But I think I'm okay."

"And about your friend … Max?"

"It's the least of my worries … Still, I think the thing that's bothered me the most is that he was the one who ended it. Dad may have been taken from us, but Max *decided* to leave. It was a *decision*. That, I think, has been the hardest for me. When someone decides they don't love you anymore. It makes you wonder what, if anything, was real in the first place." All of a sudden I felt naked in front of my mother. I let go of her hand and covered my mouth. "God, I feel so stupid."

"Don't feel stupid," she scolded, pulling my hand back into hers. "It's okay to feel love for someone who is no longer there. It's okay to hold on to it for a while, but you can't let it stop you from living."

I dropped my head to the table, and looked at her from its flat surface. She looked so large from down here. A giant, even. Wise.

"I didn't think you liked Max," I said. "That time you both met was so awkward and weird."

My mom sighed deeply. "I didn't know how to deal with it, Will. You surprised me and I didn't know how to react. It was so different. It's not the life I would've chosen for you, but I love you, and more than anything I want you to be happy."

I lifted my head from the table. "When I came out to you in the hospital you said something that's stuck with me. You told me 'It's a very lonely life.' What did you mean by that?"

"Did I?" My mom looked down into her cup. "I don't know much about being gay, Will," she said. "I have a second cousin who is. Ted. He lives in Calgary. You never met him. I only met him a handful of times. He got into drugs at a very young age. Began to steal things from home. He ended up being hospitalized for depression after a couple of suicide attempts.

I don't know where he is right now, but I know he was never, ever happy. And I don't know if it was because he was gay, but it definitely made things harder for him. And I don't want things to be hard for you."

My mom's eyes began to well up. "I know you haven't had it easy." She began to cry. "I wish I could have provided a father or brothers or sisters for you. Someone else so you wouldn't be so alone. I realize you only have me, but I feel like the luckiest person in the world to have you. I honestly don't know what I'd do without you."

I started to well up too but refused to let go, holding in the rush of tears lining up behind my eyes.

She wiped her face. "Do you blame me?"

"Blame you?" I asked, incredulous. "For what?"

"For not giving you a family."

I pulled my mom towards me and held her close. "Are you insane?" I said, trying to lighten things up. "I couldn't have asked for better. It may have been the two of us, but it's all I needed."

My mom pulled herself away and, grabbing some tissues from the table, began to dry her eyes. "Still," she sniffed, "life is a lot more interesting when you have someone to go through it with. Whether it's Max, or someone else you have feelings for, I don't want you to be alone."

"I'm not alone, Mom," I told her. "And besides, I'll always have Angie."

WALKING BACK HOME I FELT shaken, but also liberated, to have had this conversation — to have the answers to the questions that, until this week, I didn't know I had wanted to ask. And my mother had had questions for me too. It felt so surprising, and otherworldly, to have had this talk with her.

I thought of what my mother had said about how interesting life is when you have someone else to go through it with. Is that why I missed Max? Was my life more interesting when he was around? But I had begun to imagine life without him now, and what I had once been so afraid of was now no longer strange and upsetting. It was life without my mother that frightened me more. For who am I in this world if I am not my mother's son?

I am the one in remission. I inhabit the space in between. Inside there is a decrease in pain, but the threat still exists. It hides, attaching itself to what it can until it's ready to reproduce once more — leaving me helpless and sick with grief. Love is what this illness has invaded. I imagine my own biology, the cells triggered by thoughts of Max, of my mother, being invaded by dark, beautiful circles that are its own undoing. Do my good cells recognize the danger when the sickness shows up in a corner of the body, unusual and mischievous? Do they fall in love with its strange beauty? Risk an interaction, knowing full well the grief it might later bring? And is it the same when HIV enters the bloodstream? God knows what risks I have been putting myself at for love. Is the body aware of how dangerous it is? For when you think you have beaten it, tamed it into submission, it can lie there, undetected for years before showing up and wreaking havoc again.

Our bodies must be very lonely to court these things. It's futile, I suppose, to try and control my cells. To warn them about potential dangers and will them into different shapes to avoid harm. But in remission I am the victim. I cannot change the way my body works, the way the world spins forward. And no matter how hard I try the end result will be the same. I am destined to lose the people I love.

He was alone, attractive; standing by the bar with his beer. He must have been a couple of years older than me. It was hard to tell with what he was wearing: baggy brown cargo pants, scuffed-up sneakers, and a large red T-shirt that ran over his belt. From where he stood, about twenty feet away, I could see the libidinous grin that hung out on the side of his face, curling up towards his right eyebrow. He stood there, staring at me, his hands in his pockets as if he was waiting for the next bus and I was his ride. There was a look. And then another. And before I knew it I was asking him to light my cigarette and chatting him up under the loudspeaker by the bar.

I don't remember his name. He was thirty-three, francophone, and the manager of a downtown clothing store. His voice had a guttural quality, a turbulence of wear and tear from too many cigarettes or too many nights spent in loud clubs. As he spoke I noticed a small, dark blemish on the inside of his lower lip. I suppose it could've been a beauty mark, a tattoo, or an ink smudge; but I didn't ask him about it. Whatever it was made him appear lustful and licentious, as if this rogue blotch were some sort of dirty secret about to roll off of his lips.

We spoke in French, for several minutes. Or rather he spoke and I listened. Stupid stuff about the club and his job. Soon we stopped talking and just stood there, side by side, watching the men circling the bar. In silence I drank faster. I no longer took sips, but gulps; and I drew the bottle to my mouth five, six, seven times in succession before one of us spoke again.

"Tu veux partir?"

I chugged the rest of my beer, picked up my jackets and followed him out the door. Outside felt extreme and wide. It must have been around 8 p.m. and the streets were full; the whooshing sounds of traffic and the laughter of people passing us by collided with the extreme buzz of alcohol and cigarettes in my head.

"Chez moi ou chez toi?" he asked as we walked down the street.

"Your place," I said.

He lived on the edge of the Village, about ten minutes up the hill towards La Fontaine Park. I could hear and understand him better now, his voice less raspy outside the bar. He spoke, telling me one thing after the other about himself in a drunken progression. He had been out celebrating with colleagues. A promotion. More money. More hours.

We continued to walk north, crossing through intersections, avoiding traffic cones set out in the street to mark off a deep pothole. Lights changed. A bike zoomed by. He took me though back alleys, behind houses. We walked like two kids heading to the park, at a brisk but clumsy pace, overtly physical and swinging from side to side.

I told him I liked his haircut, how freshly cut and hot he looked. And his smile. I told him I liked his smile. "Je n'aime pas mon sourire," he said, embarrassed. He felt his grin was too wide, his left incisor too jagged. I looked at his face from the side. It was true his smile was bent, but I still found him attractive; and when I looked at him I could see the kid he once was, awkward in class photos at ages five and ten.

"Do you speak English?" I asked.

"A lit-tle bit," he replied, his accent as crooked as his smile. He told me he spoke better Spanish. And German. Took Spanish in high school; dated a German. The German language is so soft and gentle, he said, and I thought he was being funny. He wasn't. He told me that, when whispered, the language sounds so soothing, so loving, so erotic, and then he whispered a bit of German into my ear.

HE CLOSED THE DOOR TO his apartment and I was all over him, chewing at the bottom of his lip as if I were trying to get the dark blotch to run out all over me. I was too rough, though, and he yelped and pulled back. "Attention," he said. I laughed, embarrassed. Instead, I let him lead, and he parked his tongue in the crook of my neck as I looked down the length of his hallway. Through the doorways that ran off of it I noticed how dark and sparse the rooms were. From where I stood I could only see a couple of simple pieces of furniture: a table, a television, a sofa. He pulled me towards his bedroom. It was just as bare. Four pale walls with one unevenly hung, dog-eared, heavy metal poster; a mattress, with no base, in a mess on the floor; a bookshelf with about a dozen slanted titles; and one naked window facing his bed.

I don't remember the sex as much as how he tore into me.

With his tongue. His finger. Ripping me apart to devour me like a peach, rimming the stone. I noticed, despite my being drunk, I had no trouble keeping hard. My cock rode high onto my stomach in a way that made it feel as if it were not mine, but a prop in our sex. I didn't do much; just let him do the work. He seemed content, losing himself in my body. I lay back and watched the angled shadows on the wall, my eyes eclipsing every now and again.

"Whoa!" I said all of a sudden, sitting up straight in bed. "No, no, no," I chastised him to his own guilty chuckle. I had felt the tip of his penis, wet and slippery, push momentarily in. "I don't do that." He listened to what I said and then came down to my chest, tearing at my nipple and rubbing up against me. We must have been at it for another ten minutes before it was over, and when he came it was with a gasp. And then I came too. I couldn't see anything but could feel it on my stomach. The warm collusion between us turning cold as he lay on top of me.

With a lunge he got up, panting, and wiped himself with a shirt on the floor. With his back to me, he quickly pulled on his underwear almost as if embarrassed to be naked. "Veux-tu de l'eau?" he asked on his way out of the room.

"Sure," I groaned, grabbing the shirt and wiping myself.

In his absence, I could feel my hangover dissipating. The drunkenness slammed out of me. I could feel my body as if I had not been in it the last half hour. My backside was sore, my chest moist with sweat. I felt like crap. I could hear the guy in the bathroom, then the kitchen; the rush of water and the snaps of cabinets. "What the hell am I doing," I muttered to myself.

I got up and pulled on my underwear and jeans and, in so doing, began to gaze sideways at the titles on his bookshelf. There weren't many: one on art history, another on architecture, a couple of photo books and a German translation of *Le Petit Prince*.

"Qu'est-que tu fais?" he asked as he entered the room, handing me the water.

"Looking at your books," I said.

"Ils sont même pas à moi," he said, grabbing me from behind and kissing my neck. "Ils appartiennent à mon chum."

"Ton chum? You have a boyfriend?"

"Oui."

He explained to me how he had had a boyfriend with whom he had lived for three years. They had broken up seven months ago, but were now seeing each other again (and other people too). He told me he would be moving back in with his boyfriend in a couple of weeks and this apartment had been a temporary home, where he had stayed while they patched things up. I gulped down the water and took another look around the room. The seven months looked disastrous. In the shabbiness of this purgatory I could see this guy's sad attempt at a new life. The deficit of his relationship was this crappy one-bedroom apartment where he had been held prisoner for half a year, slowly forced to acquire new furnishings that would now most probably be passed along to the next tenant.

"As-tu un chum?" he asked me.

I couldn't help but use laughter as an answer as I pulled on my socks. What do I tell him? Do I tell him about Max? And what the last few months have been like? How about James? Do I try to put into words why I didn't call him back? Do I tell him about any of the other boys I have fallen for over the years? The ones who didn't work out? Do I tell him about the crazy junk I've been through? That I lost my mother three days ago and have spent most of the week wasted, yet came here to get fucked? "No, I don't."

I looked for my shirt and found it by the trash can. As I reached for it I felt the furry nuzzle of a cat, purring around my leg. Suddenly it hit me. Elizabeth! "Shit! I have to go."

The guy looked at me, comically, as I patted myself down to make sure I had my keys and wallet and didn't forget anything. Soon I shot out of the bedroom and into the hall where I pulled on my sneakers.

"Do you want my num-ber?" he asked, water glass in hand.

"… No thanks," I said, tying up one of my laces.

"Non?" he asked, surprised. "Comment ça??"

"… What would be the reason?" I said, tying the other. "I mean, you have a boyfriend. Thanks, it was fun, but I gotta go."

"Est-ce que je peux te le donner quand-même?"

Without waiting for my answer, he took out a piece of paper to write down his number but I stopped him. "No," I said, laying my hands on the pen in his hand. "I'm not going to take it and pretend I'm going to call you. Thanks and all, but … Il faut vraiment que j'y aille."

He looked at me as if I were crazy. As if the sex we'd had should have made me feel something else. I zipped up my jackets and turned away from him, trying not to let the cat out as I opened the door and sped down the stairs.

MY MOTHER'S OPERATION HADN'T GONE well. The surgeons had opened her up, removed some stuff, and closed her back up again. The doctor told us the next day there wasn't much they could do. The damage to her system was too great, the cancer was everywhere and the best they could do was try to keep it at bay with chemo and radiation. "With some luck we can slow it down," he had said, "but I'm afraid that is only a short-term solution." We both listened in her small room of curtains, my mom swollen and slow with morphine. They had waited until she had sobered up to tell us, but still, in her face, I saw elements of that confused look she had five minutes after an injection of painkillers. I felt numb; cornered in by the news. There was nothing I could do but sit by her side and wait for her to be well enough to leave the hospital. My mom was tired and spent most of the time sleeping. Throughout the day she soared through pain and euphoria, sometimes grasping at visions.

My aunt Mary had flown up for the operation. It was good to have her here, even if it was only for a couple of days, sitting in the hospital room next to Angie and me. Over the next few days we watched with discomfort as my mom lay stoned in her bed. I didn't recognize her under that cloud. I'd watch as she drifted in and out of consciousness, watch the fear in her eyes alight when she hallucinated, hear the dry, raspy sounds of her breathing as her body rose and fell under the covers. She was in pain, and in those brief brutal moments I could see her anger, her sadness, her fear and desperation. The doctors had tried everything they could, tried to fix the body to keep the soul inside. But the body is relentless. And there was nothing I, nor she, could do to stop it.

AROUND FIVE O'CLOCK IN THE morning the phone ripped me out of a heavy sleep. I jumped up from my bed and grabbed for the phone in the dark.

"Hello?"

"May I speak to Mr. Ambrose, please?"

"Yes, that's me."

"Mr. Ambrose, this is the Royal Victoria Hospital. It's important you come down to the hospital."

"Is it my mother? Is she okay?" I asked.

Whoever it was on the other line didn't sound sure. "I'm sorry, sir, I don't have that information. All I know is that there is a change in your mother's status. Can you please come to the hospital?"

In the dark, the phone sandwiched between my shoulders and head, I reached for my socks and jeans. "I'll be right there."

THE NURSE ON DUTY STOOD up as I approached the desk, circumventing the counter to reach me. I recognized her from the night before when I had asked her for an extra pillow. "Hello," I said, breathless. "I got a call telling me to come to the hospital. Is something wrong with my mother?"

The short, dark-haired girl grabbed me by the wrist and led me several steps over to a small alcove of orange seats and pulled me down beside her. "Mr. Ambrose," she said, "I am very sorry, but your mother has passed away."

I froze, looking down at the table full of ripped magazines, my bottom lip trembling as she spoke. The thing I had feared most was happening. I could feel the reality of the situation closing in around me, trying to break in. Whatever composure I thought I had slipped away as the tears began to sputter out in coughs. The nurse squeezed hold of my hand. It was all that kept me from falling over.

"It was very sudden," she said. "A pulmonary embolism. It stopped her heart. We did what we could, tried to resuscitate her, but I'm afraid it proved impossible. She didn't suffer. I'm very sorry, Mr. Ambrose." The nurse did not let go of her grip as I sat there, breathing in through tears, struggling to let it sink in.

"Here, let me get you some water," she said, letting go of my hand as she went over to pour me a cup of water. I wiped my eyes with the corners of my sleeve as I heard the cup flush itself full. The nurse handed it over and I took a sip. My throat clenched as the dull, tepid water made its way down. I had known this was coming, but I didn't think it would be this quick. And no matter how much I had tried to brace myself for the impact, I felt shattered.

I placed the cup on the table beside me. "Can I see her?"

"Do you think you're up for that?"

I didn't think to answer and stood up. The nurse made a signal to someone at her station and led me down the hallway, away from the bright fluorescents of the waiting area towards the dim corridor of patients' rooms. Some doors were wide open, the hush of people sleeping barely audible over the swoosh of the nurse's scrubs. As we reached the end of the hallway she opened a door. "Follow me," she said, and took me down a darker passageway. In here it was all equipment and machinery, the hum of a ventilator or furnace churning through the hall. We passed a brightly lit room, a break room I supposed, where I caught the eye of an orderly, a tall black man dressed in lavender, as he plunked coins into a vending machine.

"She is in here for the time being," the nurse said as we arrived at another door. She opened up the room. Inside, the room was bare, cold, and quiet. All I could see were the wheeled legs of a gurney standing in the centre of a string of curtains. The nurse grabbed hold of one end and pulled the curtain open to reveal my mother, lying in her nightgown, her body diffused and lifeless. I lost it then, crying as I moved over to the bed and grabbed her hand. It was cold and smooth, the tips of her fingers already turning black like ash. I saw no sign of trauma, no sign of violence. Her eyes were closed and her jaw was slightly opened, her face deflated into the pillow.

"I'll give you a moment and wait for you outside," she said.

The nurse closed the door behind her, leaving me on the edge of the gurney, beside my mother's body, her hand in mine. I sat for perhaps two minutes, not more. It was long enough to have one last look. I would have thought I'd want to stay longer, knowing this would be the last the time I would be in a room with her, but no, this was not something I wanted to remember.

I'd known the situation was bleak, the outlook grim, but I had expected we would have more time. Instead, a dislodged blood clot had moved up from her swelling legs into her heart. A self-destruct button. Almost as if her body knew it was time, began to shut itself down. The cancer revealed, the game over.

Before I left the room, I removed a piece of medical tape attached to her arm where an IV had gone in. I peeled it off and put it into my pocket. I then stood up and with tears in my eyes I pulled back her hair and kissed her on the forehead.

I SAT IN THE WAITING room and watched the images move on the TV in the corner. It was some kind of live French morning show and the host stood there, cue cards in hand, as some shorter man spoke animatedly about the city's botanical garden. Spring was coming, he said, and families could now take part in *Le temps des sucres* — a celebration of maple syrup. It would also be the last time to catch the treehouse exhibit, featuring maquettes of homes designed by environmental architects. The short man went on for about ten minutes, spouting this PR junk about the gardens, its opening hours, and admission prices. Outside, the light in the window behind these two men matched the rising colour outside the window in the waiting room where I sat. The corner of the television screen said it was 7:33 a.m. That meant it was morning. But it didn't feel like morning. Each time of day leaves its own impression — is born out of the hours before. So what did that make right now? And what part of day belonged to the last few hours I had passed through? These blackest of hours that did not belong on the face of any clock?

When Angie arrived I had been sitting in the waiting room for almost an hour. She came down the hall, hurriedly. I stood up and she ran into my arms, crying for both of us. Angie helped me collect my mother's things. The orderlies had already changed the linens, leaving no sign she had lain there. No indentation in the mattress, no stains on the sheets. The wastebasket empty, the morphine drip gone. The room was sweltering with electric heat even with the window cracked. We twirled around once or twice with bags in our hands, making sure we'd missed nothing, and then left the sterile white of the hospital room.

When we hit the outside it was bright and I was surprised to find it was still morning. Angie hailed us a cab and we piled in and left for my place. Back home, my apartment looked as it did in those frantic moments before I had left. Drawers open. A light on. When I'd left this morning, I'd left innocent, not knowing what I knew now. I propped the bags on top of the kitchen table.

"You want some tea? I'm going to put on a pot of tea," Angie said, making her way to the stove. While Angie was busy fiddling, I dove into one of the bags and searched for my mother's phone book. Inside I found a small, pink, plastic notebook about a half inch thick and in the shape of a postcard. I only needed one number. My aunt Mary had returned to Florida the day before to tend to a couple of things once it had become clear she would need to stay longer. Now I had to see when she could come back for a funeral. I thought of my aunt, in Florida, beginning her day, unaware of this call she was about to receive.

I left Angie in the kitchen and went into my room with the portable phone and closed the door.

ABOUT TWENTY MINUTES LATER, I hung up the phone. I got up off the bed and reached for a tissue to blow my nose. The pockets of my jeans felt tight so I removed the weight of objects from them: my wallet, keys, receipts, watch, a crumpled ten-dollar bill and the small piece of medical tape I'd swiped from the hospital room. I opened my nightstand and placed the tape inside a box of keepsakes, alongside lucky pennies and extra keys.

I left the room and found Angie outside, on my balcony, smoking.

"So?"

"My aunt's going to look into coming next week. There's no rush now. I don't know when we'll have the funeral … Give me some of that."

Angie handed me over her cigarette and I took a long drag.

"I'm so sorry, Will," she said and tugged on my shoulder.

I was squinting, looking outside at the sun. It was going to be a beautiful day. I was afraid of it. I felt alone. Like a shortwave radio broadcasting a signal that can never be received: What is my position? Do you read me? Over.

C
 h
  a
   p
    t
     e
      r
17

When I was young, my mother used to take me to the Notre-Dame-des-Neiges Cemetery to visit my dad. We'd go on Father's Day, his birthday, sometimes on Remembrance Day, but we stopped going when I was around nine or ten. I don't remember much of that time. I had no real questions about death. It was something that happened to other people — old women who would have tea with my mother while I played with trucks on the floor.

I was two when my father died, so I have no recollection of his death or funeral. In fact, the only memorial service I had ever been to was for my grandfather. I was about seven at the time, but I still remember the horror on my mom's face when she got the call he had passed.

As with my father, I only have a vague recollection of my grandfather. There is an image in my head of him propping me up on his knee for a photograph, but maybe that's not a memory.

Maybe it's the photograph I'm remembering, tucked away somewhere in my mother's photo albums. I remember the wake and the mass, watching his old friends and family members cry. Their mourning seemed alien to me. Even when we visited my father's plot there would be no real reference of grief for me. I didn't remember my dad the way my mom did. This cemetery was just a place — a beautiful place — that held the remains of departed friends and family. We came with flowers, we prayed, and then we left. And life pretty much remained the same.

Soon the mundane exercises of living — groceries to buy, homework to check, laundry to do — took precedence, became much more pressing than communion with the dead. That happens, I suppose. Although we mourn the loss of a loved one, at some point we start to forget. The pain dulls and life goes on: my mom had to work, I grew up, and the needs of the living outweighed the promises to the dead.

IT TOOK MY MOM'S FIRST bout with cancer to get us back to the cemetery. We went one November day, rode the Number 11 bus up the hill towards the grounds' main entrance. My mother didn't seem anxious, sitting across from me; but I was, fidgeting in my windbreaker and sneakers on the steep ride up. Mom had brought with her a wreath and some gardening tools and had packed a Thermos full of black coffee that all sat in a jumble by her feet in a plain canvas bag. It had been over a year since she had first been diagnosed, and here we were, on the other side of that year, a little worse for wear but still healthy and very much alive. Recent tests had shown no sign of cancer in her body, and we were thankful, but it had left its mark. My mom had lost a lot of weight and now swam in her clothes. Sweaters that had once made her chest look busty now fell flat from her shoulders, colliding with the jewellery hung about her neck. Stress had thinned out her hair and made it grey, and I noticed she had begun to tie handkerchiefs around her head to hide it.

As the bus approached the iron gates of the cemetery I got up and rang the bell. We got off the bus and walked up the winding path towards the reception area. It was late fall and leaves were everywhere. Some sections of the lawn were clipped and clean while others, especially the spots with no graves, were piled with fallen brown-and-orange leaves.

"Do you remember where it is?" I asked, grabbing the canvas bag from her.

"Yes, I think so," she said, leading the way. "I remember it being on the west side, not too far from the side gate." I heard effort in her voice, weariness from the small incline. "If we get lost, we can head over to the main office for a map."

Walking towards the family plot we were greeted by the grand mausoleums and columbariums where the city's once-wealthiest rested in stone crypts, magnanimous rocks buried into mounds of earth. These funeral vaults were obscured by massive trees, their strong roots snaked around the foundations like errant elephant trunks. They all seemed excessive, opulent, in their ornamentation. One final public appearance that was as much a reminder of the brevity of life as it was a tribute to vanity.

Behind these rocks lay the modest stones of the middle-class. Checking the dates on some of the graves we passed, I noticed many wives had outlived their husbands. Also interesting, I found a man who had been buried between two women: one wife who had died at the age of twenty-five, and the other who had taken her place.

The premature deaths of children were marked in one huddled section on much smaller rocks; blackened, weeping tiles that struggled to escape the long blades of unkempt grass. Grey Nun Orphanage, I was able to make out on a nearby plaque. These gravestones looked like chipped teeth. They announced the names of children caught unawares by the quick hand of death. Aged twelve, eight, three. Strange they be so young, I thought, as the dead always seem to be much older than the living.

"There it is." My mother recognized it right away. I had forgotten how large our family stone was: a pillar of dark granite with a Celtic cross on top that was at least five feet higher than most of the rocks around it. It was oddly shaped. Other graves were adorned with flat stone tablets that stood from the ground tall like the backsides of chairs. Ours danced around itself, an outpost or a lighthouse. The stone stood crooked, jutting out at an angle. "I don't remember it being like this," my mother said, touching the pillar. "I think it might have been knocked or something. Maybe they had to move it?"

"Could anyone really knock over anything that heavy?" I asked. The stone must have weighed 1,000 pounds.

My mom knelt down, took out her tools, and began to chop at the base of the stone, pulling out the dead weeds and leaves that had gathered there. I stood back and contemplated the rock, my hands in my pockets. Etched on its face were six familiar names: two of my grandparents, two of my great-grandparents, my father, and a great-aunt. Still, the rock seemed a little too large for our family.

"Why is this plot so huge?" I asked.

"I don't know. Your great-grandparents bought it many years ago. I guess they were expecting to have more children and grandchildren than they did."

"How much room is left in there?"

"Enough … I'll be there. You, if you want. My sister might,

unless she decides to be buried with her husband's family in Florida."

And that was it. Short. The full extent of our remaining family.

My mother lifted herself up off the ground, tossing the weeds and dead leaves into a plastic bag she had brought with her. I stared at the six names on the stone. "Where is everyone else?"

"Like who?"

"I don't know. There has to be more than these six." I thought about my great-uncle, who had died in the Second World War. "What about Uncle Alan? Where's he buried?"

"He's in here, I think ... There are at least five other people buried here."

"... Under here?"

"Not everyone is marked on the tombstone ... I don't know why. I suppose no one got around to adding their names. They all died so long ago. But there must be a record of it somewhere. I'm sure the cemetery knows."

My mother proceeded to list off the names of the people she was sure were buried beneath us. I was amazed that inside of this nondescript plot, buried in crates, one on top of the other, were the combined remains of my father, two of my grandparents, two of my great-grandparents, several great aunts and uncles, one of my third cousins, and a friend of the family. After all these years, their coffins must have eroded clean away, I figured. Each one mingling into the next, creating a dry soup that year after year continued to fertilize the green ground upon which we stood.

A chill ran through my body.

"Do you want some coffee?" My mom took out the Thermos and a couple of small Styrofoam cups and proceeded to pour coffee into them, handing me a Ziploc bag full of sugar and Popsicle sticks.

We drank and wordlessly contemplated our family's stone. I looked at each name, the departed's time on Earth parenthesized between two brackets. Staring at all the letters and numbers I strained to see if I could hear any of their parting words — the silent ones that whispered their proud accomplishments, hidden desires and unfulfilled dreams. I listened for them and heard nothing. And it was all the same, row by row, beside and around us. Family members buried together, side by side, together in death as they were in life.

Standing beside my mother, I thought of the scene in *Torch Song Trilogy*. The one where Arnold and his mother recite Kaddish at the family tombstone. I thought of the blow-up they have in the cemetery; how Anne Bancroft yells at Harvey Fierstein about his "need" to always discuss his sexuality.

It was remarkable how my mom and I didn't fight. Angie had told me she thought that was strange. For her, she said, arguing is a way you let people know you love them. Angie stressed how much she loved her mom, but there was not one week that went by where a simple conversation didn't end with the two of them having words. "It's not healthy to keep your frustration in. It's got to go somewhere."

I thought back to *Torch Song Trilogy* and smiled, remembering how I'd first come across it on TV in French, my mom knitting on the couch beside me. How I'd somehow found out what the film was and secretly rented it in English. And then how, while watching the credits, I had discovered it was based upon a play and gone out to find a copy of that play. In so doing I'd fallen upon a gay bookstore on St. Laurent called L'Androgyne that I soon began to visit on a regular basis. There I had discovered a whole library of books different from the ones my mom brought home and I'd devoured each one, cover to cover.

Such a long time ago, I thought to myself. I was a completely different person then.

It's November, 1999. The year 2000 is right around the corner. Everyone is excited about the new millennium and I am eager for it too, eager to leave the illness and fear in the last century. In January I'll be entering my final semester at Dawson, and although applications are due only in March I have already begun to look into university. I have decided to become a teacher: English, History or Geography. I haven't told my mother this yet, but I know she'll be happy.

One other thing I haven't told her is I've begun to think about moving out. Confident the worst is behind us, I desperately want to pick up where I'd left off. I'm twenty-two now and feeling as though I'm having a second coming out. It feels great to be out and about with Angie again. Many nights the two of us stumble back to her place where I crash on her sofa, thinking of the handsome faces that passed me by. I've been thinking how great it would be to have my own place, my own home, where I could have a personal life. Where I could bring home a boyfriend.

I looked to the empty space beside me and wondered who would fill it. Of all the ghosts in the cemetery, it was a living soul I was waiting for. Arnold recited Kaddish for Alan at the family plot. Who will I bury? Who will bury me? Who will lie next to me in the afterlife?

Family was so important to my great-grandparents that they'd saved a space for my mom and me in the underground. Yet I felt closer, in some ways, to those I wasn't related to. People like Angie and her friends. Even the familiar faces of the people from the bars I didn't know, who I may never come to know. In the end they weren't all as pompous and cynical as my first acquaintances, Shaun and François. And there were times — like when watching the gay pride parade, or dancing in a crowd into the wee hours of the morning — I felt a sense of kinship with these faces that rivalled the ties of blood. It was as if we were all war buddies, perpetually celebrating a victory, who had each other's backs.

But with my mom it was greater. I'd go to war for my mom. It would be strange not to live in the same home as she. And I hoped, when I did decide to step out on my own, she'd understand.

WE FINISHED OUR COFFEE. MOM placed the wreath on the stone and said a silent prayer. I packed up our trash and we began to make our way out of the maze of tombstones and towards the Number 11 bus stop.

On our way out of the graveyard I felt as if each stone was trying to get my attention, trying to get me to read its epitaph and tell me its stories. But if they were reaching out, I couldn't understand them. All the deceased ask is to be remembered, but I can't do that. I can't tell their stories because I never heard them.

So, what does that mean for my mother and me? Who will be around to remember us? Who will tell our stories?

Chapter 18

I was hit by the stench as I entered the apartment. In the kitchen I found the garbage can knocked over, its contents spread along the floor in clumps of half-eaten trash. "Elizabeth," I called out, but she didn't come. I searched the apartment, checked under beds and in closets and finally found her, wide-eyed and petrified, hiding underneath the couch. "Come on ... come on," I tried to entice her with the calm motion of my hand. She wouldn't budge.

I got up off the floor and made my way to the kitchen, retrieving the bag of cat food from one of the upper cupboards. Almost immediately, in a Pavlovian frenzy, Elizabeth sprang out from under her hiding place as the familiar sounds of kibble rustled in the folds of the bag. I quickly poured some out into one large overflowing mound as she stuck her face deep into the stream, gorging on the food encircling her head and falling onto the floor. She crunched away, louder and raspier than I had ever heard her eat. She took in big mouthfuls, inhaling the food in a harsh whistle. I placed the bag on the counter and then checked her water bowl. It had been five days since I'd been by to check on her, but thankfully I had filled up a large dish the last time I was here. It was almost empty now. I filled it up with fresh water and then collapsed back on the floor to watch her eat. "I'm so sorry, Elizabeth," I said from where I sat, not daring to touch her.

Aside from the feeding, the apartment was still. Every object remained in its place, hushed and frozen, locked into position the last time my mother had touched it. From the floor of the kitchen, I could see into her bedroom: the bottom of her bedspread, the books sprawled upon her dresser. She'd never walk into that room again.

In the kitchen I could hear the fright of the appliances, the rising dread of their immobility. There was a consistent sadness in the arrangements on the counter too, a state of misery in the dishes on the rack and the towels by the stove. On her fridge, I caught a glimpse of her latest to-do list, neglected and unfinished. What was I to do with this stuff? The frames, plates and cups, clothes, candles, pills, slivers of soap, gifts, albums, coupons, toothbrushes, mattresses, and old magazines? How about the frozen meals in the freezer? All orphans. All mementos in some way. I didn't want them. I didn't want to give them away either, but throwing them out felt like the wrong thing to do.

I grew sick thinking about how I would one day have to re-enter these rooms. Walk in and out of them. Put things down, pick things up. I may have grown up in this apartment, but it felt strange — hateful, even — to be here now. The apartment had no more heart. That had left with my mother.

Looking at the garbage on the floor, I figured I should clean up the mess, check to see what had spoiled in the fridge and throw out the trash. But I couldn't take myself up off the floor. In fact, I wanted nothing more than to wait until Elizabeth had finished and then take her from here, leave this third-floor collection of rooms on Hôtel-de-Ville and its objects and never come back. But that was impossible. Already I knew I'd have to be back Monday morning. My aunt was scheduled to return the next day and I knew she'd want to begin sorting through my mother's things. There was a lot to go through.

As Elizabeth's bites began to slow down, I could hear, underneath, the calm, sharp ticking of the kitchen clock; the second hand moving forward at a steady, insistent pace. Tick, tick, tick — each second heartless and unkind. The apartment, in its own timelessness, mocked me. It tormented me with its faithfulness to my mother, its power to remain unchanged by her disappearance. And as I sat in limbo, on the floor, I began to feel the pull. Invisible cables falling down around me like power lines. They were everywhere. They met and crossed, clawed and looped, like a net or a grid or the boxes of a calendar, a never-ending sequence of squares representing the days, weeks, months that I am trapped in. In its relentlessness, time was dragging me with it, inch by inch, into the future, and I did not want to go. I could hear the rush of blood through my head, the sound of it as it sped through my veins, shooting in and out of my thumping heart. I wanted it to stop. I no longer wanted it pumping and coursing through my body. No, I wanted it outside, along with my veins and heart, the lines of my entire circulatory system ripped out and hung to dry like the wash in the back alley. Vile, stupid life. Elizabeth crunched away as the clock persisted, each second a cruel reminder, like the pills my mother took, that life was finite, that time continued to be counted, and that each second separated me further and further from what I once had.

Suddenly, I leapt from the floor and opened one of the kitchen drawers. Inside lay a tangle of tools and utensils: a tape measure, a whisk, a marker and ruler. I found the hammer and pulled it from the nest of instruments and climbed atop the kitchen counter. With one vicious blow I smashed the clock dead in its place. It fell from the wall and onto the floor as Elizabeth darted from the room. I jumped down and continued to pound it into the tile. But it wasn't enough. In the aftermath I could hear the steady advancement of time echoed in the other clocks in the apartment. Taking the hammer I moved from room to room, splitting the one in the hallway in two, destroying the clock radio on her nightstand and then mine, finally pulling the life from the electronic displays on the TV and VCR.

I returned out-of-breath to the kitchen and dropped the hammer on the floor, following it down with my knees. I listened for more and heard it on my wrist. Tick, tick, tick. The watch my mom had given me. I opened the metal clasp and slipped it from my wrist. Staring at its face, I pulled out its knob, stopping it at 9:23 p.m.

INSTEAD OF GOING HOME, I found myself walking to the Metro, each step automatic. Elizabeth was balled up inside her cage and we were competing for space with the weekend revellers, men and women heading home from their evenings in bars and restaurants. At Berri Station, a mass of us got off and I took the escalator down to the Green Line to switch trains. Once our car arrived, I pushed my way to the front and grabbed one of the free corner seats, placing Elizabeth at my feet.

Two stops later, a pair of tall men got on the train and congregated above me. "Je te jure," one said to the other in French.

His accent was strong, foreign, maybe from the south of France or Northern Africa. "Ce type a une dent contre moi. Il m'a même pas regardé dans les yeux. J'étais là, dans son bureau et c'est comme s'il parlait à la bibliothèque ou aux plantes pendant que je restais là à attendre comme un imbécile de pouvoir lui expliquer que …"

"Mais c'est pas vrai," the other one interrupted. "Je me mets en quatre pour te trouver ce boulot, je mets ma réputation en jeu et toi, t'arrives toujours en retard. Mais qu'est-ce que tu crois, Pierre? C'est un cabinet d'avocats!" I could tell the two weren't arguing. Despite the nature of their discussion they spoke like brothers, a sense of frustration underlying perhaps a sibling rivalry. "T'aurais pu t'excuser au moins."

"Je vais pas me mettre à genoux pour récupérer mon poste. Sûrement pas devant ce type." I rolled my eyes. These men spoke to each other as if they were the only two in the car, while the train barrelled along and everyone else sat in solitude, staring at our hands or each other. "C'est un monstre. Je sais pas comment tu fais pour le supporter. Faudrait l'éliminer."

"C'est un très bon chef. C'est sûr que s'il faut montrer un peu de fermeté, il est là. Il s'est pas rendu aussi loin dans la vie en étant gentil."

"J'arrive pas à croire que tu prennes sa défense contre moi, ton propre frère. Qu'est ce que tu penses que papa dirait, hein ?"

"Shut up."

The man stopped in the middle of his outburst and he looked down at me, puzzled. "Pardon?"

I too was surprised to find that the order had come from me, but looking at him, staring at me in annoyance, I continued. "Shut up," I said once more, before letting three more go in a volley from where I sat. "Shut up! Shut up! Shut up!"

"… T'as un problème ?" he barked at me.

"What is *my* problem? What is *your* problem? Do you think this is your own private car?" I was speaking in English, not caring if they understood a word I was saying. "Do you think everyone here wants to listen to what you have to say? Why your stupid brother lost his job? You should have the common decency to respect your fellow passengers. We're here, sitting quiet, minding our own business. While you think it's okay to air your laundry in public."

"Fuck you!"

So he did understand English. "No," I said, turning it back on him in anger. "Fuck you!" With these words I stood up in the crowded vehicle. I had become enraged and I could tell that my intensity had frightened these men.

A quiet pause descended upon the car as all eyes were on me and the train pulled into Frontenac Station, slowing down to let the people off. Thankfully, it was my stop. I picked up Elizabeth's cage and, despite it being so crowded, everyone made room as I exited the car. I wiped my eyes with the sleeve of my jacket and made my way, forcefully, above ground.

MAX ANSWERED THE DOOR IN sweatpants and slippers, the television chattering away behind him. "Will," he said, surprised. "What are you doing here?"

"I need to talk to you," I said, out of breath.

"Is everything okay?"

I placed the cat's cage on the floor beside me. "I need to tell you that you were wrong."

"What are you talking about?"

"When you left me. You made a mistake."

"Will," he started, placing his hands on his hips and lowering his head.

"No," I stopped him, my voice forceful yet composed. "Let me finish."

Max rolled his eyes, the look on his face one of grumbling patience.

"You don't know how crazy the last five months have made me," I said, looking into the past. "How hurt I've been. Your leaving turned my whole world on its head. You were smart enough to let me know how you felt that day, but I didn't get the chance to."

Max shifted his body onto the frame of the door. He opened his mouth as if to speak, but he said nothing.

"Well, I felt shocked. Sad. Angry. Here I thought I was in this wonderful relationship with someone who loved me as much as I loved him, but I wasn't ... It's sobering to find out that the most important relationship you think you've had didn't mean much to the person you had it with."

"That's not fair," Max spoke up now, arms folded and brow furrowed. "Our relationship did mean a lot to me. You can't blame me for wanting something else."

"All right, what did it mean to you? Tell me. How *do* you feel about me? And if you wanted something else, then what the hell have the last two months been about, huh? Nothing? Anything? Or are you killing time until *something else* comes along?"

Max had nothing to say. I wondered if I was being fair bringing up our recent trysts, for I was as guilty of them as he was. I stopped myself, tempered my anger, and tried to channel Angie. "No, Max. You didn't get bored or fall out of love. You gave up."

"Gave up? Do you think it was easy for me?"

"Of course it was," I said, drawing out the words. "I suppose it's not all your fault, though. Your father messed with you so much that you've learned not to rely on anyone for anything. It would've been much harder for you to talk to me and try to make things work. But instead, you decided things weren't the way you wanted and you could do better, so you dropped me and went to look for the next guy."

Max wouldn't meet my gaze. He stood there, listening to what I had to say, arms still folded and staring at my knees.

"You know," I continued, thinking suddenly of James, "someone told me recently that the only way to make a relationship work is to keep trying not to destroy it. Well, you destroyed it, Max. And it was beautiful."

There. It was done. Everything unsaid now out in the open. I suppose I had got my point across, but it didn't make me feel any better. Max remained quiet, and so did I. Elizabeth shifted in her carrier, the TV still blathering in the background. I looked behind Max, into his kitchen, and noticed the clock on his wall, still stuck at 4:37, and then I looked down to my wrist, the watch hands frozen at 9:23.

"You know," I said, exhausted and defeated, "I came here to yell at you. To tell you how I felt after all this time. But this has been my fault too. The last couple of months I've been deluding myself, thinking if you'd only spend more time with me you'd remember how great everything was and want me back. I was hoping to stop things from changing, to have some control over the present. But I can't. No matter how hard I try, I can't stop the world from moving forward. I can't stop anyone from leaving …"

I stopped myself, and tried not to cry. "Max, my mother died this week."

A hand flew to cover his mouth. "Oh my God," he said, moving to comfort me.

"No," I whined, shrugging him off my shoulder. "I don't

need your sympathy … I've said what I came to say," I wiped my eyes and picked up Elizabeth. "I have to go."

"Will, wait!" Max shouted the words almost as an afterthought as I hurried down the stairs. It wasn't enough to keep me there.

C
 h
  a
   p
    t
     e
      r
19

A week later I looked down at Parking's dance floor, staring once more at the throngs of men below. The last seven days had been crazy ones and not something I wanted to remember: the emotional return of my aunt, the small but intense service for my mother, the clearing out of her apartment. Angie and her friends had stepped in to help, packing up the boxes and bringing them down to the church's van outside. I loved them for that. Angie also told me that Max had called her that morning to see if he could do anything. I shrugged and didn't tell her about my visit to his place.

I was at the club after having seen my aunt off to the airport, which was equally gut-wrenching, and I was feeling the need to erase as much of the last few weeks as possible. I had decided to do it without booze, though. I needed a break from drinking, perhaps even a permanent one.

Water bottle in hand, I noticed two men below me slow

dancing at the edge of the dance floor. Two hands up, pointed together, they twirled around to whatever song was playing only in their heads. I caught myself smiling, remembering all the times I used to sit on the bleachers at k.o.x. and study the strange movements of the boys in the room.

At some point I moved downstairs to check what was happening in the basement. As always, the DJ was playing a mix of songs from my youth. New Order, The Cure, A-Ha, OMD, Depeche Mode. I laughed as I heard him play a cover of The Smiths' *How Soon is Now?* The version sounded frantic, as if it were being sung by two underage girls — their high-pitched voices whining over the familiar melody. Is nothing sacred? I thought. But then again, why not? The kids dancing seemed to like it. Kids. When did I start calling them that? It's true that more and more I was feeling older in these spaces. The crowd always getting younger.

In many ways it feels as if I've always been stuck in the past. I listen to the same music I did when I was fifteen, the bands I was first introduced to on Angie's cassettes. I still head down to the Village on my bike and poke my head into one or two bars on weekends. Why does all this still hold some fascination for me? I suppose I must find some comfort in these surroundings, in these songs. But in truth, it's getting boring. These are the same songs we danced to last year, and the year before that. So why do I keep coming here expecting things to be different when everything ends up sounding the same?

I DECIDED TO CALL IT a night, go home, and attempt a good night's sleep. But before leaving, I went to take a leak. Inside the downstairs bathroom I noticed the stall dividers had been repainted. I went into the one stall I remembered housing the graffiti I had once been so captivated by. It was all gone. The walls were now awash in a deep shade of blue and those quotes, those impassioned vestiges of someone's failed relationship, were buried in a dark sea of latex. What had the walls once said? The only phrase I could remember was "Meeting you was a blessing and I don't believe in God." I did notice, however, people had already begun the task of covering the walls with new tags. In the corner, not too far from the trash can, in a tone so dark it almost disappeared into the paint, I saw a new message. "Fais-toi s'en pas," it said in bold. "Ça va ben aller."

"Don't worry. Everything will be all right."

I WALKED OUT OF THE bathroom and immediately ran into James.

"Hey, you!" he stopped me, sporting a smile. I hadn't seen or spoken to James since that moment on his doorstep two months ago. He was alone and looking good, dressed in dark slacks, a dress shirt, and a tie.

"James," I said, looking down.

"Will. I wondered when I'd run into you," he said with polite composure. "How've you been?"

"… I've been better. Listen, I'm sorry I didn't call. I haven't been making the best choices the last couple of months. Maybe you're right. Maybe there is a big part of me that's frozen."

"Well, into each life a little snow must fall."

"You're not pissed?"

"No, not really. I had a feeling you might not call. Like you said, you did seem a little lost. I knew I'd run into you again."

"Yes," I said, feeling unsure about my absolution. "You're all dressed up," I noted.

"I was at the theatre tonight," he said with flair. "No one dresses for the theatre anymore, so I decided to put on a shirt and tie, but dressed it down with these." He drew my attention to his green sneakers. "You like? I seem to remember your stylish disregard for winter."

I smiled.

"It's nice to see you, Will." James poked the neck of his bottle into the left side of my chest. It lingered.

"So." He drew the bottle back to his lips. "You're quite the kisser. I thought of that kiss for days afterwards."

I felt embarrassed and turned red. No one had complimented me on a kiss before. "Gee, thanks," I said. James was standing close to me. I knew it was loud in the bar, but it felt awfully close.

"I think I'd like to try it again," he said, placing his hand on my hip. "That is, if it's okay with you." James moved in and kissed me on the mouth, his touch sending currents through my body.

"James, I think I am going to get going," I said, pulling away.

"Can I come with you?"

I wasn't sure if that was a good idea. "Really?"

"I'm not going to let you slip away this time."

I BROUGHT JAMES HOME AND took him straight to bed. If he noticed the strange piles of boxes in my hallway he didn't say anything. James's bare body felt cold under the sheets as I moved in beside him. "Brrr," he said as the blood in my body began to share its warmth. "Maybe I shouldn't have worn those sneakers. My toes are frozen." He shivered again. "This winter has been crazy. I keep waiting for springtime to come and save our city."

It would officially be spring in three days, but you couldn't tell from all the snow outside. "This has been the longest winter ever."

"They're all long," James replied. "It wouldn't be Quebec without a long winter, right? Shit — what the hell was that?"

Elizabeth had made her presence felt in the room, jumping up in the blackness to the centre of my bed. "Oh, that's my cat, Elizabeth."

"Hello, Elizabeth," James said, scratching her chin. "You scared me. I thought I was under attack." James found my face in the darkness and began to kiss me. "Or maybe I'm *about* to be under attack. Ha, ha, ha." His laugh melted into my mouth.

Pulling back, I stopped him. "James, if it's okay with you, I'd rather if we didn't."

"Is everything all right?" he asked, trying to hide his disappointment.

"I'd rather not rush into things. I think it'd be best if we took it slow."

"Okay," he said, more content with the idea as he laid back. "I think I can manage to keep my paws off you for a little longer." I could see him better now in the glow of the blue coming through the blinds. James looked serious in the dark, older and more staid than his twenty-four years. I marvelled at the weight of his chest as it rose from the sheets, two dime-sized nipples located amid sparse curls of hair. "So, tell me more about yourself, Will. I don't think you told me what it is that you do."

"I'm a high school teacher. Geography."

"I loved geography as a kid," James said. "I used to want to be an explorer, like Indiana Jones. One year, for my birthday, my parents got me a subscription to *National Geographic*. I loved the pictures of people and cities from around the world. And

I'd stare at some of those pullout maps for hours. What grades do you teach?"

"Seven and eight."

"How do you like working with kids?"

"You mean teenagers? I like it for the most part." I thought of the group card I had received from one of my classes when word had got out about my mother. "I have some pretty great students. They can surprise you sometimes ... But enough about me," I stopped. "I don't want to talk about work. Tell me more about you."

"What do you want to know?"

"Why are you studying to be a doctor?

"Well, I've always been fascinated by the human body," he said, tracing a finger down my arm. "The way it grows, the way it works. I used to play doctor all the time as a child. Not *doctor, doctor*, but doctor, you know ... the real thing. I want to help people."

"That's noble," I said. "Any idea of what you want to do once you graduate?"

"Pediatrics," he said as if there were no doubt. "I love working with kids. They're wonderful beings. They're so innocent. Or, maybe that's not the word. They're like this blank slate, or ... I don't know. They're more themselves than any of us. None of this learned bullshit. I love that kind of innocence."

I asked James if he had worked with many kids before, and he told me about his recent residency at the Montreal Children's. "How sick are those children?" I asked him.

"Pretty sick."

"Did any of them ... die while you were there?" I asked.

"Yes, some of them did die. One child, who had emphysema, died on my last day. It was very sad. He was such a cute kid. Really shy. I met his parents, too. Wonderful people. It's heartbreaking what some families have to go through. But he was lucky to have such great parents. They really were there for him."

"I don't know how you can be a doctor," I said. "How you can be responsible for the life of another person. Or lose patient after patient. Doesn't that frighten you?"

"I don't think 'frighten' is the word," James said, sitting up in bed. "I'm very much aware of the risks involved in treating people. You don't want to do anyone harm, so you take precautions. You *mean* to do them good. I see it that way. Because maybe if I wasn't there, they wouldn't be doing so well."

"I don't think I could handle it," I said. "Having to tell someone his or her child or parent wasn't going to make it. Are you close with your family?"

"Yes," James said, resting his hands behind his head. "I don't see them as often as I'd like. My sister lives in Toronto and my brother, who's younger, lives at home with my parents in Halifax."

"Are you out to them?"

"Yes. It's hard to keep a secret like that in Halifax, especially when I was dating Tim as long as I was." It was the first time he had mentioned the ex-boyfriend by name. "I realize I'm lucky. They've been cool about it. What about you? Are you close with your parents?"

"Well, I … I never knew my dad. He died when I was two. And yes, I was quite close with my mom. But then she died recently."   .

"Oh, I'm so sorry, Will. That's terrible. What happened?"

"Well, my mom, she had colon cancer …"

James winced.

"… And it came back. It metastasized and she had the surgery to remove it, but there were complications and she ended up dying from a blood clot."

James sighed. "I'm so sorry, Will," he repeated. "Cancer is such a bitch … When did she die?"

"A week and a half ago."

James shot up straight in bed. "Oh my God. What?" He took a moment to stifle his shock as Elizabeth ran from the bed. "Holy shit. Are you okay?"

"I don't know. It's all so recent."

James could have said anything. I half expected him to get dressed and tell me he had to leave, but instead he shifted closer to me and grabbed my hand under the top sheet. "Shit. I … Shit! So, since the last time I saw you?"

"Yeah …"

"Was there any warning?"

"No, it happened fast."

"And the blood clot, did that happen …"

I stopped him again. "Actually, James, I don't know if I can discuss the details right now. Sorry. I know I brought it up, but can we change the subject?"

"Yes. Sure. It's just, I … Yes. Sure…. So. So … uh, funny running into you tonight," he struggled.

"Yes. I needed to get out and blow off some steam."

"I can imagine. I … I was happy to see you tonight. When you hinted at having gone though a rough period, I had no idea you were referring to something like this. I mean, now I understand why you didn't call … It makes complete sense. Here I thought, when a guy doesn't call it's because of a fear of intimacy, or their own personal bullshit. But no … I guess there could be other reasons too … Gosh, I can't believe …"

I turned around and kissed James hard. Not out of any

specific desire for him but, in all honesty, to shut him up. I could tell his awkward fumbling would continue if I didn't curb it, so I leaned into him, pulling him close to me. My hand danced down his side to the fleshy flank of his buttock. I cupped my hand around it, pulling his thigh up to my hip as I bored into him with my lips.

James kissed back. His body responded but he tried nonetheless to reason with me. "I thought you didn't want to do anything tonight."

I didn't answer, just kept on kissing until his reluctance gave way to submission.

ONCE WE WERE DONE, JAMES continued to kiss me in his shaken state. Slower and slower his heavy breaths began to dissolve into the pillow. Before long he'd be asleep, stirring every so often to draw me in closer under the covers. In the aftermath I noticed how cold the room was. I got up from the bed to take out another blanket from the closet, and found the afghan my mom and I had made. With a deep sigh, I took it down and placed it on the bed to cover us.

Slipping back beneath the sheets, I realized the balls of my toes were frozen too, and so I placed them, snugly, into the backs of James's heels. He grabbed my arm across the covers and kissed it, gently leading me to sleep with him.

Chapter 20

"Your grandmother had it."

"Did she?"

"Yes. You should get checked out too," my mother had said. "There was a girl in the waiting room there, not much younger than you are."

"I thought you said I should wait until I'm forty?"

"But as it runs in our family ... And if I have it, and your grandmother had it, then other people in our family probably had it too. I don't know for sure what everyone died of. To be safe, dear, you should make an appointment."

"Audrey Hepburn died from it," Angie said to me at another point along the way.

"I didn't know that."

"She was young, too. Sixty-three. You should go get tested, Will."

James would later say the same thing to me one morning

over breakfast. "Will, you should make an appointment for a colonoscopy. Just to be safe. As we get older, many of us develop polyps in our colons. Normally they're small, harmless, benign. But they can turn into cancer if left unchecked. Think about how things might have turned out differently for your mother had she been checked sooner."

It was odd how quickly James felt comfortable being upfront with me. Inasmuch as I had resisted dating him, I now found myself helpless to. I responded to his messages, accepted his invitations. He was around and I didn't ask him to leave. Life had become quiet, and I was afraid of that quietness, the emptiness that held those advancing seconds. James filled up time in a way that comforted me in my loss. Even though I didn't know if I could give him what he wanted, I felt no guilt in taking what he offered.

He spread marmalade on his toast. "Talk to your doctor. Tell him about your family history and see what he says. You trust him, don't you?"

"Yes."

"What are you afraid of, then? Having something up your ass?" he smirked.

"It's not that." I jabbed his shoulder. "I remember when my mom used to get it done. It was all so strange and painful. And there's the awful prep work too — the fasting and the flushing." My mother had had three or four colonoscopies in her life. Over the years she had become an expert in cleaning her colon. I had only ever done it once, as a nervous preparation for a lousy date, but whereas I had used one of those over-the-counter enemas, she'd had to drink vile liquids and take laxatives.

I felt uneasy asking my doctor.

"So, Will," he asked, "has there been any recent change in your or your family's health?"

"Yes. My mother passed away a month ago. Colon cancer. Well, from a blood clot as a result of the surgery. But honestly I don't think she'd have been around long had she survived the recovery. It was her second time. Stage Three."

"Oh, Will. I'm so sorry," my doctor said with an impassive gravitas only a health official can make sound sincere. I had started seeing Dr. Mazer the year I turned twenty, deciding I wanted a gay doctor with whom I could discuss everything. Above his desk hung pictures of his partner Eric and their dog Samson. "How are you coping?"

I was tired of having to answer this question, but had become adept at changing the subject. "I'm okay ... It's just, the cancer was awfully aggressive," I said, trying to sound more scientific than sad. "My mother had been in remission for many years and then, just like that, there was this recurrence. It's also what killed my grandmother, I think, and maybe several other of my relatives, too — I don't know."

Normally, he told me, they'd wait until my forties to test me. But since my mother's cancer had been aggressive, and she had been young when first diagnosed, Dr. Mazer thought now would be a good time to have me checked out. "That way," he said, "if everything is all right, we won't have to do another test for many years. Does that sound okay to you? We don't do the tests here, Will. For that you'll have to call the hospital." He gave me the number. "It might take a couple of months to get an appointment. They'll remove anything they find and we'll go over the results together. Here," he said, handing me some literature. "Why don't you take these pamphlets."

I recognized them, the standard in colon cancer literature. "Thanks, Dr. Mazer, but I think I know what to expect."

"Yes, I suppose you do ... Will, would you like to talk to

someone about this? Do you have a support network? I can refer you to someone if you like."

"No. That's fine, doctor. Really."

He didn't press. We did the other battery of tests: ear, throat, chest.

"I'd like an HIV test," I said as he examined me.

"Yes, of course," he said. "Are you sexually active at the moment?"

"Yes."

"Are you having safe sex?"

"I've started seeing someone. We're safe, but I haven't always been. I had sex in the last few months without a condom, several times — both as the active and passive partner."

Dr. Mazer made the necessary scratches on his pad, checking the boxes on a sheet for my blood work.

LATER THAT DAY, AFTER WORK, I came home to find James in my apartment.

"Hello?" I called out to the sound of music in the kitchen. James had slept over the night before and, since he had the day off, I had left him that morning with a key to lock up. I didn't expect him, though, to still be here when I got home. "James?"

"In here," he called out as I walked into the kitchen. James had his back to me, his hands in a mixing bowl.

The place was much cleaner than it had been that morning. All of my dirty dishes had been done and put away, and there was a sharp shine to the floor and sink. "Wow," I said. "What have you been up to?"

"Your bed was so comfortable I didn't want to leave it this morning," he said, turning his head to smile and greet me. "I had intended to spend the day reading, and I had my textbooks with me, but in the end I got up and began tidying. I even went to buy some food for dinner. I hope you don't mind."

"Mind?" I said. "No, I don't mind. Anytime you feel like washing my floors and cooking I'm not going to stop you." I went up to him and placed my hands on his hips and kissed him on his back in between his shoulders. "Thank you, that's very kind."

"It's a form of procrastination, really, but a part of me did feel like I was nesting."

"What's that you're making?" I peered over his shoulder.

"Spaghetti and meatballs," he said, and I smiled. I hadn't told James about my mother's recipe. Usually, by now, I would have cooked it for him, but I had yet to make James a meal. Why was that?

"You know, my mom used to make the best spaghetti and meatballs," I said. "I think it's my favourite thing she ever made ... I'll have to make it for you sometime."

"I'd love that," he said. "But the pressure's on now. I doubt this will be as good as hers." He turned to kiss me, his hands messy with the raw meat mixture. "Go, have a seat. Pour yourself some wine." He motioned towards the counter where there was an open bottle and a glass waiting for me. "So, how did you make out at the doctor's?"

I poured some wine and sat down at the kitchen table. I told James how my appointment had gone, what we'd discussed and what he had scheduled me for.

"That's good ... Do you know if he's taking on any new patients?"

"Are you looking for a doctor?"

"Yes. I figure it's about time that I get a good gay doctor who could follow me over time."

Interesting. "I thought you said you didn't want to stay here after school."

"Well," he said, turning his head and smiling once more, "the city is looking better every day."

I smiled and took a sip of wine. James went back to rolling his meatballs.

I took note of his pile of textbooks on the kitchen table. Among the spines was a magazine — an old *National Geographic*. July 2005. I pulled it from the pile. "What's this?"

"I came across it in my apartment the other day," he said, after turning to see what I was referring to. "I'd bought it for this article on stem cell research, but there are some other interesting things in there. I thought you might want to have a look before I throw it out."

I flipped through the magazine's pages, immediately locating the feature he was talking about. It was illustrated with a series of colourful photos of scientific equipment and prominent researchers. I kept flipping, skimming past stories on natural gas deposits in the West, Chinese warriors of the Ming dynasty, and the war in Chechnya. Near the end of the issue I came across an article on the Mars rovers, Spirit and Opportunity. It too was illustrated with a series of images — photos from the rovers' cameras. Everything was dry, brown, and desolate. I speed-read the first two paragraphs. The author was comparing the rovers' Martian expedition with Powell's 1869 survey of the Grand Canyon — two exploratory missions separated by more than 100 years that looked for clues of how ancient water sculpted the landscape. Each used drastically different means, each defied expectations by lasting longer than expected.

"Cool," I said. "I think I'll keep this. Thanks."

I got up from where I sat and went over to the counter to watch James work.

"Can I help?" I asked.

"Sure. Can you stir the sauce?"

I took the wooden spoon off the stovetop and stirred the simmering tomato sauce a couple of times. I then turned and admired my kitchen. And then James. James looked good in my apartment, like he belonged here. He had put his own stamp on the room. I could see it in the gleam of the stainless steel, smell it in the spaghetti and meatballs.

It may not have been my mother's sauce, but whatever it was smelled great.

Chapter

21

I had to wait two months for my colonoscopy appointment. The timing suited me fine. The procedure was scheduled for the week after classes wrapped for the summer. This meant I wouldn't have to ask for more time off from work or explain to my students why I needed to run to the bathroom so often.

"You can put these on and take a seat," the nurse said once I had been admitted, handing me two hospital gowns and pointing to a row of cushioned seats behind her. "One gown goes on the front, the other on the back."

In the changing booth I tried to discern if there was a difference between the two. No. It was only the pattern that was different. In the small telephone-booth-sized space I struggled to take off my clothes. There wasn't much privacy. I could hear the discussions of the nurses and orderlies walking around, see flashes of their scrubs as they passed by the curtain that separated me from the rest of the floor. Do I stay in my underwear? I thought stupidly to myself before pulling them off. And then, for a moment, I stood there, naked, in front of the full-length mirror I was almost pressed up against. The light in the room was unflattering. I felt bloated and hairy. Is this really what my body looks like? I slid on the first gown around the back, and put the second around the front. I tied up the strings at the side and on the top, and shuffled from the room with my belongings.

"You can put your stuff in one of those lockers," an orderly said as I emerged from the changing room. He was short and round, with dark-rimmed glasses and a lilt to his voice. "There's no lock, though, and you might be sharing them, so you'll want to keep your valuables with you."

"Thanks," I said, and began to place my clothes in one of the free lockers. I took my wallet and keys from my jeans and put them in my shoulder bag, and then moved over in my socks to the line of chairs where I had been instructed to wait.

I took out a book from my bag, but I don't know how I thought I'd be able to pay any attention to it in this waiting room. It wasn't even really a waiting room. Angie was in the real waiting room. Waiting for my procedure to be over so she could escort me home. No, I was on the other side of the wall, sitting in the corridor of the hospital's gastroenterology department. The same place my mother had come.

"Mr. Ambrose, would you follow me, please?"

I went into a room to the right and sat down with another nurse. "I need you to sign this waiver," she said, handing me a form on a clipboard. "It's a standard document. I'm going to put in an IV line." Once I had finished signing, she took my right arm and wrapped a tourniquet around it, sliding in the needle that served as a line and taping it to my arm. She then took out a syringe and, placing the needle into the nozzle of the line, shot an amber-coloured liquid into my arm.

"There you go. All good. You can go back and sit in your chair. We'll call you in a couple of minutes."

As I sat back down, I could see another man being given dressing instructions by the nurse who had first ushered me in. He was much older than me — in his early sixties, I'd say — and was tall and large. I had seen him come in with his wife while I sat in the waiting room with Angie. I was by far the youngest person there, and people seemed to look at me with a mixture of curiosity and pity. What is this poor young man doing here, the looks seemed to say. The man's wife couldn't stop staring at me — a jet-black dye job in a smart tweed suit. She held a novel at her knees, some trashy romance she had yet to crack.

Sitting in the corridor, I took out my book again and flipped through it. The man came back out with his clothes, looking as ridiculous as I'm sure I did, and was instructed to place his belongings in the locker. He smiled as he sat down one seat over from me.

"Hello."

"Hello."

"Are you next?" he said, smiling.

"I don't know," I said. "I think so." My appointment was for 9:30, and it was already half past nine. "Is this your first one?"

"Excuse me, what? Oh, yes! Yes, it is. You?"

"Yes."

"If you don't mind me saying so, you seem awfully young to be here."

"Preventative," I said. "It's in my family."

"Mine too," he exhaled, grabbing his kneecaps. "My brother. Died last year. Never told any of us what he was going through. Kept it all to himself. He was only fifty-eight for Chrissakes!

And me, I've avoided seeing the doctor most of my life. Now I know that's plain stupid. Good for you for getting this done young."

"Mr. Jones?" said the nurse with the form on the clipboard. "Will you come with me, please?"

The man propelled himself from his chair. "Good luck," he said as he passed by.

"You, too."

The corridor was tight and busy with people who each had a task. People made small talk, one of the orderlies sang a pop song under his breath, another passed by with a cart of what appeared to be equipment in a plastic bin. Could these people see how nervous I was? Was I even visible to them?

"Mr. Ambrose," another nurse called from down the corridor. "If you will come with me, please." I followed him down to another room, a wide vault with a door spanning half the length of the wall.

"Hello, Will," the doctor said with his back to me as I entered the room. He was examining images on his computer. Scans? Videos? Another person's colonoscopy? "I'll be right with you."

The nurse was already leading me to the gurney, fussing with me as if I were a bride. "Can you please hop up on the gurney here and lie on your left side?" I did as I was told. He covered my lower half with blankets. "Thank you."

"So, Will," said the doctor, now to my right, "from what I understand, there is nothing bothering you. This is only a routine checkup to see how things are going." The nurse was reaching for my right arm. "We are going to give you a mild sedative. Nothing too strong. We call it a type of 'twilight anaesthesia.' You will feel very relaxed, and if you're tired you may sleep." I watched the nurse inject two additional syringes of solution into my system. "We've done many, many of these procedures before," he said, "but I do have to warn you there is the slightest risk of perforating the bowel. But I wouldn't worry about it. You might also feel some mild cramping if I have to blow in air to inflate the colon, but really you shouldn't feel anything."

A TV was turned on in front of me, light and movement on the screen.

"You can watch the entire procedure on the monitor if you like. And I'll let you know what we find."

I remember thinking to myself: When does the anaesthesia kick in? Why can't I feel anything? But then the endoscope was inside and feeding images to the screen. Looking back, I must have been stoned because I couldn't feel a thing, and soon I became entranced by the images — a kaleidoscope of light and shadow. The surface of my colon's walls looked like the insides of my mouth, soft and pink and wet. The endoscope travelled up the tunnel, twisting as it went, aspirating any bile or remnants of the prep.

I was mesmerized. These were my insides! I was seeing the unseeable! It reminded me of the EKG I had had as a child. This was much different, however. Whereas before it was only lines on graph paper, now it was the real thing. Actual moving images of the inside of my body.

I watched as the endoscope climbed through the rings of the colon, searching the shiny pouches and folds for cancer or its beginnings. It might have been the drugs, but I began to imagine the procedure as the Mars expedition, the expensive piece of robotic equipment surveying the alien terrain like one of the rovers I read about in James's magazine — its camera transmitting images back home.

Soon, the doctors had made it all the way through and

the camera started to move backwards, stopping to check the corners but moving towards the entry. "It seems we have found a polyp," the doctor said, stopping the scope and inspecting some sort of growth. It was small and round, pink, like a piece of discarded chewing gum. "Nothing to worry about, Will. Most polyps are benign, but they should be removed. We'll remove it and I'll have it tested."

I could now see part of the endoscope, like it was a hand in front of the camera. Suddenly it reached out and lassoed the polyp, snaring it in its grip. "I'm isolating the growth," he explained, tightening the base of the lump. "And burning it off. Don't worry, you shouldn't feel a thing." I watched amazed as the doctor burned off the suspicious lesion. So small, I thought. Is this what you looked like in my mother's colon? Huh? You abnormal group of cells ...

I wondered what my mom had seen during the four or five times she had her colonoscopies. Had they looked like mine? Or did she stop looking at the screen after that first one? My mother would never have contemplated the inside of her colon had she not had this problem. But for the longest time it was the subject of much discussion. It was poked, prodded, flushed, rinsed, snipped, stretched, excised, and in all its exploration it remained as painful and awkward as it had always been.

I don't know if, given the fact I'm gay, my mother had ever considered whether or not I'd had anal sex; or why anyone would really want to. Not that all gay men do it, but I do think most parents must wonder, at some point after their child comes out to them, if they do. It seems like such an automatic, irrational fear. People are afraid to talk about the asshole. Somehow it's the most shameful part of the human body. It's inelegant. And it remains silent in its inelegance.

And in that silence people die.

When I first came out I never thought I would contemplate death as much as I did when I thought about sex. HIV, and its consequences, have hung over my couplings the way they do for most gay men. When I came out those many years ago I felt invincible to all but this one thing. I believed gay men had been given a special pass and it was only HIV we had to watch out for. Eluding it, we'd live forever. Still, to this day, whenever I hear of a young gay man who has died before his time, I think of AIDS. And whenever I find out it wasn't AIDS that killed him, I am taken aback. I know accidents, sudden illnesses, diseases, take us at different ages, but I am stunned each time it happens to one of us. Other dangers are indeed out there, willing to take us out early. I didn't realize how close the enemy was. Cancer has been an unwelcome member of my family.

Chapter 22

Angie and I rode the Number 11 bus up the mountain and got off at the cemetery's iron gates. The trip wasn't unfamiliar, but this time I knew where to find the stone: up three rows past the grand oak tree, on the left, by the fence. The family plot had the markings of recent disturbance. The monument was still askew, but the earth below it now bore the telltale signs of transformation. The ground was soft, loose and brown, scattered with thin patches of glowing grass, fine and light. And a new name had been carved into the side of the pillar: Katherine Ambrose.

We had brought some flowers with us from the market, and tools to plant them in the ground. They were small and purple and, as delicately as we could, we tucked them into the edges of the earth where the soil met the stone. Angie and I didn't talk much. When we did it was perfunctory. "How deep do you think it should go?" and "Do you think anyone will water them?" After we were done we said an improvised prayer and packed up our stuff. On the way out we passed by the central chapel, birds rushing around the spire like souls awaiting redemption.

We hopped back on the Number 11 and rode it along the winding road, back over the mountain towards home. Halfway, I impulsively got up and rang the bell. Angie looked at me, puzzled, as the bus pulled to the side of the road and I gestured for her to follow. The bus left us at the top of Mount Royal.

From this vantage we could see the entire city. It was a bright spring day. The parking lot of the lookout was flush with people taking advantage of the warm weather to admire the view. It was April. Spring had come to Montreal, uncovering the city and discharging its inhabitants from their bleak hibernations. Below, neighbourhoods spread out before us like fallen rocks, the solid three-storey buildings of the Plateau and Mile End and, scattered beyond, Park Ex, Rosemont, and Centre-Sud. The heights of these short buildings were insignificant in comparison to the natural vastness of the horizon. The sky glowed a bright blue as a white stripe ran across its bottom, touching down with the crumbling ground. And there, staring at me from across the great expanse, in the distance, the constant tower of Olympic Stadium.

"Angie," I said. "You know how you believe it's how a relationship ends that matters? I think you're wrong. You have to be, or I will never be able to get over this. I don't want to remember how it ended. I don't want that image to stay with me. I want all the other ones. The great ones. I can't let how it ended with my mother affect my memory of her."

Angie remained silent. She reached out and held my hand.

"I'm afraid I'll forget her. Afraid I'll forget what she looked like — not like in pictures — but who she was. The dents and creases in her smile, her laugh, the smell of her hair when I kissed her on the top of her head. I'm afraid of it fading … I always seem to hold on to the wrong kind of memories."

Up here on Mount Royal I can see the appeal of angels, why humankind believes in them. I'd like to believe I'm being watched over, protected. From above, the world seems understandable. There is a clarity absent on the surface. I suppose every now and then it's necessary to get out of ourselves, to look at everything from above.

JAMES SLEEPS SOUNDLY BESIDE ME, the lungs in his chest expanding and retracting with quiet force underneath the sheets. Watching him sleep I feel as if I might love him. It's possible. I like him. A lot. He makes me laugh. And I continue to learn new things from him. He challenges me. His body turns me on. I know it well, how it works. I am as comfortable sleeping beside him as I once was with Max. It's now the end of August and we've been seeing each other for five months. I'm not sure how I got here, how it happened, but I wish I had left behind breadcrumbs.

I know it's dangerous to compare loves, but I can't help it. It's hard not to size up the people who walk into your life and wonder how long they'll be around: a day, a decade, a lifetime? The last few months with James have been wonderful. We spend much of our time together. We cook. Watch movies. He studies and I read. James is helping me reset the tick of my heart. I don't know what will come from this but a large part of me wants to see it through, find out what type of person I can be with him.

In the bright light of morning, James starts to rouse from his slumber, almost sensing I'm awake. He crawls out of his nocturnal stupor to greet me. "Good morning," he says, emerging from the sheets red and raw like a newborn. We share a deep kiss hello, and with it comes the warmth and funk of familiarity. We have a big day ahead of us but still find time for a sloppy romp on the mattress, James's lithe body exposed in the white light on top of me.

We shower, eat, and head to the Jean-Talon Market. He is going to show me how to pickle cucumbers today, a family recipe. Tonight we're going to see *Cats*.

"Did you hear?" James asks while examining a basket of apples. "Pluto isn't a planet anymore."

"What?"

"Apparently some scientists at this international astronomical association got together and decided they were wrong. Pluto should've never been called a planet. It's just a chunk of ice and space debris. So our solar system only has eight planets now. Isn't that wild?"

"Really?" I say, gobsmacked. "Where did you hear that?"

"On the news. They announced it just the other day."

"Wow," I say, paying for the fruit. "You think you know your own universe."

"I wonder what they're going to call it now," James says as we move over to the next stand. "I mean, they have to call it something if not a planet."

"I'm sure they already have a name for it, whatever it is."

Suddenly, across the stall, I lock eyes with Max. He is standing in the next row, a canvas bag of greens in his right hand. "Max," I say in response to his grin. James looks up as Max walks over.

"Will. How are you?"

"Good," I say, and then ask him the same. We don't lean in for a kiss hello, invisible lines keeping us apart.

I introduce him and James. They shake hands. "What are the two of you up to?" Max asks.

"James here is teaching me how to pickle cucumbers," I reply.

"A top-secret family recipe, so don't go sharing it," James says, jabbing at me with his index finger. "Oh, I think I see the secret ingredient. Will you excuse me? Nice to meet you, Max." James takes off to give us a moment.

"So, are you two …?"

"Yes," I say, looking over at James as he heads towards the herbs. "Five months now. He's younger than me, but definitely the mature one."

"He's cute."

"We're going to see *Cats* tonight."

"*Cats*? I thought you hated Andrew Lloyd Webber."

"The tickets were my mom's. She and I were supposed to go together. It feels wrong not to go."

Max places a hand on my shoulder. "How are you doing?"

"Okay," I say, a little uneasy; but then simply: "I'm fine."

"Well … It's good to see you, Will."

"You, too. Take care, Max." I lean in to hug him, no more invisible lines keeping us in place.

"so that was max?" james asks me after he's gone. I nod and leave it at that for the time being. I've haven't told James everything about Max yet. I'm not sure why that is. I trust him. Perhaps I just want to move on.

Later that night James and I head to Place des Arts, our hands smelling like dill. We enter the building from the street and walk up to the grand entrance of Salle Wilfrid-Pelletier. James looks handsome in his beige blazer and red sneakers. I hand over our tickets and we make our way through the hall to find our seats. I can't help but think about my mother as we do this, wonder if there is an alternate universe out there where another Will is leading her to her seat.

The lights soon darken and I almost forget what we're here to see. The curtain opens on a junkyard and a bright glowing moon hanging in the centre of the sky. The moon is large and perfectly round, with craters casting light shadows on its surface. The show is silly, and doesn't make much sense. Songs of *Jellicle* cats and their *Jellicle* moon. We're introduced to each of the cats, and are told one of them will be chosen on this night to be reborn. It's a ridiculous conceit, but my mother would have loved it. The singing, the dancing, the over-the-top emotion. I keep looking over at the next seat to imagine her reaction. Thankfully James is there. A wide grin as he is caught up in the show — enjoying it for me, for my mother.

All of a sudden Grizabella comes out to sing "Memory" and I find myself recoiling into my seat. Grizabella is an older cat, a female who has seen better days. She looks ragged, sickly, and I can't help but think again of my mother. At intermission I collect myself and try to joke with James. I even begin to forget my sadness as the show starts up again, but then Grizabella comes out at the end to be chosen as the one to be reborn, the one sent to the "Heaviside Layer." The big cat Old Deuteronomy walks her around the stage and up to a junkyard tire, which slowly begins to ascend towards the heavens. He points to a spot in the sky and suddenly a metal staircase descends from the rafters. Grizabella boards the staircase, looks behind her, and disappears into the night sky.

One last number closes the show. I alternate between clapping and wiping my eyes as the stage goes dark. James grabs my knee as the lights come back up and the cast returns for the curtain call. In groups, the cats take their bows. We stand to greet them. At the very end Grizabella emerges to roaring applause. It's a surprise to see her, a shock she has not really left this world.

Programs in hand, we leave the theatre through one of the emergency doors. Outside, on the steps to Place des Arts, James and I are greeted by a full moon. It looks more real than the one onstage, hanging there, glowing in the night sky. It makes me think of Pluto and its decommission; and the New Horizons team, only seven months into their voyage. What do they think of the news? Do they even care? It'll be 2015 by the time the spacecraft gets to its destination. Who knows what other discoveries will be made in that time.

Is anything truly permanent? Can anything ever be when your own universe can surprise you with something new about itself — correcting a fact you were taught to believe your entire life? The teacher in me wonders what they will do now with the old textbooks, the ones that count the planets in our solar system as nine. The little boy in me feels betrayed by the astronomers, the curtain pulled further back on the limits of science. But the lover in me is optimistic, content that something so cold and distant is perhaps more understandable.

A
c
k
n
o
w
l
e
d
g
ements

I WOULD LIKE TO THANK Marc Côté for his hard work and dedication, for playing the perfect game of KerPlunk with my book and helping to remove all the errant straws without letting the marbles fall.

Extra special thanks to Peter Dubé who played an instrumental role in bringing this book to life. I'm grateful for your friendship, your guidance, and all of those beers in dark bars.

For the heart-to-hearts and their professional advice, I am indebted to Elise Moser, Neil Smith, Elizabeth Robertson, Jennifer Warren, Nairne Holtz, Marie Hélène Poitras, Michael V. Smith, Linda Leith, Daniel Allen Cox, Bruce Walsh and Meryl Howsam.

Many thanks to Lori Schubert and The Quebec Writers' Federation. *The Geography of Pluto* was developed under the QWF Mentorship Program.

For reading the manuscript in various stages of evolution,

and their feedback, I'd like to thank my friends Alison Cook, Ashley Diener, Ahmar Husain, John Custodio, Yvette Rambour, Valerie Pospodinis, Atif Siddiqi, Irena Malyholowka, Anastasia Kitsos, George Baylor and Jeffrey Silverstone.

For their talented eye and generosity, I'd like to thank Paul Specht, Vincent Fortier and Craig Therrien. For help with technical terms and translation I'd like to thank Michael DiRaddo, Jennifer Malarek, Fred BG and Sophie Cazenave.

Big thanks go to my parents, John and Elizabeth, my brother Mike, and my sister-in-law Hiromi. Thank you for your love, trust and support.

And lastly, thank you Greg Chisholm. You are my star. I love you.